Midheaven

Midheaven

Ken Kuhlken

THE VIKING PRESS   NEW YORK

Library of Congress Cataloging in Publication Data
Kuhlken, Ken.   Midheaven.   I. Title
PZ4.K94956Mi   [PS3561.U36]   813'.5'4   79-23760
ISBN 0-670-41757-2

Printed in the United States of America
Set in CRT Compano

Grateful acknowledgment is made to the following for permission to reprint copyrighted material:

Dell Publishing Company, Inc.: A selection from *Crime and Punishment* by Fydor Dostoyevsky, translated by Constance Garnett. Copyright © 1959 by Ernest J. Simmons.

Harper and Row, Publishers, Inc. and *Olwyn Hughes*: A selection from "Sheep in Fog" from *Ariel* by Sylvia Plath. Copyright © 1965 by Ted Hughes.

Ludlow Music, Inc.: "The Big Rock Candy Mountains" collected, adapted and arranged by John A. Lomax and Alan Lomax. TRO © Copyright 1947 and renewed 1975 by Ludlow Music, Inc.

FOR ADA

Part One

My name is Jodi. I live alone now on the western slope of the Carson Range, five miles up the mountain from the highway between Incline and South Tahoe. Each morning I climb the hill and watch the tour boat make its turn toward Emerald Bay. It cuts a wake through the choppy water, surrounds itself in foam and sets a straight course southwest toward the peaks they call Desolation. There the snow has stayed all summer, a dozen shades of red when sunset meets the fog from the lake. It will be there still in the last days, when the earth is scorched and the rivers boil. And halfway up Mt. Tallac is a cross of snow all through the year.

Charley's dad built this cabin where I stay to hide, cramped between the hill, two mossy boulders and a row of second growth fir. Vines and manzanita from the hillside cover the roof, drape the southern window, which looks out on the meadow, and take second root between the granite stones in the path around the cabin. So far no one has found me here but chipmunks, mosquitoes, butterflies, a doe and Charley.

The cabin is split pine and fir logs and scrap boards which Charley's dad (Walker we call him—I'm not even sure if Charley knows his first name) salvaged and dragged up the mountain. It has a loft in one end where I sleep. In daylight I draw a tarp over the window so no one who might pass on the creek road can see its reflection. The land is Toiyabe National Forest, but loggers have been here; the big trees were cut years ago all the way up to Marlette Lake, and the road has washes and fallen stumps that only hikers can cross. No one will find me here unless I meet him at the road·

A cast-iron stove and a mat on crates and plywood fill the end of the cabin near the door, opposite the loft. It's a small cabin, fifteen feet long and ten feet wide. The floor is bare split pine with splinters still, and the cracks in the walls have never been caulked. I fill them with rags and socks and cardboard, but the wind always finds more. There is a full-length mirror on the north wall. I don't know how Walker brought it up here, or why. In the evenings I sit by the stove and stare at the mirror. Once, boys thought I was pretty. My legs are long and my eyes are large and nearly black, so people used to watch them and not notice that my nose is too thin and curls up too much at the end, that my lips are flat and wide and there is a gap between my two front teeth, which makes me afraid to smile. I used to be tan but now I'm just dark; my skin is cracked and dirty and I never comb my hair. I should cut it off. I'm very ugly, but I don't care. No one will come up to see me but Charley.

The day I came up in June I thought Charley was following me. I hitched a ride out of King's Beach with a man who said I seemed disturbed because I couldn't sit still or keep my hands from my eyes; he offered to share his bed. I told him I'd scream, and when I did he dropped me at Sand Harbor. On the first ridge I looked back because I thought I heard Charley's voice, but I couldn't see him, so I knelt in the dew to watch children hopping from campers and dashing across the asphalt to the beach while drivers slammed their brakes and lay on

4

their horns, and I cried because I was grown up and had
no faith, no family, nothing.

Up the road I thought I had lost him. I busied myself
with remembering other days I had made the climb and
watching rustling bushes for deer or stray dogs. Then I
wondered if the rustling might be Charley; I cussed him
and threw stones till I felt foolish, as though there were a
crowd watching. Then I stopped still, covered my eyes. It
was at one of those times I first heard a screech from far
up the mountain, then a whine like the wind through a
tunnel, only quivering, like the falsetto of a human
voice. I watched for a squirrel to perk up its ears or for
birds to stop flying and look back, but only I seemed to
hear it. I scrambled up toward the voice as if it came
from the end of a rainbow, ran too fast and staggered,
tripping in ruts and scraping my arms and hands, wiping
the blood from my forehead so it mixed with sweat and
dripped into my eyes. A motor sputtered behind me. I
slid down a bank to hide. A trail bike skidded around a
corner, spun, then righted and blasted back down the
road.

At the edge of the stream where I stopped to drink
was a bird with one wing unhinged in the water. I had
never seen such a bird before, the size of a large hawk,
with white wings and a golden belly. A bloody groove
parted its head, its eyes were crossed and its beak spread
wide as if in a gasp. I ran from it, buried myself in high
grass and pounded my fists in the mud. Still I was sure
Charley was watching me from the trees or was already
ahead, knowing where I'd go. "Kill me, Charley!" I
screamed. "Please kill me! You've killed people before! I
don't believe it's hard!" I waited, so tensed and silent
I heard insects splash in the stream, but Charley didn't
come. No Charley, no Phillip, no Jesus anymore. Evil cir-
cled above me, vultures behind the trees; it lay hard be-
neath me, the hard earth, and I prayed to the God I didn't

5

believe in anymore, for hours, till the sun was straight above.

Then I climbed dizzily, giddy, and by instinct I made the right turns. I tore into the cabin, exhilarated as with a second wind, alone, really alone for the first time ever, as different from being away from home as thinking is different from believing; and I promised myself to cast off everyone. I was heartless and proud. I swept the floor and shook out the blankets, dragged the mattress out to air, scraped the windows and washed them with a bucket of water from the creek. Charley came just before dark.

He found me in a corner of the loft, curled up and facing the wall. "Go away, Charley," I whispered.

He climbed up and reached for my hand but I jerked it back. "I looked all over for you," he said. "Down at the pier, your folks' place, Hidden Beach, the hot springs, even at the church. I knew you'd be up here but I didn't want to think it. It's not the right place. Too much happened here."

"I knew you'd be right behind me, Charley. I can't ever get rid of you, you or Paul or my dad. Poor precious Jodi needs a man. You hang on like ticks but you can't change a damned thing!"

He backed away, hung his legs off the loft, threw his boots tenderly at the far wall. "I can go down if that's what you want. I just brought food and some of your clothes."

"Well, you didn't have to come," I said. "I can do all right by myself."

"Sure you can, Jodi. You can sit up here and think all summer. That's just what you need, lots of time to think. And you can run in those same jeans, eat bark, kill deer when they come down to the creek. If that's what you want."

Charley stayed on. He hung shelves, cleared brush for

6

a path to the dam he built upstream. He gathered logs and kindling, transplanted wild bulbs to a garden by the door where he said they would bloom next spring. Every few days he went down the mountain; in Incline he slipped into my folks' house when they were gone, took my sweaters and jeans, pajamas and ski caps and warm socks; in King's Beach he sold what he could for money to buy me books and writing tablets and tubes of oil paints and canvases, to stock the shelves with canned food and corn meal and peanut butter and dried everything. I didn't thank him; I snubbed him and ignored him and pouted and moped in the cabin while he tried to talk me into climbing trees so we could sit on branches like we used to do, squealing noises we pretended would call bears or elephants or whatever I wanted. Some days I walked off alone, but never far from the cabin, not to explore or think, not even to cry, just to remember Phillip and how they destroyed him, so I could keep on hating.

Charley built a platform in a fir on the ridge from where we could see the lake, matted the boards with dry grass and sat there at dusk after he finished working, picking off pine cones with a slingshot and calling for me to come up, but I never would. He said that he told my folks I had gone to Mexico with the Children of God and asked me to write a letter to tell them I was O.K. I told him to go to hell, that I didn't need his suggestions.

Now the aspens in the grove upstream have begun to turn, and the last wild flowers, mouse-ears and monkshoods, have wilted. The hummingbirds left the creek in the meadow a few days ago and only a few butterflies stay on. The chipmunk with a broken and dragging tail, who used to follow behind and nibble while I picked wild mint, left or died. The flies and mosquitoes are dying, the crickets sing softer and farther down the mountain and the wind wakes me in the mornings. Nights fall earlier, I sleep later, the mountain prepares for winter and I get lonelier every day.

I drop the tarp over the window each morning; then I make oatmeal or millet and coffee and sit on the bank to eat before I go down to the creek. I wash my face in the creek and clean dishes or draw faces in the mud; then I turn back to the cabin and try to read the books, but the words jump out, dive away, and nothing means anything. I make tea and climb the hill, sit on the bench in the outhouse and watch the sailboats tack along the shore around Dollar's Point, leaning toward the public beach and the pier. I can't see the pier, and the boats all turn back west from the cove, on their holiday.

In the afternoons I stay in the cabin and sketch landscapes in charcoals, always of the lake, the hotels, the highway, the western peaks behind and above, shaded by faces in the clouds. I wad up my sketches to start the evening fire. Or I hike up the mountain and shout for echoes. At night I sweat by the fire and read my journals if the words stay still, until they exhaust me. In my sleep I'm plagued by nightmares, and sometimes I wake up in the meadow.

Charley lives in King's Beach again. All week he works with Pancho building block walls, and on Saturdays he always comes up, brings what I need and asks what I've done. I tell him what I can remember, which isn't much, because most every day is the same. I'm not angry with him anymore; I've become kind enough to forgive the one person who has proven that he cares for me no matter what I've done and will do. But when he asks me to go back down with him, I scream at him to leave and call him names even though he's my only friend.

I'm only eighteen years old; six months ago I was still a girl. I'd go back if I could. I'd run back home before the snows come and my father would pet me and hold me so

8

tight that I'd cry till the pain was gone, till I believed he loved me again and had hurt enough to be terribly sorry. Then I'd dress up warm and run down to the beach by the marina, skip stones on the lake and dig channels for the tiny waves to run up. At dark I'd climb the road and we'd all watch television or play cards while my mom painted. At bedtime I'd kiss my family good night, my brothers, too, and Charley if he was over, then curl up in clean sheets with flowers, watch the shadows of branches on the ceiling and wait for tomorrow, when I could take my dog Sherlock on a picnic by a fishing stream above Emerald Bay.

When I wake up at nights I try to remember my dreams so I can guess what they mean, decide what to do, how and what to think about to keep myself well. But usually all I can recall is the feeling, revulsion and nausea, when the nights are cold. Winter is coming. I don't believe I can make it through the winter.

★　★　★　★

September 26, 1971

I'm Mr. Oswald's office assistant first period. Sixth period he teaches my senior English class in British literature. Already he has lent me two books, poetry of Walt Whitman and William Blake. He's friendly to me, very kind. Last year in Miss Waterman's class we were reading *Moby Dick* aloud, taking turns around the room, but Miss Waterman took all Ahab's parts. She paced the deck comically. She's older, maybe fifty, pale, with tight red curls and long flowery dresses, a bum-cast Ahab—peering over the railings and tugging her hair.

Jerry stood up and waved.

"Yes, Jerry?"

9

"Miss Waterman, how come he calls the whale a head? Does Ahab think that whale smokes dope?"

She bit her lip and turned back to the reading. Jerry blasted a fart.

Miss Waterman slammed the book on her podium, grabbed Jerry by the collar and pulled him outside, as she often had before, but this time they didn't come back; Mr. Oswald from next door came in instead. He took up the book and asked what page. A dozen kids shouted different numbers. He sat on the table and chuckled. He seemed frail, his shoulders slumped and his forehead wrinkled, but I admired the gentle humor in his eyes and the thoughtful way he flipped through the pages till he found a favorite passage.

" 'There is a wisdom that is woe; but there is a woe that is madness. And there is a Catskill eagle in some souls that alike can dive into the blackest gorges and soar out of them again and become visible in the sunny spaces. And even if he forever flies within the gorge, that gorge is in the mountains; so even in his lowest swoop the mountain eagle is still higher than other birds upon the plain, even though they soar.' "

Mr. Oswald told us to write this journal, not like a diary, to be stashed away, but as though we were writing it for the world, with things we think important though we might not know why, so if we were to share them we'd all know that our problems aren't only ours and we aren't alone in our troubles or questions, or in our joy. I'll write it for guidance, even if only from myself, charting the places I've been so I can guess, or plan, the next stop.

I resent school this year even more than before, though the work won't be hard; I have art again with Mr. Lopez, who lets me come and go, sketch outside on the grounds and run up to the faculty lounge for his coffee. I resent having to come every morning and be where they say when the bells ring. I disrespect authority, which my

10

dad says is healthy, to a point. Mount Rose is a small school and most of the teachers and counselors know us by name and reputation. Our senior class is just eighty-five kids, a quarter the size of our freshman class the year they bussed us to Reno. Mount Rose has birch trees and Japanese tuft grass; from spots on the grounds we can see past Incline to the lake, but the buildings are beige and modern, matching the meadow like a tugboat on a lily pond, squashed between Jeffrey pine and fir and a row of chalet townhomes. Our high school is Incline in miniature, a brick pressed into a garden world. But it's better than Reno, better than most places, so far.

On our way to the assembly the first day of school, Coach Fabriano handed out copies of the school rules. For tardiness we'll serve time in detention class; for unexcused absence we'll be suspended; for drugs or alcohol we'll be expelled; for referrals anything can happen. Two years ago we had to wear skirts or dresses except on Fridays in May and June, and we couldn't wear backless dresses, spaghetti straps or see-through tops. Last year we could wear hemmed shorts, but no T-shirts or anything without bras. This year the boys can wear trimmed beards and we all can wear sandals and T-shirts, but no halters or tank tops or patched jeans. Next year they'll decide that mustaches can't be braided, girls can't show more than one breast bare, and panties must be worn with short skirts except on the Fridays of football games. If they let us go naked they'd regulate our suntan.

Mr. Furby introduced the coaches, last year's lettermen and lastly the teachers. We already knew about them, that Mr. Koslowski's daughter had a Mexican abortion; that someone caught Mrs. Wenzel in the boiler room with Lloyd, the custodian, during a pep rally; that Miss Waterman was really divorced; that Mr. Oswald sent his shirts to the cleaners, never flunked anyone and for a bookish man was suspiciously friendly with Coach

11

Bracken; that Coach Bracken wore red jockey shorts and picked up underage girls in South Lake. Like most common knowledge these things were probably lies. At the assembly Aaron came to squeeze in between Jill and me. He stuck his hand down the back of my jeans, so I rammed him with my elbow and ran out the aisle and down the steps and back to the halls, where I was given my first referral this year for being where I wasn't supposed to be.

Till last week Aaron was my boyfriend. His father is a corporate attorney and flies his own airplane. Aaron treated me the way he did the rest of his gang, as a foil for his wit and arrogance, one he could touch where he wanted. At lunch in the patio beside the cafeteria he'd lean on my shoulder, talking with the boys about football and how fast they could drive the thirty miles to Tahoe City, and rolling their tongues at the breasts and butts of girls who passed by.

When he came last year with his haughty black eyes and glib New Jersey talk, Aaron was so smooth most every girl was after him. His folks bought a place in Incline above the country club, with colonial chandeliers, redwood decks, sunken tubs and so many rooms I can't remember what all of them look like. They have another place in San Francisco. His mom and dad switch back and forth, one here and one there; they don't even know where they live. Aaron comes and goes.

He was in three of my classes last spring. He threw the javelin on the track team and the coaches stopped him in the halls and struck up friendly talk because they'd heard he was a powerful fullback. With his suede coats, turtlenecks and hand-knit sweaters he stood out like a prince against the boys in sweat shirts and ski parkas. His dad bought into a restaurant in South Lake and he worked there some nights as maitre d'. They let him drink in the bar, so we'd start out our nights there with candlelight and lobster, bourbon for him and daquiris for me. Then we'd take his M.G. up the highway toward Monitor Pass, pull off and kiss, fool around and drink more till I was dizzy and begged him to let me do the driving back down. On the way he'd tell me about his uncle who fought for Palestine and explain the theory of the expanding universe, watching the stars as if he owned them. One night he found a motel room.

He was the first boy I slept with. I hadn't been cold before, I guess I'd done most everything but screw, but the pill seemed so premeditated and screwing so final, as if I'd die a little because there'd be nothing left to try. And for so long I had imagined I'd sleep first with Charley. But Aaron didn't even question that we'd do it, so we did. I was tight and I hurt and my fingers were so cold even afterward that he jumped when I touched him. We finished before midnight but I told him I wouldn't go home, because that would seem like a lie. I tried to wash myself out while he went for more wine; then I drank till the room spun giddily. In the morning I was sick and bruised on my thighs and my breasts.

At home I saw my dad in the upstairs window; he stomped through the front door while Aaron pulled away.

"You sleep with him, Jodi? You're in the big time with a society brat, sports car, etiquette? Be a hooker like your friend Jill! That'd show more class. I'll bust his pretty face, Jodi!"

My mom came out. "You don't know what happened, Ronald. They might've been in a wreck or anything."

"Jill's not a hooker," I said.

"Shit!" my dad muttered and turned away.

I followed my mom inside. "He didn't sleep all night," she said. "But he shouldn't blame it on Aaron. Your father's jealous of anyone refined, anyone with money. I don't mean to sound crass, but there are worse things than money, especially when you have talent."

"Jill's not a hooker, mom," I said. "She only asked the

13

man for a place to stay. He just gave her the money, so she took it, and that was two years ago."

"I won't even ask what you did last night, because I don't think I'd be proud."

My dad's car squealed out of the driveway. I ran to the door. "Where's he going?"

My mom rolled her eyes and started up the stairs. "To gamble, maybe. This upset he might begin again."

From then on, when Aaron came over my dad ignored him. Aaron tried to tell him sports jokes and ask questions about construction, but my dad didn't laugh and usually left the room. Aaron told my mom about art galleries in London and Amsterdam, and she brought him tea with honey. When he brought me home, always past midnight, my folks would both be waiting, my mom to hear where we'd gone, my father for the night I'd tell him I'd dumped the snob.

Yesterday was the first warm Saturday since school started. Jill picked me up about one and said she would stop by Charley's house. Glenn took our money for drops of psilocybin; then we giggled in the car, waiting for the chills and sunspots to come on, and by the time we walked to the point at Hidden Beach, they did. We were alone and the rocks were hot, the sailboats speeded and the wind stormed wonderfully back through the pines. There was a low mist across the lake and when I spit on the water it steamed. Jill jumped in first and screamed from the cold. She was so lovely I stopped to just watch, brown still from summer and graceful, kicking softly, magnified through the water. Then she dove and I watched her all the way down to maybe eight feet. She stayed under for minutes, it seemed, and when I helped her out she was blue. "You're blue, Jill! Look how blue you are!"

"Yep," she said. "It's *so* cold. I want to go again. C'mon." She tugged at my arm and I cannonballed in behind her, swam out past the first shelf where the currents

14

rolled up even colder from black water, then backpad-
dled and watched the fast clouds, floating dreamy and
high as a saint, till Jill called me in.

We stayed too late, nearly till sundown. In the car I
told Jill about the country club dance Aaron was taking
me to that night, the young folks rubbing arms with the
middle-aged folks and trying to find something to say,
the old folks dancing crookedly. I had been there before.
Aaron was due to pick me up. I told my mom to tell him
to go on ahead, that I'd walk over as soon as I had had a
bath and all. Aaron knew I despised those dances but he
always pushed me to go with him, as if he were already
thinking about business contacts or whatever he'd need
to make films, which he plans to do—his dad bought
him a thousand-dollar camera this summer—or like an
apprentice to the landlords and embezzlers who are
buying up the lake. If I stay here and live long enough I'll
either join them or wind up their servant. All of us will
be one or the other.

I lounged in the bath, fingering my hair, massaging my
feet, scribbling with my nails on the soap bar, loving the
shooting chills and twitching lips I still had from psilocybin and swimming so cold. I ran the hot water till it was
gone and then I rubbed down, dried my hair, put on a T-
shirt, black panty hose, my oldest sandals, and a long
chiffon dress. Downstairs my mom said, "You can't wear
that!" but my dad snickered.

I jogged across the golf course and entered the hall
through the garden door. The ballroom smelled like roses
and cigars. I spotted Aaron in back with his father and
two men in matching blue blazers. A waiter stopped to
stare at me and I skipped across the floor and took Aaron's arm. "Hi. Sorry I'm late. Hello Mr.—"

Aaron whisked me away into the hall by the kitchen.
"What the fuck is with you?"

"Nothing," I said. "My clothes are just for fun."

"I don't need a fool, Jodi."

15

I turned lightheaded, from running I supposed, but I caught my balance. "All right."

"All right what? You're going to go home and change?" He held out his car keys but I pushed them away.

"No. I don't need you, either. I'll go ask your daddy to dance. He likes girls."

He shoved me against the wall, so I kicked him. He slapped my face hard, so I kicked him again and ran out through the kitchen and away. Across the golf course first I cried, then laughed, then I was only tired. I won't go out with Aaron anymore. I won't go out with anyone who uses people, anyone who is proud.

★ ★ ★ ★

October 6, 1971

A rumor says that Incline has the highest per-capita income in the country. Its beauty draws the bosses, the corporations who own lakefront condos, and the bankers and doctors and insurance executives who buy up the homes for their summers.

Carpenters and laborers live in King's Beach, a half hour's drive north, in Tahoe City at the top of the lake, in Truckee halfway down the mountain to Reno—anywhere housing is cheaper—and drive to Incline to build the condos, A-frames, chalets and shopping malls for the others. Always except in rain and heavy snowfalls we can hear hammers and power saws from sunrise till last light and sometimes beyond. I don't like the riches, the shops where pant suits can cost $500, the velvet couches and chandeliers, the speed boats and the fenced-off beach club that hoards a quarter mile of shoreline south from the marina. One day wealthy people will own all the beauty everywhere and poor families will be pushed out to cities like Bellflower, where we came from.

16

Bellflower is south of Los Angeles, with hot streets and thick air, and a public pool with guards and fist fights. My brothers were always in trouble for stealing or breaking windows or hanging out at the bowling alley after dark. Danny was twelve and Mark was ten the summer of my seventh birthday when dad came home one night laid off from his job, saying to hell with this place, it's not fit to live, the small house, the dangerous streets with cars racing and teenagers shouting dirty words.

Our house was sold before I believed we'd leave, before I'd said goodbye to my friends; I didn't understand how it could be that I'd never see them again. I missed my friends terribly, even while we were packing, missed the neighborhood and my grandma. We stored our toys and furniture and mom had to drag me to the car, where I cried the whole first day. My dad held me beside him while he drove, told me there were wonderful places in the world, that he'd find the most wonderful and make it our home.

By morning we were in the big trees; we stopped beside a river for breakfast. There were great flying bugs and children throwing stones into the river. While I sat moping Danny came and told me something he had read; some folks cry, he said, and some folks are brave and the brave ones keep looking for happiness. I believed him, believed it was a special secret only grown-ups knew. That day I played games in the car and watched the trees grow taller, thicker and greener.

Tahoe was the first place we camped, in the park above Emerald Bay on the southwest shore; there were streams and waterfalls, squirrels and woodpeckers and the energy of living outdoors. Each night after dinner, while my brothers and I bedded down in our tent, I heard my mom tell my dad he shouldn't go gambling again, but he went anyway, driving twenty miles to south Stateline. Mom worried that he might lose all the

17

money he made from the house. Finally she convinced him to pack up, but we stopped again in just forty miles, at the campground on the lake at Sand Harbor, where the road leads up to Walker's cabin on the mountain.

Mom tried to talk Danny and Mark and me into telling dad we wanted to move on—away from the casinos, she meant—but I couldn't say such a thing. If we left we'd never find a place so grand, with the mist from the lake in the mornings so thick I could hide. When it burned off I'd swim out so far mom would shout for me to come closer, but I'd act as if I didn't hear and pretend I was in the center of the lake with no ground beneath me ever, that the water went clear through the earth and the mountains all around were great castles where princesses lived and I could climb over the clouds.

My dad found a job driving a Caterpillar, building roads, and we rented a house in Brockway, a block from King's Beach, just a mile from north Stateline, where my dad went to gamble once a week. Dad gave me a puppy for my birthday and every day I took Sherlock to play in the woods past the end of our street. I brought along bread for bluejays and squirrels. I hollowed a bush for a playhouse. I climbed for pine cones, cooled my feet in the creek and panned for shiny stones I pretended were gold or diamonds. I taught Sherlock to fetch sticks, to hide without barking when my mom sent Danny to bring me home. Sherlock and I tracked deer through meadows and low brush, tiptoing over cracking twigs, and I blamed Sherlock when deer turned and ran. Each evening I picked new wild flowers for our table.

On weekends we drove to new spots around the lake. Every side road seemed to lead to new lakes with bright deep water and green shadows, new rocky streams and waterfalls and pools. I climbed and slid while my dad and brothers caught brook trout and my mom painted the landscapes in watercolors. I'd sneak away and follow Sherlock after rabbits and toads, stare at the bees while

18

they gathered and the field mice on their haunches watching for hawks. On the way home we'd stop at the public beach for a last swim while dad cleaned the fish in the oily water around the boat launch at the public pier. Then we'd cook in our yard and eat fruit salads; the weekend would finish too soon, but the next morning I'd be up early and off on my own in the woods, while Danny and Mark took their balls and bats to the school yard.

Past the dead end a few streets down was a pool in the creek where I swam every day after lunch. I never brought a towel or change of clothes, so I lay in the sun to dry. One day my brother Mark followed me there and snatched my clothes. I chased him back to the street but he was gone, so I ducked back into the woods to hide, but after a while I stopped caring and went on my usual way, following the creek to the first big meadow. Sherlock ran circles around me and gave back his stick, so I threw it again into the trees on the hillside. He scampered to fetch it then barked furiously and turned tail, squealing back down. I picked him up and crept to the hill. "A bear!" I screeched and backstepped fast.

It was a brown bear, a cub about five feet tall. He hopped from a log and swung his arms as he squatted. I threw a pine cone, whopping him square on the nose. He pawed at his nose, then grunted and moved toward us, so I whipped his face with a stick, grabbed Sherlock and took off running back to the creek, down the path and into the street. There some boys were taking turns on a coaster. Laughing, they pointed at me. I ran into a shed that had pots of dirt and fertilizer and spiders on the walls. One of the boys peeked in. "Get me some pants," I begged.

The boy was older than me and kindly-looking, with thick blond hair and a dark tan. "I'll give you my jeans," he said, "because I only live next door—if you let me feel your thing." He made me spread my legs, stuck in his dirty finger and wiggled it around. It hurt and Sherlock growled, but when I pushed him back and asked for the jeans he ran away. I pounded the dirt in a fury and swore to myself that I'd hurt him someday. His name was Paul. Last July he married my girl friend Maggie.

In October that year we bought our house, a mile up from the lake at Incline, on a dirt road off the new Mount Rose highway that carried up over the pass to Reno. I could climb through the window of my room and up the rock chimney to the roof. Above the trees I could see across the lake to Sugarpine Point, Rubicon Park and most of the western shore. Through the clearings I could see to the village in Incline, to the stretch of new highway where my dad was working and to the end of the dirt road, to the paintless, tar-roofed shack with cardboard for window curtains and a great carved wooden sign on a pole in front, three feet long and crafted with care and patience: WALKER.

Our home was a gift from my dad to us all; there was a room each for my brothers and me, a study where mom could paint. It was what he'd promised—the best place in the world. Sometimes after supper when I was supposed to study I'd climb down the chimney, cut through the woods, cross the highway, run straight to the beach and watch the waves flatten and the lake turn slick when the last boats docked. Home lights blinked through the trees up the hill and from the far shore. The stars joined them and I'd fall on my back in the sand and watch, clap my hands and breathe deep of the air Mark Twain said the angels breathed. When I saw a strange light or shadow, or the first snowflake, I always thought it was an angel.

Charley taught me to ski on old wooden skis on the hill behind the shack where he and Walker lived. My dad called it dangerous there so he took me on Saturdays to Squaw Valley, just down the mountain from the northwest shore; he rented good skis and bought me lessons. My brothers came, too, but I picked it up faster. I loved to turn sharply in front of them, look back and watch them tumble, let them leave the lift at halfway, then ride to the top myself and still pass them by.

For Christmas my dad took off early all week and brought us little gifts every day, candy or underwear, bright shoelaces for our boots, colored Wiffle balls we couldn't lose in the snow. He stayed home every night all that week and my mom baked cookies and fruitcakes and I helped her frost them and licked the bowls. Grandma came up and each night we spent an hour decorating the tree just right, each tinsel strand separate from the others and the lights tucked way inside so we could see just their glow. If Mark misplaced an ornament Danny slugged him, but my dad stopped it right off because he didn't allow any arguing at Christmas time. On Christmas morning my dad made breakfast, the only time all year, and we said grace, the only time all year. I wanted to pass out the presents but my dad asked me to sit on his lap; I loved him so for being my dad and bringing us here that I couldn't say no. Danny started with smaller gifts but I was squirming so much my dad told him to bring my package from the garage. I held my breath till I saw the package, then jumped and tore off the wrapping. My own skis.

Charley came over after breakfast and we all drove to Squaw Valley. Danny and Mark got off at their halfway slope, but Charley in his old wooden skis and I in my new ones with snap-off bindings and red boots rode to the top and slalomed like partners down the two miles, up one bank, then across and up the other, then raced down the last slope and Charley let me win. My dad was waiting. He clicked off a whole roll of pictures. It made me afraid to grow up, because no year could be so fine.

Now apartment buildings are blocking our path down the hill, and from the roof I see King's Castle, the newest casino hotel. There are sand traps and water hazards in the meadow across the Mount Rose highway, our road is a paved cul-de-sac, and the banker whose car hit Sherlock summers in an A-frame where Walker's shack used to be. Everything is changing, and I'm trying to remember back to the feeling I had when Danny told me brave people find happiness. I need to feel brave. Another change is coming. There seems to be more joy in my memory than in the days that I'm living now, and I'm afraid of leaving what I've been—a child who believed in her heart that good people would live good lives and bad people would be sorry.

Sometimes I feel as if I'm at the top of the world looking down, as if what I do is visible to anyone looking up and it's bad for everybody. I hate feeling that I've grown up before I want to, before I have the wisdom to decide what I want to be, how I want to be. I believe I can make the world what I want it to be, see it however I choose—if I can only choose.

* * * *

October 15, 1971

Nothing is simple, since last year when Charley came home from the army. I used to have lots of friends, used to like parties and dancing and dating around. Now I avoid most people but Jill, my family, Mr. Oswald, Mr. Lopez and my friends in the house in King's Beach— Maggie and Paul, Pancho, Charley.

Last spring Aaron took up most of my time, but during the summer he went back east to visit relatives with his mother. Since I was still Aaron's girl, though beginning to turn angry about it, I spent most of my evenings alone at home, in my room painting portraits in oils of imaginary people with sharp features meant to tell about their hearts and souls. But they didn't work, I couldn't control them, so I tried pastels and ink drawings of mythical landscapes like scenes from childhood or mes-

22

caline. During the days I went with Jill to Hidden Beach, where we all went nude till patrol boats came.

One day at Hidden Beach, Paul, Charley's friend who had married my girl friend Maggie, was stoned on speed and downers, goofballs. He was on the point blowing his harmonica when the patrol boat whipped in and a cop with a bullhorn told us all to freeze. Paul dove into the lake and tried to swim to the rocks in the north cave, but the boat circled back and picked him up. Then they spun back close to our rocks and called for someone to bring his clothes. Maggie did, but Paul threw them overboard and bounded onto the deck grinning. So they cuffed him and took him to the sub-station naked.

Once Paul had been quiet, considerate, till he crashed his motorcycle and nearly died because a broken rib punctured his lung; then he flunked out of college in Carson City. When he came home he turned into a reckless doper, eating handfuls of pills, washing them down with beer, going foul-mouthed and looking for fights. Except when he was with Maggie—then he was a gentleman and brought flowers and things. She believed he was troubled but not forever, believed she could help him. A week after their wedding he dropped acid and wouldn't come down; all through the first day he sat as if in a coma, only now and then muttering something about molecules in molecules in molecules and reaching out his hand for them. He stayed up all night and cried all the next morning. In the afternoon he smashed a chair on the kitchen sink, then ran off alone to the public beach, stole a rowboat from a buoy. Maggie watched him row till she could hardly see him; dark was coming, so she called the police.

Lots of kids turn from drugs to Jesus, like Paul, claiming, like Paul, that they had to go through hell to find heaven because our world had gone stale, desensitized, had spared us the harshness and ecstasy of life as it was

23

meant to be. In August Paul came to Hidden Beach most every day, but fully dressed and packing his Bible. He stopped at each group, begged us to put on our clothes and turn away from that place and drive it out of our minds. He said we'd all die and be punished, the same as if we were all in a pile screwing, or beating each other with whips, or murdering babies.

Most kids laughed him off but I didn't. Jill warned me that his kind get their hooks into you and before long you don't know what to think; they split you in half. You can't do anything that makes you laugh or feel good without thinking you're evil; then you turn into a bitchy old woman and preach at your friends, so before long you have no friends except other fanatics and bitchy old women. Jill's sister lives in Eureka with Jesus freaks who own a bakery. She writes long letters calling Jill scum for what she does but beautiful because God still loves her. Jill hates her sister. I tell her I listen to Paul because nothing makes me laugh as freely or feel as good as it used to. She says it's probably hormones, that I should go see a doctor.

Paul and Maggie live in King's Beach on Fox Street with Charley and Pancho, because once they were all friends and still they're all poor. King's Beach, just a mile through Brockway from Stateline, is on the lake, like a village, old enough so it deserves to be here, modest, with old homes and cheap motels, pensioners, families of workers and young people, small lots and houses up next to each other as though sparing the forest.

Maggie isn't happy because Paul isn't fun anymore; he crams his heart with the Bible and calls her hardened because she won't believe that what he tells her is true. And he won't compromise. He threatened to throw out her stereo unless she got rid of her rock albums, so she took them to her mother's, where she listens on the sly. She goes there often now that she's pregnant.

Pancho lives in a shed out back. His real name is Marlon, which he left behind in Boston, he says, a few years ago when he finished college and first went to Mexico. Most winters he goes back to dive for oysters with Mexican friends who built him a grass-roofed house by a delta where a deep river meets the Pacific. Up here he does gardening. Sometimes he plays his guitar and mandolin at nightclubs or small cafés, and he sells the weed or hash oil or vials of psilocybin he brings back from Mexico. He doesn't talk much, unless I ask him questions; then he speculates, elaborates, gives me lists of books by Baudelaire, Basho the poet, Malcolm Lowry. He laughs at Paul's faith and writes songs to tease Paul:

> "I'm stoned on Jesus, praise the Lord,
> ripped on the gospel, swinging His sword.
> So long, mama, adios, dad,
> I'm goin' to heaven where *nobody's* sad.
> Come on up and bring old Unk.
> Be like me, a Jesus punk."

Often I go to the house after school or in the evenings, usually with the idea of talking to Charley. Once I thought he knew all the answers, but now he's turned cynical, worried and old. He sits on the porch drinking beer when he's home, like my dad on his hemorrhoids' worst days, as though he'd been breaking rocks all day in the sun and there was nothing to look forward to but more days of the same. So I leave him alone and talk to Maggie if Paul isn't home, but if he is home he takes me off from the others and reads to me from scripture. I try to open my heart so I can hear the words and imagine that Jesus is speaking. Jesus is tall but he slouches like Mr. Oswald and always seems ready to laugh at himself; though he's serious, he's also shy.

I told Charley and Pancho that I need to decide what to do when this school year is gone. Charley says I have two choices—one, to do like my brothers, leave the lake,

25

go to college. Danny is still in school in San Francisco, but Mark only made one year and now he's in the army in Germany. Theirs was the active choice, Charley says. The other way is passive, what Pancho calls the Zen choice, to stay at the lake and let the world pick for me rather than trying to force my will upon it. My dad would call that doing nothing.

I could teach skiing. There should be snow soon; the almanac calls for it early this year. I'll ride to the top and take off down the back sides cross-country till I meet a road, then hitch back around to the lifts. It might be dangerous, because there are no worn trails and no telling what's beneath the snow, no telling when there is a gorge or canyon where snow isn't packed and you could fall in, with no one around for miles, and the back slopes sometimes have avalanches.

But my dad says that when your time comes you could be anywhere—in bed, bowling, eating brown rice—and zap, you're dead. Besides, when I'm skiing I feel control over everything, the only time I can call what I want to do and the world will cooperate, rise up where I want and fall where I want. I feel I can jump over hills if they get in my way. I'll ski a lot this winter.

If I don't go away to college my dad will scream that I'm wasting my brains and my mom will moan that all my talent has come to nothing. She thinks I could be a fine painter, but I don't know if I want to try anything that takes such devotion. I wonder what good it would be for me or anyone. Charley says he can't answer; Pancho says I might be forcing something which should just grow. Maggie says to do anything but marry; Paul says that nothing but the Word deserves devotion. If I can find the nerve I'll ask Mr. Oswald.

* * * *
October 23, 1971

Once a railroad climbed Incline Mountain. High-piled flat cars crashed down the slope with lumber for the mill that was on the first meadow up from the lake, by a stream which carried log chips and burned garbage that turned the water brown and foul for a mile down the shore. Thousands of men, including Charley's granddad, worked for years strip logging the forest from the shoreline to the divide, leaving the stumps and logs rotten and the beaches black with soot from the smokestacks.

Walker used to tell us a story about an old man named Lutes, a hunter and trapper Walker's dad had known when he was a boy living in a camp with his Washoe mother. Years later near the mill two Washoes were murdered by loggers and soon afterward one logger was shot by a rifleman. Loggers suspected Washoe revenge but the Washoes blamed it on Lutes, a wild man, and soon the loggers began to find words like "justice" and "God's wrath" branded on trees. They posted guards, organized posses to search the mountains, but found no sign of Lutes; only when they guessed he was dead or gone and dropped the guards did Lutes kill another, dead aim, one shot in the head.

Some loggers quit and others refused to work the high slopes, so the company brought in hired guns from Virginia City. The hired guns played cards and most always won because they had enough silver to bluff the loggers and if they cheated, no one had the nerve to call them. But one night Knute, a friend of Walker's dad, came in from drinking and punched a gunman named McQuarry. McQuarry shot him six times. Walker's dad buried Knute just up the road from where our house is now. In the morning McQuarry was missing and Walker's dad moved away. He took a job with the railroad in Truckee and met Lutes there, an old man living in Chinatown with a Chinese woman. Walker's dad asked him why he killed the loggers at random. Lutes was stoned on opium. Lutes wouldn't talk. The Chinese woman told Walker's dad, "I think he forgot."

Charley told me Walker's stories were true, as far as he knew, because each time he told one it came out the same, no matter how much he had been drinking. My mom used to say that though you didn't know whether to believe the stories, you couldn't accuse him of lying, because it was sure that he believed himself. Mom used to worry about Charley, that Walker couldn't teach him to live in the world the world had become. Mom used to ask Charley to tell her about his mother. Charley said she was slender, with red hands which scratched his skin, and sometimes she'd take him away for a while, days or weeks, he couldn't remember because he was only five when she died.

Charley was my brothers' friend from the day we moved to Incline; he was between their ages, four years older than me, and the only other boy on our dirt road. Even then he was working, though he was only eleven—selling newspapers at a corner in Incline, digging weeds, cutting wood, shoveling snow. My dad admired him, though he despised Walker and wouldn't let him come to our house. But Walker came anyway, to see me or my mom or my brothers, and when dad was home they fought over petty things like my dad claiming that a broken bottle of Walker's punctured his tire, or that Walker's yard was a fire hazard. Walker laughed it off, which infuriated my dad, and sometimes I thought he'd start swinging and I was afraid for them both, because though Walker was much older and slow, there was power about him, an aura of the indestructible.

When Charley had time he played with my brothers, or with me when my brothers were gone or even sometimes when they weren't, which made Mark jealous, so when Charley left Mark would call him a pussy. When my dad was working on some project, like clearing the yard or building shelves, Charley always showed up to help him, while Danny and Mark ran off. In the evenings when Walker was gone Charley would come visit, play basketball in the garage with Danny and Mark, play cards or board games, climb to the roof with me and watch the night and point out landmarks on the far shore. Often he'd stay late, till after I was in bed, till he heard his dad coming home. When I wasn't too tired I stayed awake to listen. The breeze would rustle the tops of the pines, down on the highway a car would pass and when the noise died away I'd hear a whistle from the end of the road, coming closer, then in a grumbling voice:

"In the Big Rock Candy Mountains
you never change your socks,
and little streams of alcohol
come trickling down the rocks.
Lawmen have to kiss your butt
and grocery clerks are blind.
There's a lake of brew, malt liquor, too,
with naked girls to guide you through
the Big Rock Candy Mountains."

That was Walker, who claimed he used to own the lot where our house sat and acres surrounding it; who claimed he had founded the first casino at north Stateline, on a stump by the hot springs, just him dealing poker; who claimed his great-granddad had come to the lake in 1844 and could've staked claim to the whole basin and had the Washoes and Paiutes to back him up, but he wasn't the kind to want to be king.

In the mornings Walker was gruff, dirty, with bulged eyes and the look of a man just knocked on the head, but later in the day he stood tall, was playful and funny, even to the sheriffs who came to his house if there was a burglary around, though they never took him in. Charley said Walker wasn't a thief, that the rich guys told the sheriffs to harass him. Sometimes Walker worked at carving signs or odd jobs, but he was past sixty and called himself retired.

Charley worked more than Walker did, to buy himself clothes, lunches at school, sometimes food for home, anything else he needed, skis, a bicycle. When kids at school made fun of Charley because of his dad he fought and was beat up badly sometimes, but he always told us it was from football or soccer. Once a gang of kids attacked their shack with stones and firecrackers. My dad and my brothers and I ran over to stop it. Charley was outside with a split lip; then he ran away and stayed away. Walker didn't drink for a week, looking for Charley, but he wouldn't call the police. They couldn't have found him. Charley knew the forest too well. He came home on his own.

My folks let me go everywhere with Charley. He was my protector on long hikes up Mount Rose, in the summers to tumble and climb trees and boulders, in the winter to find a free slope we could hike up and ski. I loved and admired him and wanted to grow up to be like Charley, strong and gentle, a hard worker. I saw him as a pioneer, as though he'd been in the mountains since his great-granddad. I thought he knew everything and I told him everything about me—when I had my first period, when my breasts began to grow, when I fell in love with Paul McCartney, hoping Charley would be jealous. He never laughed at me. When I started dating, when I first let a boy feel me up, I told him, hoping he'd think I was old enough for him, but he didn't ask me to shows or dances. Then he was gone, drafted.

When he got the notice he came to me. "Everything I hear about that war tells me I shouldn't go. But if I don't, I'd be an outlaw, watching for some F.B.I. guy who might pull up and snatch me away. Besides—I mean, I know Walker wouldn't know about it unless he gets better. Better . . . yeah. He can't even spit over his chin, but in this I feel I ought to do what he'd want me to do. I bet if I didn't go I'd feel like a coward, like my reasons were just rationalizing, you know what I mean?"

I was a kid and stupid about those things so I said he was right, he should probably go. I thought he'd be a hero. While he was in the army I was the one he wrote to, because he had no brothers or sisters or girl friends and his dad couldn't read anymore. When he needed to bitch, when he needed to talk, when he needed to cry, he wrote to me; from Fort Ord, where he had to repeat basic training because he did time for a night gone without leave; from Fort Polk in some bayous with swamps and water snakes, where they showed films of V.C. traps and lectured on V.C. tortures and Charley said he was one of the few not moved to kill; from An Loc and Pleiku, from patrols where he wrote beneath bridges, stopping to shoot into the brush and never knowing whom he had hit, whom he had killed; twice from hospitals, where he stole morphine Syrettes to take back to base camp; from Sydney, Australia, where he got the crabs. I mailed him almonds and sketches and the easy answers of a fifteen-year-old: that his war wouldn't last, that when he came back things would be just like always, only better; and I sent pictures of me in tight sweaters and swimsuits.

He came home last year with scars on his legs and ribs, and too quiet, as if he was worried or frightened, and always on guard. He drank too much, took pills too often with Paul. Before, he had dreamed of skiing in Peru or of buiding a home with a hundred cherry trees, but now all he wanted was a woman to live with. He didn't come to see me very often and usually I didn't know where to find him. He slept in different places, some on the south shore, and he was gone a lot to San Francisco. He wouldn't tell why he went there, which hurt me, but not nearly as badly as that he didn't ask me out or try to kiss

31

me; I believed he didn't even see me as a woman, though I had filled out and grown up and worked so hard to seem older for him. Then Maggie told me that Charley was buying heroin in San Francisco and selling here what he didn't snort himself. I called him and told him that scared me. He said he wouldn't spike it, for fear of a habit which he couldn't support and stay half-honest, but I told him selling was bad enough, that I already knew a girl younger than me who had gone through withdrawals and now was back shooting again. Charley hung up. A week later I slept with Aaron, Charley's opposite, suave and shrewd, an aristocrat prick.

Next time I saw Charley he had found his woman. She waited tables at Harry's on the south shore. Her name was Maria but she had red hair. She was older than Charley, nearly as tall as Charley, made-up and slinky in high-heeled boots and velveteen tops. Her hips were always squirming. Once when they came to our house she hung like a purse on Charley's arm. My dad took Charley aside and told him to grab his coat and run fast and far, that Maria was a potential shrew or worse, but Charley wouldn't listen; he said she had brains and loyalty, that she came from Detroit, where they all dressed like that. When Charley found a job with the phone company they took an apartment in South Lake, just a few blocks from the hospital where Walker stays. Charley called once to tell me he was happy, again to tell me he was happier, again to tell me he hit a keno jackpot, again to tell me he quit drinking; he drove over to tell me they were having a baby.

Charley wanted to marry but Maria didn't; she claimed she had never missed taking the pill, that a child was the last thing in the world she wanted, that the first was a Volvo and the next a corral full of horses. Her doctor had offered an abortion but Charley went wild, was still wild when he told me. When his dad died he'd have no family, and he had sworn a thousand times he'd never kill anything again, not a stink bug, he said, or a mosquito, but a minute later a spider crawled past and he smashed it in a rage.

He went back to drinking and one afternoon on the job he jumped a light and slammed the rear end of an L.T.D. His blood alcohol was high so the phone company called their insurance void and sued him for $8000. About the same time Maria left him.

★   ★   ★   ★

November 5, 1971

Tonight I went out alone as usual. My dad was complaining because he can't find an easier job. Though he's a foreman, he still has to drive when operators call in sick; he says his guts are loose from thumping around on graders and his organs are scrambled, not to mention his hemorrhoids. My mom thought she'd be happy because she found work in a gallery in Incline, but she comes home nights grumbling, exhausted from smiling all day and praising paintings she'd rather see in a bonfire.

They call me depressed because I don't talk much. My mom asks if I want to see a doctor. They say I'm pale and that I've let myself go because I wear the same jeans and sweat shirt to school every day, because I haven't been sketching and they know I sign my own sick cards some days and hitch to Squaw Valley. Trying to find new excitement, I ski recklessly; I run up the banks and cut back too sharply, leave the slopes and shortcut through the trees. If there were jumps, I'd try them. I lose control, then find my balance. On the weekends I don't pay enough attention. When I reach the lower slopes there are always beginners who chop in front of me or freeze when they see me bearing down; I've sent a lot of them tumbling.

Tonight I hitched to Stateline and walked through

Brockway to King's Beach. There were men drinking wine in the park and I thought of Walker, whom Charlie and I used to find there most every time we went looking. A ski boat was lashed to the pier. A few water skiers keep on through the winter in wetsuits—the lake is too deep to freeze over—and I read of one who skied too far out, got too cold and drowned. I'll try waterskiing some day in the winter.

I walked up to the taco stand for a soda. Across the street was the tavern where Walker used to drink; there was loud country music inside now and a younger crowd. A guy who works on my dad's crew whistled and then waved at me, yelled that I should come over. I waved back and shouted no. Then down a block I saw Mr. Oswald crossing the street and turning into the drugstore. I thought of going down to see him but I was in a mood to be alone with my thoughts, of simpler times before Jill had found other friends and called me boring, before I had to dodge Aaron and his bunch at school. They glared at me as if he had told everything we did and described every lump on my body—the thoughts would have been uglier each time they came back around, if I had let them pass then. So I took my soda and walked back to the pier.

I took off my boots and sat at the end of the pier, dangling my toes in the water that was so cold now it burned all the way up to my knees. Moonlight from behind me carried over my shoulder and glistened on the sand beneath the water, five feet down. In deep shafts of mines in Virginia City, Walker had told us, there was seepage which miners used to think drained through channels from Tahoe. Stories said they found a man in a shaft, drowned and bloated, who had fallen from a boat on the lake. Soundings claimed the lake was deep as the Carson Valley, and engineers who believed they could tame anything searched for the channels, drew plans for drilling and plugging and using the water to work the

34

mines. Walker said one dreamer went down in a diving bell and never came up.

Tires screeched somewhere and my heart began to thump so strongly it seemed to rattle my ribs. I clamped my arms stiff to my sides. Then lights flicked off everywhere and the moon went black. I jerked my feet from the water, tucked them beneath me and scooted back, afraid I'd slip in. I rubbed my eyes, pinched them tight, then opened them. I could see, but blurred, so all the dark colors in the lake, the mountains and the sky, all the blues, blacks, greens, shades of gray, the white lights and yellow lights from Sugarpine and Dollar's Point mixed like spilled oils and ran into one drab brown. I smelled sewage, like what once came from shore drains, and the stinking breeze whirled around me, watered my eyes, caught in my throat till I choked. I stood up dizzily, turned the wrong way, and fell off the pier.

I screamed and grabbed for the planks but my hands slipped each time till my fingers finally caught a knot or crack; I brought my elbows up, but I couldn't pull farther because my legs were numb and too heavy. I thought I was paralyzed. I thought it was a stroke, from clotted veins or God's wrath for something I had done or hadn't. But it was in my mind, I convinced myself, trying to calm myself, but it backfired; it was a more fearful thought, the most fearful, to be toyed with and tugged by some demon in me, not me. No control, no choice. I was frantic. For the first time since church with my grandma in Bellflower, I prayed. Lord, get me out! Lord, take me home! Lord, teach me to swim again! I gave one more pull, scraped my breasts, stabbed a splinter into my side and flopped on the pier face down and sobbed till I heard footsteps. Someone was standing over me, with brown shoes and corduroys, and between his legs King's Beach was bright as ever and the neon blinked above the taco stand.

"Jodi, you're very wet."

"I just fell in, Mr. Oswald. I just fell in, I'm O.K. now."

He made me put on my socks and boots, and he took off my jacket and gave his to me. I asked him to walk with me to Charley's house, only three blocks away. Across the beach, across the highway and around the corner he held my shoulders and walked with his hips against my waist to warm me, because I asked him to. He didn't question me, because he knew I'd tell him just what I wanted, and he knew, because I had told him at school, that I couldn't make sense of my mind these days. At Charley's gate I gave him his jacket. "Mr. Oswald, do you believe in God?"

He shook his head solemnly. "No, Jodi. I've never found a cause to."

Paul and Pancho were gone. Charley was drinking. He made me take a hot bath, called my folks, who said I could stay over because it was Friday night and Charley's truck wasn't running. Maggie loaned me dry clothes. They asked how I had fallen in but I wouldn't tell them much. I wanted to talk to Paul, but when he came he was angry and went to bed. Charley kept drinking and watching me as though sooner or later I'd tell him what had frightened me, but I wouldn't, afraid that after what he had suffered, the war and Maria, he'd think me silly and self-indulgent for letting my nothing troubles push me so far. I was embarrassed to confess how much he had hurt me, and afraid it wouldn't be fair to him. Besides, I was still half-shocked, and found it hard to speak. When he ran out of beer he brought me sheets and blankets, put oak on the fire and stacked nearly enough to burn all night. I'm writing in the kitchen. I won't be able to sleep.

*　　*　　*　　*

The plants, the rocks, they all have their motives. There is no fear, only running, no sorrow, only breathing and death. I have a fern I keep near the stove and sprinkle with water when the air dries. One day I singled out a strand, began to poke it and flick it with my thumb, because it was growing faster than the others. The second day it turned yellow and the third day it died. Its choices were fewer than mine. When a hunter stalks a doe she runs scared, but only because it gives her more speed. And when she drops and looks up puzzled at the hunter she doesn't see death, but she dies, anyway. Everything dies too soon.

Yesterday I was looking for a can of spinach. It wasn't on the shelf as I remembered, so I rummaged through the boxes Charley had brought. There were cans of everything but spinach. I shrugged it off but later I was searching for a sketch I drew of Danny the day Charley told me Danny was engaged. I wouldn't have thrown that away but I couldn't find it, either. Then last night I looked in my journals for an entry remembering my first trip to Marlette Lake, an hour's climb from the cabin, from where I can pass to the divide and stare down across Carson Valley; but the wind is so damnably strong and the ground so slick with ice that I don't go there anymore.

That day at Marlette, five years ago, Danny and Mark were fishing with bait and my dad was trying flies. I dug a channel back to denser ground, thinking I'd make mud to pack on my arms and legs to keep off mosquitoes. But a few inches down I dug up the charred rocks of a fire ring and a skin lashed with rawhide. Inside were a handful of pinion nuts turned black and hard as pebbles, only a half inch high but etched with tiny faces in the finest lines, round noses and notches for ears. I guessed it was

37

magic and I ran them down to my dad. "The work of a bored Indian," he said, so I wrapped them back in the pouch and didn't show them to anyone else for fear they wouldn't be excited.

I checked each date in my journals twice, but the pages were gone. With all these things missing I decided there could be a thief, someone hiding out like me in a cabin as hard to find or a cave or the shaft of a half-dug, never-worked mine. The air was restless, as if someone were near. I tied up my robe, took up my hatchet and slipped outside. There was no moon and only the tops of the trees were in starlight. I climbed the hill, scanning the brush, the meadow, the far hill for movement, but only the leaves quivered in the wind, softer than most nights. I called hello, then cussed myself for giving up cover. Something rattled on the far hill, rumbled, then thumped on the road.

I wasn't afraid. What used to be fear was apathy now since the trembles and the cold in my fingers and the lumps like choking on meat became customary, like fingernails, like insect bites I wouldn't scratch. Once my grandma told me that when we've lived all we care to, the pain turns to irritation and passion gives way to mild curiosity. She called it peaceful, but I can't, because moments of hope come back, hope for a love, hope for a faith, hope for a change of heart and a will to go back down the mountain. I have hope in the nights before Charley comes; then I bundle and sweat, refuse to sleep because the dreams are too hard to decipher, and things without meaning are torment to me.

In dreams my mother paints flowers, then paints them again when they fall from the canvas. Danny buys cocaine, then pours it like salt on a sandwich. Phillip flies airplanes to seed the clouds with stones; he has nosebleeds, a dog and a shaggy beard. Maggie diapers Bambi with clothes I left in King's Beach and the baby burps blue steam. Condors and parrots roost in the meadow and mailmen come to my door with boxes of fruit. Sometimes I dream myself waking up, walking laps around the cabin, then dream myself back to sleep.

On the nights before Charley comes I refuse to watch those things. I burn tall candles, watch their shadows on the wall, and make up my own dreams in which I laugh with Charley, race him to bed, and we wrestle and pinch and draw so together that I see myself through his eyes, and I'm lovely, not a hag anymore. I ask him about Maggie's baby and Phillip's beard and he says it's all true, so it doesn't need to mean anything. I tell him he's too soft, so I stuff him in my mouth and blow him up like a balloon. Then I'm ashamed. But when I hear him come up the path and he steps inside, his arms full and his pack loaded with all that I asked him to bring, I can't laugh or remember how we used to feel. I treat him like a delivery man. He's too good for me to love.

I raised my hatchet and kept to the path because my feet were bare. Thin ice cracked too loudly. The creek was high from the rains and the bank was slippery. I found the thing that had rolled, a stone as big and round as a soccer ball and grown over with wiry moss. I sat on the stone and buried my feet in the mud to warm them. A meteor crossed the sky above Emerald Bay; another came from the north, dropping, and fell so near it seemed I could hear it crash. I wondered if it was really that close, or could still even be on fire. I ran back to the cabin for boots and warmer clothes, filled a thermos with tea and decided I'd chase the meteor, since I wouldn't sleep anyway because Charley would be up in the morning.

There were no clouds or snow though it's already November. On the road I had to stop every few steps to kick off the mud. Up the hill and down along the creek nothing moved but the water and leaves. A mist rolled up from the basin, high at first so the stars showed dimly, then crawling up the ground as if the earth steamed, until there was nothing but me and where I stepped. I could've been anywhere, in Alaska, in Norway, drifting on the Arctic Sea. I might step on the star any moment and be burned through the soles of my boots, or be ravaged by a pack of timber wolves. It was all the same. My flashlight glared back off the mist and into my eyes.

It will be like this in the final days, I thought, when everyone runs wild and no one can see a thing. Their eyes will be hooded and their flesh hot as fire, their sins tied around their feet like balls and chains, all of them screaming to die and longing to kill, insane and bitter because their hearts will be judged wicked and none will know why or remember a time when she might've changed. They'll remember the times when they asked for the Lord and the Lord chose not to answer. Their hatred will swell with righteousness and if they're allowed a last word they'll swear they were framed.

I stopped at the high point where the road branched. I knew that down the bank was the aspen grove, where the leaves were softer than beneath the pines. I slid down blindly, scuffed across to where the trees began, poured tea, and lay down and sipped it slowly. Dampness seeped through my jeans and warmed inside them. I closed my eyes, willing to sleep if it came, but I was startled up by a sneeze close by. I shifted to my knees and crawled backward. Out of the mist an old woman hobbled.

Her neck was long, her trunk bundled in men's shirts with rolled-up sleeves. The top bands of a dozen shirts made her waist immense and a sugar sack was tied to it by a rope belt. She cleared her throat, spit and lit a rusted lantern. Her hair was black, tangled and caked with tar, and her nose was sharp and broken. She kicked a clearing in the leaves, then stepped out of sight. I burrowed into the mulch and waited, but she came around behind and nearly stepped on me. I knew she saw me, but she kept on to her clearing, gathering twigs; then she fired

40

them off. Her eyes were dull amber and her loud skirts were charred at the hems.

She folded her legs, sat by the fire and reached beneath her skirts for some tiny dolls as tall as a hand, fashioned from sticks, dry grass and pinions. While the fire burned down she wove pine needles into pencil-sized spears, stacked them in her lap, then hung the dolls on sticks in a circle around the fire. One by one she lit the spears, lit a doll with each spear, so they sputtered, flamed, and collapsed to the coals.

The fog rolled over her and I ran for the bank, up to the road and far enough till I felt safe; I rested and wondered. When my grandpa died he was sitting by a window. He called my grandma and told her he saw a light. He pointed outside and said the light was burning for him, then he fell off his chair. For weeks my grandma came back to the window and stared at each light, trying to find the one, but there were thousands of lights outside that window.

It was nearly dawn, I guessed, and Charley was probably packing already. The fog was thinning, as it does toward morning, and I hurried along. The wind had switched and blew from the southwest and I could hear a truck backfire, perhaps on the south pass to Carson. I was proud and excited, having lasted the night and seen the old woman.

Back at the cabin I lit the stove, stripped and put on the robe I always wore for Charley. Then I lay down and thought about him, remembered him tan and strong the summer before he was drafted, when he took me along cutting firewood from dead trees off the back roads behind King's Beach, when he was grown up and smart with ideas about saving money to buy a lot and build a house of his own, a patient house, doweled and thick-walled, with windows and porches where the sun rose and set. I was fourteen and I loved him. He let me use his chain saw, steadied it for me, whistled a song, picked me up high. When I was sad he'd tickle me till I smiled.

I met him at the door and took a box he was carrying. He kissed my cheek and told me my eyes were swollen. "I was up all night," I said. "I went up the mountain to look for a meteor, but instead there was an old woman in the aspen grove. She burned dolls, Charley. She was big with black hair and bare feet. She might be a gypsy. There could be gypsies here. Pancho said he saw gypsies in Mexico, big women with their own language and covered wagons. He said they had lots of gold teeth, but this one didn't have any teeth."

"You should look out, then," Charley winked. "I heard gypsies can steal your underpants off you while you're standing up."

"Then I won't wear underpants. Charley, can you go to my folks' house and get into my bedroom again? In the closet shelf, on the far north end, toward the window, there's a little pouch with a rawhide string. I want to see it. You know that gypsy might be stealing. There are things missing that I'm sure were here."

"What things?"

"The canned spinach you brought me and some pages from my journal, and a sketch I drew of Danny when you told me he was engaged."

He slipped out of his pack and sat on the floor. I brought him tea while he stared at me. It felt good, having someone stare. I wanted to know what he'd been feeling and how he was living, where he was working and if he saw much of his son, my first unselfish questions in weeks.

I sat down beside him. He put his hands on my knee. "When was Danny engaged?"

"I don't know," I said. "You told me about it. You said you were there when he told our folks."

Charley shook his head. "I haven't even seen Danny, Jodi, and I didn't bring any spinach. You must be mixing

42

real stuff up with your dreams. Everybody does that sometimes."

I stomped to the door and kicked it open for him, "You're lying, Charley! I can tell what's a dream!"

★   ★   ★   ★

December 12, 1971

Last Saturday there were snow flurries and a bitter wind, so Squaw Valley wasn't crowded. Beneath the new fall was hard fast ice. While the wind was downhill I made a dozen runs; then it shifted opposite so I decided to try the back, down to a road from where I could hitch home.

There was a full storm on the way; the clouds were darkening, and the snow came heavier and wet so it slapped hard against my face. With the new snow covering landmarks, it was useless to look for a trail, but any way down there would be some road. My legs were sore and my back stiff from skiing hard all day. Ahead clouds split to show a flare, like sunset, though it didn't seem that late. There was a cedar grove straight ahead, so I slowed and snowplowed through it, turned with my poles and bumped over branches, then sidestepped up a hill. Below was the green roof of a cabin and smoke from a chimney, which meant a road close by. The slope was gentle and the clearing wide, a summer pasture. I pushed off strongly, used my poles till I was running so fast the snow popped loud against me. I thought of stopping at Charley's and asking him to come up tomorrow, to kick off his moodiness; I'd offer to pay for his ticket and we'd race all day for dinner and I'd even let him win.

I hit something beneath the snow. I flipped head first, rolled on my shoulder. My bindings broke free but my foot caught in ice and my leg tore all the way from the hip; then I skidded and stopped, angry and hurting. The first time I stood up I fell; then I braced my leg rigid and

43

dragged back up for my skis. Downhill I used my skis for a crutch. My ankle and knee hurt so badly that I moaned loudly to try to make it a joke, but it hardly worked. There were drifts waist deep where I fell, and ice packed down my sweater. I was tired to death of everything going wrong.

When I came near the cabin a dog ran out howling at me, and a woman was waiting at the door. She gave me shots of bourbon and cookies and let me call my dad. He yelled at me because I had promised him a hundred times not to go off the back of the hill. The woman made coffee and spiked it; told me her husband had run off for Texas saying his mother was dying, what he said every year, and when he came back winter would be over and her savings gone. She said her son was my age and she asked for my phone number so he could call me and meet me skiing, but I said I wouldn't be skiing for a while. My dad came with blankets and made me wrap up; then he carried me to the car. I thought he was angry but he turned up the heater, tore my pantleg and kissed my red swollen knee. At the hospital he hassled the nurses because we had to wait so long; he followed along to X-rays and into the room where the doctor told how ligaments healed very slowly. He watched all the time they fitted my cast and let it dry, from my toes to above my knee.

For three days I moped in the house. My dad bought me crutches but I refused to go to school. When my mom came home at lunch I was on the couch thinking I was hateful and my heart was ugly, I had nothing to lighten my life, nothing to care about. When my dad came home in the evenings I was still there. I refused to cook or help with anything, said my leg hurt when I moved. I took about ten Darvons a day, pounded on the cast because my leg hurt beneath it, and made my dad help me upstairs. At night I took more Darvon and lay awake staring at the frosted window, on dream trips to ice castles

44

where witches kept reptiles and the antlers of bucks were poison, and out in the field was a man frozen, whom I would bring in and thaw by the fire.

Wednesday evening Charley came over. I guessed my mom had called him. He said we could go for a drive around the lake and my dad offered his car because the cab of Charley's truck was too cramped for my cast. Charley stopped for a six-pack and he asked me what I'd heard from Mark and Danny, how my leg felt, how long I'd have the cast, what I'd do now for thrills, more questions, about boyfriends, about Aaron, about school, but I only answered briefly and told him to speed up. He did, on the high turns west from South Lake, before the road to Fallen Leaf, till it was slick and dangerous. I told him to speed up more, but he pulled off and took my hand. "Jodi," he said, "I know you've got troubles, and I know I have for a long time. They seem worse than most people's because they really are, because we let them be, because we don't want to miss out on anything. But I swear to God it's better that way, because one day we'll be so strong that nothing can take us down, maybe twenty or forty years from now, or tomorrow, and the worst that any trouble can do is make the day come sooner."

I told him he was up to his ears in bullshit, so he laughed and yanked my seatbelt tighter and tore off the last forty miles to his house at King's Beach, where I told him I'd stay. He was working graveyard at Harry's and still had to dress and drop off my dad's car. Maggie was watching the news. She was just beginning to show pregnant. When Paul came in and flipped off the television without asking, Maggie got mad and went to her room. I called Paul a fascist but he said that Maggie would spend her life at the television if he let her, that he didn't like to be stern but he didn't know how else to stop her. His voice and his manner were so much softer since he had found Jesus, compared to his blustering ways on pills. His voice made his words sound true.

He asked if I'd like him to read; then he opened his Bible to Psalms. I sank into the corner of the couch, searching for a hiding place. I knew he was trying to win me, same as always, but now I was falling into terror as I had on the pier, defenseless, frightened that the next moment would find me drowning in the power of something which might be good or evil or neither but no way would it be me, some devil instead, in a stolen body and stolen mind. The back of my neck seemed on fire and my breathing went fast and shallow. The cast on my leg was a ball and chain. If I'd had both legs I'd have run for sure.

" 'Let your eyes look directly forward, and your gaze be straight before you. Take heed to the path of your feet.' "

I was afraid to look up, believing there were two great Gods standing over me, two fathers, beseeching, threatening, looking upon me with love and repulsion. My fingers turned cold and I needed to touch something to make sure it was there. I grabbed the couch, then pressed on the sides of my head, then folded my hands.

" 'For the lips of a loose woman drip honey, and her speech is smoother than oil; but in the end she is more bitter than wormwood, sharp as a two-edged sword.' "

I cried from fear, from exhaustion, from three days of Darvon, from the pain in my leg and the shame of having fallen for Aaron. Of all the boys I knew he was the last I should've valued, stinking of pride and greed. But crying did no good. I still felt the heat from above me, the pressure of hands trying to pull me up, and I was no match, I had no choice, I had to pick one or the other and give myself away.

Paul took me by the shoulders. "Try Jesus, Jodi," he said, "He loves you the most. The other is darkness forever," as though he could read my mind.

I leaned into his hands and he laid me softly on the floor, face down, because I couldn't kneel. He stood praying silently.

"I'm sorry," I whispered. "Jesus. Please make me well."

Paul bowed over me and pressed down my head with his hands. " 'In distress you called, and I delivered you; I answered you in the secret place of thunder.' "

Now in the days I read the Bible, though my mom cocks her head comically and my dad says I should do schoolwork and leave the Bible for nuns. At nights I talk to Jesus and He answers in gusts of wind and the vision He gives me to see through the dark and the woods to the lake and the stars. Tomorrow I'll go back to school.

* * * *

December 22, 1971

I'm dying for this cast to come off so I can move freely again, jump and run and bend just even walk. But even so, I'm thankful for the accident now and I haven't missed skiing. I've stayed home and read the whole Bible, Job twice, and I've spent the last week on Revelation; the horseman and Babylon and all the numbers keep me awake puzzling, angry as if it were a foreign novel with the last page untranslated. Paul has codes he's taken from books, and Pastor Sandoz at the Community Church refers back to Daniel and clears up some things, but even he still has questions about Revelation.

Mr. Oswald is kind to me. Because of my leg I'm excused from gym, so I go to his classroom, and at lunch I go again to avoid the cafeteria and the tables outside where my old friends are talking of dates, parties, gossiping, things I don't do anymore. If I sit with any of them we're all uneasy and if I sit alone I feel them watching. I believe they're talking about me, and kids from church or the Campus Life club come up and greet me with beatific smiles and talk of silly crap like car washes and ice cream socials; last year some of them were eating speed and brawling. Now they try to act innocent, virginal, meek.

So I eat lunch in Mr. Oswald's room, read my Bible or the books he loans me, poems about Christ and the mysteries, blasphemous books by Blake and Coleridge and Whitman, who suffered and thrilled more than I think I ever will, books which Paul calls dangerous, because faith and knowledge, he tells me, come just from the literal scriptures. Mr. Oswald listens to me talk if I need to; if I have questions he's there. He brings me chairs to prop my leg, and when he goes to the lounge or snack bar he always brings me a doughnut, an orange or coffee. He's a wonderful man, not peculiar, scatterbrained or timid or any of the things the kids call him. He's thirty years old, slim and pale, with soft cheeks, one eye bluer than the other, a high forehead beginning to wrinkle. His clothes are old but neat, tab-collared white shirts and thin ties, too formal for here, and loose as if he had once been heavier. Because he doesn't hide his love for books and passionate expression of feelings, kids say he's gay or castrated and they mimic his speech, the way he stutters and his voice cracks when he's reading verses or stories so vivid I can lay my head on my arms and dream, above the whispers and giggles around me, of a world where tongues are soft and truthful, where people touch in kindness and law is notched on each heart in words of clear meaning. I can watch Mr. Oswald and see through his eyes that our worlds are the same at those moments. But kids ignore him, laugh over nothing to make him feel foolish, and play cruel tricks.

The Monday before Christmas break he brought in a record of, "The Rime of the Ancient Mariner." The spell it cast over me, the mystery of purification through sin and repentence, stayed with me all day. In sixth period when I came into class Mr. Oswald was off on an errand and a crowd was around the record player, Jerry in the center doing something. Jerry is a wrestler and Aaron's best friend. His dad builds homes to look like German inns, his mother is on the school board and Jill has been his girl friend lately. He's homely, to me, with thin red hair and a freckled nose always raw from fights or peeling from the sun, but Jill says he keeps her laughing and buys her pendants. Someone shouted and I watched Jerry stuff something into his pocket.

Mr. Oswald passed around Christmas cookies he had bought to make it a special day. He told us to note how the orchestra complemented and counterpointed the poem, how the musical drama rose to prepare for the verbal statement; when he set on the needle it slipped to the label. Around the room there was tittering and hysterical snorts. He brushed off the needle but it slid across again, so he touched the record, picked it up and reached for his handkerchief to wipe it, but it slipped from his fingers and cracked on the floor.

"Aw, shit," Jerry said, "it busted. So what'll we do now?"

Mr. Oswald set the pieces of the record away, then walked to Jerry's seat. I had never seen him angry before, his face flushed and his eyes set hard, his shoulders tight and bent.

"Hey," Jerry said, "I'll tell you what happened, because I'd hate you to think unkindly on us. You know I'm nearsighted, well I picked up the record to read what it was. I must've had oil on my hands, from auto shop you know."

Around me were muted giggles and everyone stared and waited tensely. I had never thought I'd do what I did. "Look in his pocket," I said. "His jacket."

Jerry turned on me. "Fucking born-again snitch!"

Mr. Oswald grabbed him by the shirt. Stunned, Jerry stood up.

"It's my friend's record," Mr. Oswald whispered. He reached for Jerry's pocket, then jerked his hand back and pointed.

49

Jerry pulled out a squirt-can of oil. "Hey I didn't know the record would break, man. You're the one that dropped it. So I'll buy a new one."

Mr. Oswald fingered the oil, then aimed the spout at Jerry's pocket, at the letter with a wrestler, a football and two all-league pins. He squirted the can empty. Jerry watched, bewildered, then knocked the can from Mr. Oswald's hand and ran out of the room. Mr. Oswald turned back to his table, covered his eyes with his hands for a moment, then picked up his book and began to read aloud, too loud, almost shouting, stammering once. I noticed his hands were shaking.

At times like these Jesus is nearest, I thought, a father, a brother, not to punish but to hear out my guilt, though my guilt from snitching was foolish and sinful. Jesus was a lover to wrap me in silk and bathe me in a cold spring. With the class staring at me, hateful because I'd turned Jerry in, Jesus took me away to the sweet land where I didn't need words to tell my burdens, where they lifted and fled like bright day clouds, and I could pray unselfishly for people most precious, like Mr. Oswald.

He dismissed the class early though it was against the rules. Then he stuffed his books in his briefcase, stared for a while at the record which seemed to mean so much to him, and started to leave without noticing I was still in the room. He looked so desperate I called to him impulsively, not knowing what I'd say.

"Mr. Oswald. Can we talk?"

"Oh." He turned around, startled. "Surely, Jodi. I thought I was alone."

"Um, you live on Fox Street, right?"

"Yes."

"Which house?"

"Across from the church. The green house, green where the paint still holds."

"The little house?"

"The very little house."

"That's the church where I go. I'm there a lot, and to Bible studies at Charley's—remember where you helped me to that night?"

"Then we're neighbors."

"Mr. Oswald. Whose record was that?"

"It belonged to Biff. Mr. Beavers. Jodi, it's not—it wasn't the record. You know that, and it wasn't even the disruption of class or the fact that it showed how few people appreciated—I don't have the right to expect anyone to appreciate what we do in class. It was the cruelty, Jodi. Do you understand? You do, I know." He leaned on the table and rubbed his eyes, then watched me and shook his head as though bringing me back into focus. "God, I feel so despicable. Why did I lose my patience? Jerry still has the world to impress, so why should I care if I'm the butt of his jokes?"

"It's not you—he hassles all the teachers. I think you did the right thing. I don't know about me. I never snitched on anyone before."

"That was my fault, too."

"No, and it doesn't matter. I decided I was your friend, not Jerry's. I guess sometimes we have to do things we're not sure are right, I mean because we have to decide whose side we want to be on. Don't you think so?"

He smiled honestly, humbly, nodded, then stood up and fetched my crutches. We walked down the hall together, him scuffing ahead of me to rough up the slick freezing sidewalk, me swinging long hops against the wind. He asked if I needed a ride but I said no, that it was all downhill to my home. It was as close as I could come to running, and I needed to run, to cut myself free from studying like a monk and feel myself part of the world with all its stupid complexities, all its troubles and pettiness, feel I was more than a blunt one-sided thing. And I believed Jesus would understand. That night, for the first time this year, I looked forward to the next day at school.

There is a plan to reorganize the English department, with reading labs and writing labs for freshmen and kids who can't pass the tests, and electives for the rest of us. I've heard arguments in the faculty lounge, all the teachers taking sides, some calling electives frivolous, some saying parents would scream, some believing the labs would cost too much. On my regular run for Mr. Lopez's coffee—he put a strap on a thermos so I can carry it from my shoulder—I watched Coach Bracken leaning on the sinkboard, one eye down Miss Loftus's low-cut top, the other eye on her face politely.

"Waterman!" he scowled. "If I hear another word about moral decay, defiling the classics, filth from Hollywood, I'll glue her tongue to her dentures."

Miss Loftus nodded. "Oswald's against the plan, too."

"Not Phil?"

"So says Waterman." Miss Loftus noticed me listening. "Yes, Miss McGee?"

"Coffee," I said, filled the thermos and left. I wanted to tell Mr. Oswald, though I still felt guilty about snitching and I wondered if he'd think I was spying. But I was sick of the rumors about him, of kids snickering behind his back, of Jerry boasting outside class that morning that Oswald wouldn't cross him again. By third period I decided I should warn him. I stopped at the door when I heard Miss Waterman.

"So under the plan I'm to choose electives. What shall I choose? Shall I bone up on science fiction, read gothics, study the Beatles and hail them as poets? Or I could take folk-singing lessons. Do I look like Joan Baez? Mr. Oswald, just how many students will sign up for my class in Spenser, or the Romantic poets? How many students will take any class I offer? I don't believe we should cater to them. I believe we are guides, I do, not entertainers."

She huffed out past me and walked to her room, left him staring after her, glumly, slouching forward from the table.

"Mr. Oswald?"

"Yes, Jodi?"

"Um, Mr. Oswald, I—"

"Something's wrong, Jodi? I haven't noticed you speechless before."

"Um, I heard—you know I go to the faculty lounge for Mr. Lopez, well today I was there and I heard some teachers talking, they said you were against the elective thing next year and if that's true well the kids and everybody will be down on you, and if, well if I knew your reasons I could stick up for you because, I mean if I heard them talking, because I want to and maybe they'd understand."

His hand reached out, then dropped, and he stood up and walked to the window and stared out. The bell had just rung and kids were beginning to gather. "I don't expect to be understood," he said too loudly, like a curse.

I thought he meant to be condescending and it hurt me so, I picked up my books and started for the door, but he stopped me. "Jodi—I'd love to be understood, but I'm no different from anyone else. I try not to care anymore."

"But you said I could be your friend."

He blushed and looked down. "All right. But keep it to yourself. It's only Miss Waterman. The plan may do good things, bad things or nothing—I'm willing to try. It's so damned insignificant, all this. But she feels a fool, outdated and useless. She needs at least one friend, too. I think it will pass without my vote. I'm certain it will." He watched me for a moment, then turned shyly, flipped through a stack of papers I had graded and rubbed his neck.

I told him, "Charley says friends are a pain in the ass."

He slapped the desk and laughed meekly. I wanted to

hold him, my friend and my teacher, so wise and unselfish, so precious.

* * * *

January 16, 1972

There were secrets whispering around our house before Christmas and I wondered what gift they thought would excite me. My grandma came up from Lodi, where she had moved, and each night my dad called Danny to ask him when he was coming home. Danny always said "tomorrow," and when he didn't show up my dad called back and accused him proudly of having too many women. Dad sat me in his chair by the tree, gave me the job of sorting and hooking the ornaments and asked me to check each one from my angle as he hung them.

On Christmas morning he was up cooking breakfast, the first time all year, and as soon as I swallowed my coffee he led me out to the tree. My package was small. While I opened it he told me his news. He had found a job in Reno, selling graders and snowplows, and in a few months he could work from the lake. I supposed he meant to drive down there each day, an hour even when the roads were clear, and I stopped unwrapping and stared at him, baffled that he could be happy at such a hassle and such long days as he'd have to spend. The pay would be lower at first, he said, till his commissions came in, but he'd be his own man and travel as far north as Redding and in six months he'd be rid of his hemorrhoids, driving a company car instead of the damned Caterpillars and backhoes. Then he watched me thoughtfully while he said we'd all live with Rosie, my mom's divorced sister, in her big house in Reno. I dropped the package. He picked it up, reached it out to me, said I'd have my own room and I could finish the

54

year at Mount Rose, drive up every day as soon as my cast came off.

"I won't move to Reno. It's a pit, and school isn't all I do up here. Why don't you drive down? Why are you dragging us down there?"

"Open the box," he said.

I sat down and opened it. There were black leather gloves, fur lined and snug.

"They're driving gloves," he said grinning. "We'll buy you a car."

I didn't want a car. I didn't like to drive, all wrapped up inside a hunk of metal, not like skiing, where you can feel the air. He wouldn't buy me a motorcycle. Besides I didn't want any big gifts; what I own I should earn myself or I'd think myself spoiled, feel like a rich kid.

I kissed him grudgingly, then dragged up the stairs to my room and sat on my bed swallowing bitterness. Reno to me was as bad as Los Angeles, as far as Tibet. Nothing was green in Reno; curbs and drenched lawns and sidewalks and windows were everywhere, huge windows and chrome with the sun gleaming off like buildings on fire. Nothing was holy in Reno. Everything my dad had done for us seemed erased, because it was all here at the lake. Home was as much part of our family as he or I, like a pact which bound us together. And the months we'd be gone seemed ages or forever because if I chose to go to college I'd be leaving as soon as we came back home. I heard him downstairs bellowing, his Christmas ruined, his family split, cussing Danny for not coming home and me for being stubborn and thoughtless. My grandma yelled back, about friends I must hate to leave, but he said I didn't have any since I took up the Bible.

There was a hush. Then I heard him on the stairs. "Jodi, we'll be here every weekend."

I hobbled to the door and squeezed him, small in his

arms and sorry for my selfish thoughts. "Dad, can't I stay at Charley's?"

Charley's room was largest because of the deck out into the back yard. My dad paid for the lumber and helped Charley frame it and wall it off, divide the room and cut my door from the kitchen. Charley worked all day and only caught short naps before his shifts at Harry's. My dad trusts me now, because of the Bible he says mockingly, and he trusts Charley, thinks he'll take care of me.

The house is old, with asphalt siding and tar patches on the roof, a porch out front and big rooms, and the yard would have a place for a garden if we cleared the debris from the firewood Charley cuts and sells. I have a desk in my room, a bent rod with a curtain for a closet, a dresser and a bunk bed which my dad hauled up from our basement. At night Maggie comes in, when she has fought with Paul or she's just lonely. He made her let down the hems in some of the maternity dresses he bought her at the thrift shop, and for Christmas he bought her a one-piece terry-cloth bathing suit with shoulder straps and heavy cups. If she's gone when he comes home from work he tramps off angrily, and he expects her to cook fine meals on ten dollars a week.

When I think of my folks, when it hits me I'm on my own, I'm proud at first, then as puzzled as after I first slept with Aaron. It's as if I've left something behind which I can't retrieve, or as if I've come a thousand miles since yesterday and ahead is a world of prairies, badlands and creatures who starve in the night, as well as freedom. I think about freedom, try to decide what all it means. I can walk out anytime, at 3:00 A. M., and no one will ask me where I'm going. I could lock my room and cry alone for days, or take pills and die but no one would have the right to come in and save me unless I asked him to. Freedom could be dreadful, so I need to be strong, but I'm afraid for the people I love. I wish they all knew Jesus, for protection.

Sometimes Charley wakes me in the mornings when he's home from his shift; then we go to the kitchen and I make coffee while he drinks malt liquor. Now his biggest problem is money, so that's what he talks about most. Maria was fired when her pregnancy showed; he pays her $150 each week and he'll have to forever or she'll move to Detroit or somewhere else where he'll never see his baby when it's born. He takes all the overtime he can, most every night now with big crowds up for skiing. He hates dealing, standing still throwing aces to the rich folks and regulars while the ones who come in from Kansas with dreams and nerves slump away broke, because he deals them wrong—unless he cheats, which he says he's learning to do.

The first morning he was surly, so I kissed his forehead. He only scowled. "More doctor bills, Jodi. How can a young guy owe so much money?"

"Did you see Maria?"

"Yeah. She's over every night drinking when I come on and she stays till nobody'll buy her more drinks or this bald fucker takes her home. The baby'll come out pickled with Kahlua and drowned in raspberry douche."

I cut him some raisin bread but he took off for the back yard, so I followed him out. He was standing by the woodpile with his ax. "What do you think, Jodi? Armed robbery, kidnapping or both? Your dad has guns—does he have a pistol I could stash under my belt?"

"Let's run down to the beach, Charley. I bet I can beat you on crutches."

"Bring Paul, too, so I can drown him."

"What'd he do now?"

"Aw, the asshole doesn't miss a night saying where drinking will get me. I'm fed up with his lip. I don't need another conscience. The one I've got bitches at me enough. You won't turn into a saint, will you?"

I laughed and handed him bread. He washed it down with the last of his can, then threw the can and set a foot-wide log on its end. He raised the ax above the eaves of the deck, then slammed it down. The log split like a carrot and Charley grabbed another.

"Paul Bunyan," he said. "No. Lizzy Borden."

Last Tuesday my cast came off. My calf was clammy-white and skinny and it's still painful up the back of my leg when I walk. The doctor told me to keep using crutches for a while but I won't. I left my crutches at my folks' house, after seeing the doctor in Incline; then I hitched back to King's Beach with a banjo player who was coming to visit Pancho. After dinner Paul found Maggie smoking with them, so he dragged her from the shed to their room and soon she came running outside screaming. I caught up to her at the gate, limping, feeling crippled and caged, angry at myself for allowing self-pity.

"Damn him, Jodi! He throws everything at me at once, about God, and he says I'm killing my baby's brain cells. I only took a couple hits. I just wanted to do something I'm not supposed to. I hate him!"

While we walked down the block she kept looking back at the house. "Maggie," I said, "remember last year we just thought about parties and being pretty and what our folks would do if they knew all the stuff we did? Now it's all different and next year will be different, too. I think next year you'll love the baby so much you can ignore Paul, and maybe he'll be more mellow by then, not bother you all the time."

"Maybe he'll be gone," she said. "Sometimes I believe in God, Jodi, but I won't tell Paul because I hope he thinks I'm a heathen, so he'll have an excuse to leave me. Sometimes I hate this baby. Sometimes I think when it's born I should give it to Paul."

She turned up the street to her mother's house and I kept walking, down the block to the church steps across

58

the street from Mr. Oswald's. In his front room Mr. Oswald crossed past the window, then came back and sat down. There was a weird rush up my spine like water up the pipe of a well, and with it the thought that I hoped to God I never turned harsh as Paul, but that was nothing to pray for, that was for Jesus to decide. Behind me, leaning on me, was the church, Pastor Sandoz behind in his quarters, writing a sermon, looking up answers for counseling, or matching his logic against Revelation to fit it all in, to tell us all, so we could all believe. Across the street was Mr. Oswald with his nose in some other book looking for the same peace and fury. Both of them want the truth and the passion to find it and live it, no matter how hard it may be. Both of them want to believe they are living rightly, trying to help the world rather than tear it apart and chew it up to feed their pride.

Mr. Oswald might be reading one of the books he had loaned me, perhaps William Blake in *Marriage of Heaven and Hell*: "Those who restrain desire do so because theirs is weak enough to be restrained," which I worry might be true, because I don't believe, as Blake did, in the goodness of hell, and my desire is not weak enough to be restrained without help from the Holy Spirit. As I grow nearer to Jesus I feel the rising of passion, which I used to burn up running in the woods, going to parties, swimming, skiing, telling frenzied long stories to my girl friends, and dreaming. The way a starved man craves food or a nymphomaniac wants sex, I want everything, to be high all the time. Paul says it's Satan blocking my way. Pastor Sandoz said if I pray sincerely and follow God's word I can't go wrong, but the Word is hard and doesn't allow much for passion.

Thinking all this, realizing the sin in my desires, I still wanted to stand behind Mr. Oswald's chair, watch him turn the page, hear him sigh and watch him fold the book reverently and stack it away, then tell me the words he had found and what in them was true. I wanted to believe him, though it might be sin and blasphemy with cunning and godless poets like wolves in sleek winter coats. And I wanted to touch him.

I pushed myself back home. In Pancho's shed I sat beside the banjo player. When he slid up against me my skin quivered and tightened and I wanted so badly to stay, to smoke with him or drink Charley's malt liquor, turn hot and outrageous, so stoned I'd just do what I wanted, but instead I ran into the house, into my room and climbed into bed dressed. Paul knocked and asked about Maggie but I said I didn't know. I turned my Bible to a dog-eared page and tried to read, but the words were just letters in lines, no meaning. I tried other pages but they were all the same. Next to pride, Pastor Sandoz had said, lust was our deepest wound.

★ ★ ★ ★

January 30, 1972

Friday I mentioned to Mr. Oswald that William Blake said Jesus was holy because he acted impulsively, against the laws, but I wondered how did we know which impulse came from God and which from Satan. Mr. Oswald said that to Blake in this life there was no soul or God divorced from the body or Satan. For the rest of the day I felt my body, the little tinglings, the soft pressures and pains I usually didn't notice, the little creaks in my joints when I moved, tensions in my hand or jaw.

Blake said Jesus broke most all the commandments. Then he gave examples—Jesus mocking the sabbath and murdering those who were murdered because of him. But Jesus didn't break the sixth commandment, adultery. Adultery and love walk together so often. By evening I was thinking hard, trying to distinguish between love of God and love of men, but each seemed to follow from each; I tried to distinguish between innocent love and lust, but the two so often merge and collide. By time for the Bible study I couldn't think about the end of the world, I was worried about that night. I couldn't concentrate, so when Paul asked me questions I had to tell him to repeat them and then try to bluff the answers.

Afterward I walked to Mr. Oswald's house, but the lights were out there. I was relieved because I would not have known what to say, not known what he was thinking of me. It was hard to tell; he was kind to everyone. I sat on the church steps wondering why I was drawn toward him. For sure it was partly his gentleness, his brains, his reverence for books and ideas. For sure I believed he was poor in spirit, mournful, meek, thirsting for righteousness, merciful, pure in heart and a peacemaker, the first seven beatitudes, but there had to be more, or else I might just respect him but wouldn't want to be with him late at nights, wanting to use him for sin. I wondered as I watched his house if his loneliness appealed to me, if I also wanted to be a hermit right here in town like him, one no one dropped in on and no one tried to change; his life seemed orderly compared to mine, freer of chaos, freer of impulse and whimsy, freer in so many ways. But I knew he didn't see himself so; he was troubled as anyone else, though I believed he accepted trouble, knew how to live in spite of it. And he's handsome in a sheepish way, a delicacy in his features and the way he looks overwhelmed sometimes, like Phillip the disciple in Leonardo's *Last Supper*, at the moment when Jesus says one will betray him. I wonder if his mother named him after that Phillip. She's a Christian, he says.

Perhaps I just need someone to love. Christians who can't shake the itch, Saint Paul said, should marry. Lord, Jodi, I thought, marry? I tried to laugh to myself but I couldn't, so I ran back home and tried to sketch my feelings, but they were too abstract to translate into images. I couldn't lose my mind enough to draw. I climbed into

61

bed but I couldn't calm down. My hands kept fidgeting, reaching down my pants, scratching myself and staying there for comfort and warmth. Finally I jumped up, took my cap and gloves and ran away.

On the highway the gutters were deep in slush and cars sprayed mud as they passed. The streetlights were dimmed and in King's Beach only the tavern was open. A woman staggered out ahead of me and weaved toward her car. Men at the door laughed and called after her. I walked west out of town, wanting to run someplace where not even God could see me, just for an hour or so, wondering how far I could walk in an hour and how many hours till dawn, kicking up slush with each step and watching it splatter on my jeans. Whimpering dogs frightened me, as though they were spies sent to watch me or warn me of misery coming. From old homes on the lakeside came music and sparks from the chimneys; inside, I thought, were other folks like me who had tried to sleep but couldn't, who had prayed for vision and seen only confusion. I tried to think that Jesus would find me, calm me, lead me somewhere along the western shore, but I couldn't believe that, and I knew if I couldn't believe, that hope was no use. I tried to remember what terrible thing I had done or had forgotten to do to deserve such a poisonous mind—I had let my thoughts run free. I knew better than to do that. To keep a simple faith I had to keep simple thoughts.

I kicked through the snow spitefully, proudly rebellious and sorry at once. In Tahoe Vista I stopped to stare into shop windows. There were boots and a leather coat I wished I could buy or steal for Charley, books Mr. Oswald would love, a painting which looked in the dark like my mom's. It all seemed so silly I wondered why I was there, my left leg still weak and tiring already, driving myself, doubting my faith when all I had to do was let it be and ignore those questions. Tomorrow I might forget them. But I felt too foolish to turn back so I took off, walking faster, losing myself easily in long strides and determination, as if I'd be the first ever to walk around the lake, as if it would prove my will power, my strength and my sanity. Pickups splashed by, grinding their tires, slowing for moments as they saw my shadow, then speeding away as if to catch up the time. On a rise above Dollar's Point I climbed off the road, high enough above the trees to see the cluster of colored lights from the south shore. For once they seemed grand, like a beacon.

Before Tahoe City was a road I knew, first gravel, then dirt, then a lumpy trail to an island where the stream split for a hundred yards. Pancho used to camp there before he moved in with Charley. For two summers he was most always there at night. Jill and I and our dates would drive up and find him beneath his lantern and a halo of bugs, reading novels in Spanish. He'd sell us what we wanted and warn us to treat it gently because whatever you rushed hard came back at you just as hard, and karma was true from day to day. I tried walking up the road, past the second house where the snowplows had stopped, but ahead the forest was frightful and overgrown.

All the lights were out in Tahoe City. At the fork where the highway split off to Truckee an old man stopped and asked if I'd take a ride, not seeming curious that I was out alone, but only awake and lonely. I wondered if he'd talk me deaf, but I took the ride because my leg needed rest and my neck was stiff from the cold. The man said his name was Justin, that he lived in Soda Springs on a pension; he scratched his knee with one hand, steered loosely with the other, and didn't say more. I wondered why he was driving aimlessly, how long ago he might have left his wife and what he said to his sons, where was he when his brother died and if he

63

would ever go home. But I didn't ask him, it was no use, no one knew any answers. Silence turned dark and comfortable, the moon falling behind Twin Peaks, Idlewild and the stone estates of Homewood slipping by dimly. He made a U-turn past Meeks Bay and dropped me there.

It was colder, near morning and colder still as I climbed the grade beneath Rubicon Peak. I flapped my arms, buttoned my collar and walked through clouds of breath, relaxed and very tired. The sky past the eastern mountains over Carson was lush, richly black and seeded with rows of stars. From the grade I could see lights in King's Beach, the café, Maggie up cooking Paul's breakfast or Mr. Oswald not able to sleep. They all seemed warm and lovely. I tried hitching but the few cars and trucks passed by, tried running but the climb was too steep and my leg too wobbly.

Before dawn I made the cliffs above Emerald Bay. There is a castle on the island in the bay, a thousand feet down from where I stood. It's a small castle, a toy, the size of a cabin, and it angered me because it wasn't taller, because it had no battlements, no knights charging out with streaming banners. It was weak and brittle, so small I could crush it in my hand. It made me want to cry. I found a windbreak, sat down and watched for the sun, waited for hours it seemed. Then it rose too fast and white, hung colorless and limp as a raindrop over Kingsbury.

In the turnout was a new Harley Sportster, all custom paint and muddy chrome. The rider kicked it started and pulled away; when he saw me, he turned back. "Say, sweet thing? Jump on."

"Which way you going?"

"Around, man, always around. Easterly."

I hopped up behind him and he roared off, frightening a Volkswagen to a swerve and a near miss of the guardrail. His ponytail whipped in the wind and slashed at my nose; he slid back in his seat pinning my hips to the sissy bar. "You passing through?" he shouted.

"Sure," I said, "always."

"Now me, I live up by Cascade Lake. They call me Lucky, because I'm rich. You think it's the same thing?"

"Nope," I told him. "My name's Gwendolyn."

He turned far enough to wink. Then he lifted us up on the rear wheel and set us down hard, leaned us around the turns so my hair touched ground, and gunned it on the straightaways so the road signs blurred. I dug my face into his sheepskin back and held on tight and blind. "The road's too slick!" I shouted.

"Be cool, sweet thing. I take it every day, sleep or no sleep, stoned or sober I make it around. Cold wind makes my skin thick, makes my face hard. Feel it."

We were down the mountain in no time. In South Lake I told him to drop me at Harry's. "A gambler?" he snorted. "What a shame. Want to buy some skag . . . coke?"

Inside Harry's the machines lit red and clanged lazily after the night. Porters slouched around clearing debris, cigaret butts, keno tickets, the rules to roulette. To come into Harry's after walking around the lake was like leaving Eden for the barren and treacherous land of Nod, like stepping from purity into temptation or from childhood into greed. Couples in ski dress, just in from breakfast, were bubbly and anxious for the day, skipping past the tables where all-night players still leaned and fingered their chips as though they were doomed to stay there forever, and the dealers stood straight and bored, seeming thoughtless and resigned as hit men must be. Above, behind one-way glass, was the catwalk, the eye in the sky who watched everything from the invisible place, who could send down orders and have someone expelled without giving reason. I spotted Charley at the bar so I slipped behind a guard, ducked by the floormen and hopped onto a stool beside him. "Buy me a drink?"

"Nope."

"Aren't you surprised that I'm here?"

"Pancho called and said you were gone all night."

"That's wonderful. So everybody's watching me?"

"It's what friends are for, Jodi, and why some guys go to be hermits. You borrow a car?"

"No. I walked. Let's go someplace. Charley, I don't like you working in here."

"I don't like you hitching at night."

"I walked," I said.

In Zepher Cove he bought us breakfast, drank a half pot of coffee and told me he'd break the casino by organizing one righteous night when dealers paid triple on blackjack, double on pushes, croupiers paid twenty to one on corners and cashiers took obvious counterfeit hundreds. "Nobody is a pro, at least nobody starts that way. Half are college kids from Oklahoma; they stash five dollars of their allowance every week, drive here for the summer and stay on because Harry lets them handle five thousand a night, on a bad night. Makes them feel rich and worldly. They play the rules because nobody tells them different. I could tell them different. They might go for it. It's not hard to deal seconds, just takes practice, not hard to work the deck on shuffles. Hell, I bet they've got fifty dealers cheating for the club if you count all the shifts. I'll talk up that we should cheat the other way. Just a few of us would drive them mad upstairs. I'd love to burn those pimps. What do you think about money, Jodi?"

"I don't much."

"Yeah. You don't need it. Sing me a holy song. I don't get enough from Paul."

I snuggled against his arm. "I hope you beat them, Charley."

* * * *

February 23, 1972

There is a map of my life with the place names left blank
but the roads are drawn clearly; there are turnouts and
detours, some loop back to the main road and some zing
off to nearly nowhere, but the end of them all is the sea.
That's the way a map is supposed to look. I could throw
myself on Mr. Oswald, but if he took me I'd have
to make him believe; if he didn't it would have to be
sin, and if he turned me away I think I might blame it on
Jesus.

* * * *

February 26, 1972

Last weekend was Washington's birthday. On Saturday
my dad took me up to Squaw Valley, but I only made a
few runs. The lines to the lifts were long; most all the
skiers were drinking and loud, pushing and falling,
wound up from long drives and hangovers. College boys
bumped me and asked my name. I was clumsy, my balance was bad, and even when I found the right compen-
sation for my leg and hit the last slopes at nearly my old
speed, most of the thrill was gone.

Saturday night we left to see Danny in San Francisco,
my mom, dad and I. In the car my dad talked about next
year when I'd be going away to school somewhere, and
he wondered where I'd applied and if I was taking tests
and all. I told him I will. I slept on the floor with Danny
and his roommate. Danny woke me up and we sat in the
kitchen. He told me next year he'd go to law school in
the city and that he wanted to learn labor law, work in
civil rights and welfare rights and tenants' rights. I told

him about Charley's plan to rob the casino. He called Charley a beautiful dreamer.

At breakfast Danny told us he'll foul corporations and wedge rifts in bureaucracies when he becomes a lawyer. I loved his spirit and my dad was proud that Danny was a fighter like him. He said, "No matter if you get to be a rich lawyer, you'll still be a working man. You know that now, so don't forget it." We ate lunch in Chinatown and dinner at Fisherman's wharf; then Danny took us to a stage play, *Hair*. Those kids were grubby and loaded, on their own like me, raised up to find their own vision. My mom thought it was funny, my dad winced through it, but to me it was sad, ending with the end of dreams. I told Danny later those kids would turn to Jesus. Danny said he hoped not.

On Tuesday Mr. Oswald was out and I missed him. I wanted to brag about Danny, tell him what we'd done and that I'd changed so much that even skiing didn't matter anymore. Without him there I had no reason to be. But he hadn't left lesson plans, so I stayed to help out the substitute. Mr. Beavers and Coach Bracken came by and Miss Waterman, very upset. There were rumors and laughing in the faculty lounge and Mr. Lopez told me the plan for the English department had passed. I walked by Mr. Oswald's house on the way home but couldn't find the nerve to go to his door.

The next morning he came in late. During class he was drifty, stopping during a lecture to check his notes, which he usually didn't use at all, and when we were reading aloud he forgot to tell us when to switch. After class he started to tell me something, then said "Later." When I came back at third period he was waiting at the door to his office; I followed him in. First he sat on the desk, then moved to his chair, then stood up and paced by the bookcase. "I had a rough weekend, Jodi."

"Tell me what happened," I said. "All year I've been telling you about me and you're always so patient even though you think I'm dumb about Jesus and all, but I don't even know what you do."

"This weekend wasn't typical."

"Tell me anyway."

"All right. At our meeting Friday Biff, Mr. Beavers, was angry. I sat beside him. He looked away." Mr. Beavers is a retired marine, once a boxer, kids say, with a bulbous nose and a hearty laugh and the wit to make all the kids respect him. He teaches sophomore English.

"I'm sure he'd heard rumors. Miss Waterman tried to catch my eye but I looked everywhere else, stumped by this pitiful crisis. It's fools' business, Jodi, notions and quirks, the choice between a prison cell and a playground. I can believe in nothing compulsory anymore. Biff said, 'You all know my proposal. I should give Phillip credit for helping me with the details over the summer. Since September we've had the cost analysis and scheduling; you've all had time to consider them. The bottom line, obviously, is the failure and irrelevance of our present curriculum. With that in mind, I suggest we vote, rather than argue anymore.'

"'Just what is irrelevant?' asked dear Miss Waterman. 'Descriptive grammars,' says Biff. 'Dr. Johnson's pedanticism; Pope's mastery of the couplet. These things simply don't concern our students, and for good reason. Some are baffled by newspaper headlines. But we've been over it all.' Says Miss Waterman 'We cannot teach to the lowest common denominator, Mr. Beavers, and we cannot allow them choice. Do you suppose we're dealing with adults, that a large body assumes a grown mind? They will pick the simplest courses, we all know; we'll become mere entertainers. We owe them more than catering.' And on. The proposal passed, myself and Miss Waterman the only nays. I should've told Biff my reasons but it seemed like compromise, so I left, squeamish and vulnerable, not a state to be in when you're going to see my mother.

"My parents live in northwest L.A., too close for my mother's taste to Hollywood and Santa Monica, where she goes to watch the whores and homosexuals she needs to rekindle her wrath."

The outside door rattled and Miss Waterman called from the classroom. Mr. Oswald slipped out and left me shut in the office, hidden away, tingling like a lover ducked in a closet. I believed he was telling me things he wouldn't tell anyone else, and it was just a beginning. All year he had treated me as his equal, as though I had thoughts worth hearing and thinking about though they weren't the same as his. I had found another Charley in Mr. Oswald and though he hadn't touched me or leered at me the way school boys do, I believed he wanted to be my lover but was too kind to ask for anything I didn't believe was right. I was thrilled and tormented, hating decisions and not trusting impulse. I wished he'd decide for me.

Miss Waterman left when the next class came in, and I went to math. I tried to sit through it but I could hardly keep from jumping and shouting, so I told Mr. Albey I was sick and ran down to the rest room, locked myself in a stall and took out my journal to write. I felt like a vagabond, in deserts and red mountains where I'd wake up cold and thirsty, but I pressed my face to my lap and prayed frantically for guidance till I believed in the strength of my faith which had already borne me through doubt and anger, so now I felt safe in salvation; like Solomon I might commit horrid crimes or like Jonah I might run but still be delivered, and bring me and Mr. Oswald safe to Our Lord.

When I heard the bell I went back to his office. "You were on your way home," I said.

"Yes, home. I came in late after my parents were in bed, used my key and crept past their door to my old bedroom. It was musty and cluttered, with smells of dead flowers, old sheets and boxes of rubbish for rum-

70

mage sales. I smothered myself in the pillow. Early Saturday she was clattering pans in the kitchen, a gospel show on the radio. She didn't hear me step up behind her. I tapped her shoulder, she wheeled around, raw egg from a bowl she was holding splattered my shirt. 'Good Lord, Phillip!' she said. 'You're a clumsy child!'

"My father and I tried to talk over her screeching questions: Where did I go on Sunday evenings or did I refuse to answer the phone? What had I heard from Gary Albright since he entered the seminary? What were my latest vices? 'Phil,' my father asked me at breakfast, 'why was it they sent you home from retreat that year?' I told him, 'Gary and I climbed to the skylight above the girls' shower, but the glass was fogged,' I confessed. 'We couldn't see anything.'

" 'Bitch,' my father moaned and went after my mother, who had stormed from the room. He's a good man; I go to see him, but there's no escape from my mother. I dressed and drove to Santa Monica, for escape in the tape room in the library with Christmas songs. Later I kicked for lost change on the beach, testing my luck, and searched used book stores for rarities. A lively day. I stayed away until I knew they should be gone to evening service, then came back and read until I heard them drive in. Sunday morning she woke me for church but I courageously refused; soon as they turned the corner I packed, planning to leave a note for my father, but Reverend Albright from next door intercepted me. He had been a terror once, coming to Sunday dinner with his family, his timid wife, his autistic daughter, and Gary, on leave from military school. The Reverend would take me aside, strangle confessions from me, lies, my revenge and adventure, of sucking pink nipples, masturbating in church—I'm very sorry, Jodi."

"Please tell me, Mr. Oswald."

He stopped for a breath and stared me all over. "Lies, sneaking out nights to run with tough gangs and shoplifters, visits to sluts and whores, dreams, gambling, but he'd absolve me in the Lord's name. Now he's a cripple, panting and gray-skinned. He asked me to help him fix a faucet leak. While I worked he told me about Gary: from drugs to the Air Force, to the seminary. I suffer for Gary in there. He was my friend.

"My parents came home too soon. My father said the drive was long and rugged and I should leave. She stepped between us. Typical. 'Phillip, I've come to a hard decision. You simply can't stay there any longer. The place is a devil's playground.' I looked to my father for aid. His eyes were like mirrors; then they closed.

"She screamed after my car. In a few miles the free-way was stalled. I was limp, dull; I turned on loud music, very loud, and tried to read besides. It's insidious, how your God noses in. I found a poem in a bad choice of books for the time: 'The far / Fields melt my heart / They threaten / To let me through to a heaven / Starless and fatherless, a dark water.'

"Sunset frightened me. I left the freeway for the coast route and pulled into a turnout, paced around to find my equilibrum. Past the guardrail were cliffs and the moon behind a cloud bank, the beach a mile down. I thought of floating, jumping, dipping into the sea; then I ran back to the car, jammed it into neutral and loosed the handbrake. We rolled toward the moon but at the last possible second I tapped the brake. The front bumper barely pinged the guardrail."

The next class was coming in. In Art I told Mr. Lopez I wanted to sketch outside. He said he'd write me a pass as soon as I fetched his coffee. I ran to the lounge and zipped back with my arms out like wings, splashing coffee along the walls and windows. On the lawn I turned cartwheels. I took my sketch pad, ran out across the football field to the benches by the high-jump pits and sat down to draw Mr. Oswald's face.

"Hi, Jodi!" Jill skipped up behind me. Jerry was by the

fence, rolling up a sleeping bag. "Hi, Jodi," she said again. "Is lunch over already?"

"I'm happy, Jill. I can't tell you why yet but I'm so happy."

"She's fucking Oswald," Jerry said. "That's why."

"Get lost, Jerry," Jill said. "It's none of your business."

"Yeah it is," he sneered. "I'm ready to kick Oswald's ass and I don't want you saying I shouldn't because he's fucking your hypocrite friend."

I picked up a rock and ran to crush him but he jumped back and Jill grabbed my arms. "Get lost, Jerry!" she said. He walked off smugly toward the gym.

"Jill, I'm not fucking anybody."

She hugged me and stroked my hair. "It's O.K., Jodi. Anything's all right with me."

I slipped loose, ran to a break in the fence and away. All that hour and most of the next I walked up Mount Rose. Balls of sunlight sprang off the white mountain; all the west shore peaks and valleys quivered, reflecting in the lake, dark water.

I ducked through class and into the back room before the last bell. Jerry looked in and gave me the finger. Mr. Oswald came before the last kids left. "You're here for more?"

"Yep."

He sat down close beside me, on the table, so his legs brushed mine. "I stopped at the Sahara, cashed a check—large for me—for four hundred dollars. I'm a nickel gambler. I count cards and play strategy, but I'm not a computer. I believe in luck, fate, the small and large of the same notion. We face it to be punished or paid off. We'll get what we deserve. I won a few hundred while drinking, which I normally don't do. I lost some back and left, drove the west side, stopped in bars, three, as I remember. In the morning I fell out of bed on my head, delirious. I called in sick, drank gallons of water, tried to sleep again, but couldn't. When the worst of my headache passed I started reading papers, yours first." He took it from the top drawer of his desk. "Can I read it to you?"

"O.K." I was blushing, nervous.

" 'I thank God for trials. Without them my joy would be empty. Without them I never could climb so high. Steel bars have turned to summer leaves and blown away. The gardens I walk smell of heaven and my longest days are blessed with dreams of golden things, eternity. Someday, Mr. Oswald, the Lord will meet you, hold your hand tightly, because you are a kind man. Jesus loves you and so do I.' Jodi, I walked out of my house, no headache, my stomach so passive I ate enchiladas, up from the dead like Lazarus. I walked around town all afternoon, hoping I'd meet you."

He looked up, tried to stare, then turned away. "You must have to go, someone to meet, your boyfriend or—"

"I don't have a boyfriend."

"This Charley?"

"No."

"You don't have a boyfriend?" From his wondering eyes and taut lips I guessed what he meant. My fingers were cold. I covered my mouth. "Mr. Oswald," I whispered, then stopped. I stood up and touched his arm and then I ran out the door.

I haven't gone back to school yet, since that day. Thursday and Friday I helped Pastor Sandoz at the preschool. I won't tell him or Charley or Maggie about Phillip. I'm afraid of lust and ugliness. I don't know where to turn.

* * * *

March 7, 1972

Today was my first day back at school. Last week I was honestly sick, but I didn't tell my folks till they came up, so through the school days Maggie took care of me. It began with chills and congestion, then went to the runs and coughing. I was sore and almost delirious, staring at T.V., letting Maggie cook for me and change my sheets. Once during my fever she came in and saw me with my hand between my legs pressing hard, my finger just inside, my hips raised and my eyes pinched closed when I heard her gasp. First she started out, then she came back and bent down to hug me. I pressed her close, she was so warm and kind.

I guess she was happy to have me home, someone to talk to even when I didn't feel like talking back, someone to care for so she'd know she could do it. "Jodi," she'd say, "I wonder what this baby will be, a musician maybe, a model, or maybe an old fat shrew. I wonder if she'll believe Paul, all about God and his hard rules. I don't even know if I can love her; when she grows up and starts calling me names, maybe I'll hit her and maybe she'll hate me when I'm thirty; I'll be so pissed off because I've been dragging her around for eleven years that I'll just leave her with Paul, get my tubes tied and be a glamorous call girl. That's if I'm with Paul so long, or if not, maybe he'll take her away or if he doesn't and if he doesn't send money I'll go on welfare or get a job where I won't see her enough so we'll both feel cheated and end up hating each other for that. Or maybe people forgive easier, I don't know."

On my way to school this morning I was thinking about Maggie and families, about Phillip's family, his mother worse than Paul and his dad sensitive like Maggie, and I wondered how deep were his scars and how much all that home life really means or if we're born what we are. I gave them sick cards at school and dragged my feet to class. I hadn't seen Phillip since that day in his office. I still wasn't sure what had happened or if I was angry because he hadn't called me or walked up

75

the three blocks to see how I was feeling. I wondered if I'd look at him and just turn away or run up in front of the whole class and squeeze him. My heart was racing and my teeth had started to chatter.

Bravely I opened the door, bravely I scanned the room, but he wasn't there, so I stepped into the office. He was sitting on the desk as if he'd never left, as if he'd been waiting there for two weeks. I dropped my books and jumped at him. His arms spread and folded me in there with the door open and kids walking past. We were hidden behind the wall. He tipped up my chin and kissed me softly. I pushed him away and ahead of me out the door.

I skipped out after first period and sat through Spanish oblivious, but I couldn't go back to his office. I thought of going to gym class, saying my leg was finally O.K., but then I'd be stuck there for the rest of the year, missing an hour each day when I might have him alone. Besides, it was one of those days when you squirm at your desk, want to get out and run just because the sun's warmer than ever during the last four months and you call it a holiday, the first of the year. So I left school without even telling Phillip and Mr. Lopez, so they wouldn't mark me sick again. Tomorrow the office will call me down, send me to detention class, but I'll skip detention anyway.

I faked a coughing fit to slip past the T.A. in the parking lot, then ran down the hill and into the woods to a clearing where kids go before school to smoke. A house had burned down there before it was finished. From the chimney base on the second level I could see the lake through the trees. It seemed that spring had already started—there were buds on the vines that climbed the power pole, the trees seemed brighter green in sunlight and the air was drier than in winter and sweet with new smells.

76

I believed that Phillip loved me, that I loved him, which was what mattered, that I should bury worries and confusion back in the winter days when snow blocked the paths through the woods and the slush along the lake road soaked through the seams of my boots, back months ago when I used to wake up nights thinking I was all alone and afraid of the cruelty I saw in the world. Now I had Phillip to love and Jesus to love me, now were the perfect times, when the mountains were white and the low snows had melted, now spring had come and Jesus would take care of us all, no matter if we sinned, as long as our hearts were true.

Back at the road I ran down toward the lake. The air was electric and dust particles slid on sun rays to the ground. On a cedar a squirrel scampered down, then up again, stopped and scratched his chin, waved and called, "Hi, Jodi. Missed you all winter." I hitched on the highway, caught a ride with the second car all the way to King's Beach. I found Pancho eating lunch on a bench at the taco stand, ran up and plopped on his lap. "See what you missed all those winters?"

He let me bite his burrito. "Just think what you missed not going to Mexico with me."

"Someday," I said and ran up the road to the beach, dropped my books, kicked off my sandals, pulled off my sweater, threw back my shoulders and gulped as deep a breath as I could hold. I closed my eyes and listened. Up by the cabins someone was playing a flute, birds sang quartets in the park, swells popped against the pier, footsteps shuffled past me, a truck hit its airbrakes on the highway, a speedboat geared down nearing shore. I rolled up my pant legs and ran into the water past my knees. The speedboat swung around and crossed in front of me; the driver waved and grinned, so I waved back and yelled that he should give me a ride, but he didn't hear and sped off toward Dollar's Point. I splashed myself, wanted to rip off my clothes, run out over my head, shout and jump and go crazy. Instead I unzipped my jeans and tugged them down a few inches. The speedboat crossed back and spun figure eights. I dipped down so the swells caught my bare waist and whooshed down my jeans in a rush of chill and happy pain. When my hands turned blue and my legs cramped I came back to shore, changed to my sweater behind a bush in the park and flopped on the sand to let my jeans harden dry.

Tomorrow if the sun stays, I thought, I'll go out to Hidden Beach, sure to be the only one out there, and tan on the rocks. I remembered Phillip, that it was him I was happy about. I wondered if I should go down to his house tonight, wondered if his cares had lifted, and if he might think I'd changed my mind and run away. From the house I'd call school, leave him a message that his remedy had worked and I'd be back tomorrow. I crossed the highway and wiggled up the street with my jeans still damp. Paul was just leaving the house, so I stopped out of sight and waited till he turned the corner. Lately he had seemed always angry with me. Maggie was in the kitchen rinsing dirt from dried beans.

"Jodi, Charley and Paul just had a vicious fight. Charley was in here, loaded and feeling lousy. He just started to tell me something when Paul came in and yelled he better not catch him alone with me again. Just because I had my arm around him. Look at me, like a puffy old squaw. Charley jumped up and Paul grabbed that bottle on the counter, so I got between them and Charley went outside. It took me a long time to calm Paul down and he still was mad when he left. I looked for Charley but I guess he's gone."

I changed, then found Charley outside, standing drinking by the woodpile. When Charley is happy his eyes are golden; he stands straight and tosses his head back to keep his hair from his eyes. But then his broad

78

shoulders drooped, his hair hung tangled across his forehead and his eyes were dull like adobe. "Hi, Charley," I said. "I hear Paul almost cracked you with a bottle."

"I can't even blame him for this one. He must've seen I wanted to bust something and thought he'd give me the chance."

"That's not what Maggie said."

"Yeah, well let me think it. He's paying most of the rent."

"I could pay more rent. I could probably find a job."

"You know anybody wants to buy firewood? I've got four cords of tamarack here and I found some more trees yesterday. Lightning hit and split the whole length. You should see them, dismembered."

"Can't you lay off, Charley? You never get any sleep. Why don't you quit doing wood for a while? Aren't you paying O.K. just from your job?"

"No job since this morning." He sat on a pile and I sat beside him. "There's this pit boss named Russo who put a rush on Maria one night and I chased him off. I just didn't like the guy. He's too smooth. Now he comes by, tells me to throw faster, because sometimes I stall, you know, when it's late and they're losing big; the less I throw the less they lose. So today, he was watching and I didn't know he was there. The way the shifts go, if I start winning I'll keep winning all night; it just works that way. My table was empty, I was so hot I couldn't lose, so when this old midget guy came up I told him to go find another table. The guy left and Russo went off to get the shift boss. That was it."

"Can't you go to another club?"

"They'd check. If I did get on, they'd be watching. I'm sick of that shit, and I'm turning into a company man, anyway. Half the time I want to win. I don't know why."

"Well, maybe you can make enough selling wood. I'll help."

He popped me a beer and watched me gulp. "See, if I can get a stake, about a thousand dollars, I can make a run to San Francisco and invest it."

"Oh, don't, Charley. You'd probably get busted and anyway nobody up here needs heroin."

"They might not need it, but they'll buy it."

"That's a sweet attitude, Charley. You talk about the pigs at the clubs. Besides, you'd probably snort it all yourself."

He laughed and kicked the dirt. "That could happen."

I walked to town and hitched to Incline. At the chalets near the high school I knocked on doors and told the people my brother from law school had cords of clean fir that we'd deliver and stack for eighty dollars. But the season was over. I only found one buyer, so I tried down by the shore, but most of the condos were vacant, the houses had woodpiles, the estates were guarded by fences and dogs.

Back home Charley was gone and Paul was sulking over Maggie while she cooked. I tugged him into the front room. "Why did you say that stuff about Charley and Maggie?"

"Drop it, Jodi. I've got a temper and I'm trying to deal with it. Look, I don't like the way you play nursemaid to these people, either. You think you're doing them a favor? This place is bad news; it's tainted. Pancho sells dope out the front door, and Charley is always drunk, moping like we're supposed to sympathize. If he'd give it over to Christ it'd all work out—you know that, but you don't tell him. There's no peace here, no joy in the Lord. But I tell Maggie we'll move and she says she won't. You think I'll leave her here? Listen, I know you think I'm a nazi, but I think you're lukewarm. Which is best? The Word ain't something to ponder. It's the law."

Maggie came to the doorway to listen. "Jesus died," I said, "so we wouldn't be judged by the law."

"Yeah, Jodi, that must be it. Jesus died so you can skip

around with your tits flopping in a T-shirt. Jesus died so you can leave the door open when you're taking a shower. You think Charley doesn't get a hard-on when you go nuzzling up to him? You think Pancho doesn't? You think I don't?"

Maggie called us to dinner and we ate stiffly. I couldn't look at Paul. Part of me wanted to laugh, part of me was proud, part of me wanted to slice myself with a razor. I believed what he said, and it seemed even Maggie did because she wouldn't look up from her plate. I left the room and went to sit by myself. Charley came in, built a fire, went to the kitchen for beer, then stared wide-eyed and rigid into the fireplace. Maggie came in, started for me as if she had something to say, then grabbed her stomach, went over to Charley and asked him if he wanted to feel. Halfheartedly laying his hand on, he must've felt it kick, because he started to smile; then his smile slapped shut and he turned and stumbled outside. I made a move to go after him but I felt like a tramp, as though I used him for my vanity.

Paul came from the back room and Pancho from the porch. "Hey, Paul, I wrote you a new song. You'll love it. Listen man:

"There's a sceeter on my Peter, Sweet Marie,
and another on John's brother, can'tcha see?
There's a billion or a zillion
or at least a hundred million.
Let us pray it ain't this bad in Galilee."

I went off to find Charley. His truck was still parked. I guessed he'd be in town so I walked down. In the tavern some lady warbled on the jukebox and Charley sat at a corner table alone, surrounded by smoke like a gray aura. "Jesus, " he said. "I think I can get away from you by going to a bar, and you just come busting in like you're thirty years old."

"I'm big for my age," I said, "and shut up or they'll kick me out. I wanted to tell you I sold a cord of wood and any time you need money I can sell some things. I think I can get a hundred dollars for my stereo. Charley, you're my best friend in the world."

He shook his head and smiled peacefully. "Then we should skip out, maybe up to Vancouver, down to Mexico. Sound good?"

I think he was kidding. "You had your chance. Charley, I have a boyfriend. Mr. Oswald, my English teacher."

"So why come tell me?"

"I don't know." I sat pouting, confused and hurt. Charley was hateful. "I bet he could find you a job. I mean—I just bet he could."

Charley kicked the table. "I don't need help from your fucking English teacher. Hey, Ernie, get her out of here. She's only seventeen."

I didn't wait. I took out running. At the end of the block I stopped and stared up at the few wispy clouds. Today the sky had seemed too small to contain my joy. Now it was low as the roof of a cave. Every time I got happy somebody brought me down. The stars were flaming arrows, clouds the dreams of dead men, the streetlights fireflies from hell. For anything to be right, to be good, I needed Charley's O.K. He was still part of me.

I stumbled one block and around the corner. Phillip's house was dark. I fell to my knees on the sidewalk and prayed to Jesus for nothing, only to pray. Springtime shouldn't have started this way.

Part Two

In the grove the aspen leaves are buried. *The trunks are bare and white against the white earth sky. The stream is iced hard over and only the hard stems of thistles stand up through the snow. Some mornings when I climb the hill there are no boats at all on the lake, and swells like an ocean streak the blue water. Even on dry days the air is flecked with tiny ice crystals, as if it might freeze stiff and crack like glass. Some evenings the deer come down and knock with their hooves on the stream but the ice won't break. A small cat with a stump tail stalks around the cabin at night and screeches angrily as it runs away. Coyotes whine down the hills and howl bitterly. I cover my ears and try to be brave, but I'm afraid to be lonely anymore.*

I'm not really lonely. Loneliness is sad and longing, but what I feel is something else that comes with fear. I hate fear. Fear isn't natural. It's a hype and an intruder. It's not part of me, just as death isn't a part of me. When our cells die others replace them, just as new as the first ever were. Aging and death, like fear, attack from outside, and each night I feel them coming in.

The night before last was the coldest so far, I think. There were no clouds, the stars were stiff and the moon didn't climb. With a pain in my side and cramps just starting I watched from the window for something to move; then I gave up and drank tea, stuffed the fire and wrapped myself in woolen blankets. The cabin filled with heat and smoke. I sweated as long as I could stand it; then I threw off the blankets. My skin was slick and oily. Shadows from the fire danced on the front of my body and as the sweat dried my skin went numb, squeezed to bumps and began to shiver uncontrollably. I watched my hips quiver and my breasts jiggle, my nipples point and shrink small as a dime. A rush of wind shook the door, so I slammed the board latch and hustled around to find distraction, washing my plate, folding more blankets, boiling more tea.

When I sat down with the tea I jerked the hot cup and spilled it between my breasts. It made a red splotch and stung through the numbness. I rubbed it with my fingers, pinched it with my nails till the red turned white and the pain spread out across my chest and down my arms. I bit my tongue, rubbed my breasts and stomach hard, scraping lines in my skin from the scabs and the cuts on my hands, loving the heat from my hands and the pain, the deliverance from thinking and worry. I trembled tense and rigid, rubbing my head and my neck with one hand, my legs up and down with the other, up to my crotch and pinching, down again to my toes, between my legs and around to my rear, squeezing fast all around. But my stool tilted and I fell, laughing, and shimmied across the floor on my back, scraping and bumping my hips till I gouged my spine with a splinter and cracked my head bloody on a leg of the stove. I fingered the blood while it dried. I slept on the floor.

In the morning I dressed and went up the mountain, as on lots of other days, looking again for my gypsy. Sometimes I can hear her laugh, sometimes she screeches strange words, but when I called her she never used to answer. I had to push through waist-high snow up over the hills past the second valley, where ash-black stumps

86

are uncovered, like road signs to terrible places. I rolled down the bank and crossed the drifts in the meadow to the aspen grove.

She was waiting in a space of black dirt she had cleared, warming herself at a fire. She grinned and spit through her gums. "Come join me, little butterfly." Her rags were the colors of flowers, violet, yellow rose, the red of poinsettia. Her skirts were spread apart, shielding the fire and baring the blue veins of her thighs. Her eyes were black and cold. "Come closer," she said. "It's oh so hot by my fire." She hopped up and took a blanket from beneath her and spread it out for me. "Sit down, little miss. I've made a fine cushion. Would you like a bedtime story? There you are. You're comfy now?" She scooped a nut from the fire and tossed it to me but it burned my palm and I dropped it away. "Oh my, you're so tender. What does such innocence do to itself?" She sprang for my arm and kissed it; she stroked my arm beneath my jacket and touched my fingers to her wrinkled cheek. I tried to jump away but my legs were asleep.

She cupped my chin in her hands soothingly. "This is not your place," she whispered. "You're from Nevada, California. This is the world. Haah! Such a pity you're lost here. You haven't yet learned to love loneliness or suffer the dark nights of the soul. Haah! I have. I've spent a million. And you seek to be saved by great suffering, to humble yourself with tears and disgust. Then seek on foolishly!" She coughed and spit and spewed a wild cackle that clouded her eyes, then turned them bright blue. "Where is your Savior? And where is the one who loved you so? Haah! Follow me, little daisy, little pansy. I'll show you solace. I've found it. Oh yes I work for the day of the doom. I'm the Whore of Babylon, little sweetness, I'm the dragon, the soothsayer, the rose's thorn."

She pulled me down, lay my head beside her and ran her fingers in circles around my eyes. Her lips pursed and her tongue curled; she ripped off my jacket, peeled my sweater slowly, tore at my belt and yanked down my jeans. "Look at you there! So pretty. Naked as a snake, tender as a pink fillet. Just a child but so full of sin. Does it surprise you I say sin, my lady? Because I'm cruel doesn't mean I'm an atheist. Haah! Haah! There is no one so cruel as the fallen angel."

She left me and paced around the edge of her clearing. "You think I've come to help you? No, you found me. Or did I find you? To suffer you must know these things. To suffer exquisitely you must see clearly. You don't need medicine, miss, or distraction of tedious dreams. The truth is a gnat, my softness, a chip off the mountain. Oh, it's much too precise for a dreamer. But excuse my neglect, little miss! You've dented your skull. My, you've rent your head. And the burn on your hand. Such a pretty hand, and oh such wounds for a fairy princess. Let me serve you now, child. Let me service you." She pulled a pouch from her skirts and daubed a cream on the gash on my head. "Does it sting, little butterfly? Then it must need more. No, don't speak. Relax and love your wound. Never speak to me, little miss. You don't have a thing to say."

She spread the green stuff over my body, on bites and sores, scratches and scars, down to my toes, which were all I could see but my breasts while she pressed my head down. "Shall we talk? We should talk. We'll call it fore-play. We'll talk about killing. I kill you kill he kills she kills we kill you kill they kill. Ho hum. The killing doesn't matter. It's the death that counts. It's the dead one who suffers, not us. Suppose a sparrow were to perch on my hand. I'd squeeze it dead. It's nothing, my love. I'm a marvelous killer; like you, I had to learn the skill and the taste. I was born with a tender heart but we learn to love what we do well, our contribution. We're social creatures, after all. Some of us love to sing and some can't sing at all. You love to give yourself; you've

88

touched so many and killed more than your share. *You should be proud. But are you cold, dear one? Here, slide closer beside me. And are you wondering what I'll do with you now, my lusty princess? You can't kill me. I know karate. Haah!*

"Oh, you're the hag and I'm the bride, / you're the slave and I'm the queen, / I'm the fairy queen. *But my, you're a pretty hag. And you're afraid. Then run and scream, 'Police!' No, no. I'll make you a true woman. Close your eyes. I'm not a pretty sight. Imagine, sweetness. Close your eyes or I'll sear them with coals, I'll gouge them out and draw a circle. I'll play marbles.*"

There was crunching in the snow, a thud of something, and the rustling of my gypsy's skirts. My eyes were pinched tight but I could feel her weight above me; then she dove at my waist and bit. I screamed; she let go, ran her tongue between and around my breasts and up to my neck. *"I won't kiss your lips, little butterfly, they may be poison."* There were sores on her flesh that my skin could feel as she dropped her fat heap across me. She was hot and broke the wind; her breath was like dead things as it passed my face. I tried to tear loose but she flattened me down. *"Relax, little princess, you were doing so well."* Her fingers slipped beneath me, kneaded my hips and grabbed like a man's strong hands, then tickled down and beneath like worms. *"Lie back and savor your dreams. We'll save the truth for later. Dream yourself a halo, my love. Haah! You should bathe more often."*

Going down was easier. I followed the path I had already kicked loose. There had been no more snow. I passed the cabin and climbed the hill. The sky and the lake seemed warm and streaked with gold. The sun was low between Rubicon and Mount Ellis and frost had cleared from the air. An excursion boat was making a turn toward Homewood. I could see tourists waving to shore, hot mugs in their hands and hot breath from their lips. Straight across were ski trails, white slashes down the mountain, and black specks of skiers hardly moving. Over the pass from Placerville cars were crammed tight as chain links, some with their lights on already, slinking in and out of the trees and down into the basin to the red and green and golden lights of the casinos and warm hotels. I could hear rolling thunder, waves slapping the pilings of the collapsing pier, then the hiss and explosion of all my years past, boxed, set in rows like volumes of history and detonated. For a moment I was free, light and invulnerable. But the rest of my life, the days from here out, crawled from the rubble, a slumping creature with its nose in the mud.

I could imagine a loneliness which is delight and freedom, unburdened warmth and cover and the chance to step away, to stride around the world and watch, marveling at the throat of a toad, the prick of a thorn, the quiet power of deer escaping, spirits and angels crossing the night, above the white, white world. But in the cabin I waited for Charley, wound in my guilt, feeling scrapes and cuts and spots frozen solid, one on my side above my waist, around in the heel of my foot. There was no fire or shadows. Snow was falling again, gently and lusciously, and it seemed it would cover me over and lay the whole mountain in a drift. Charley might not make it up. I wondered how it would be to die packed in. I wondered if the smell would be musty when I'd breathed all the air.

In the morning I had kicked off my quilt and I woke to the cold. Snow was nearly up to the windows but not high enough to stop Charley. I thought I heard a bird at the window but it was only a cracked twig tapping against the glass. I wrapped up again and waited, wondering how I could greet him and ask him to stay, to hold me and give me his strength. Finally he shook the door, then knocked. I climbed down from the loft wrapped in my quilt and lifted the bar on the door. He was wet, loaded down and nipping whiskey from a wine bag. He dropped his pack and the bundle he carried and kicked off his snowshoes. "No fire?"

I wanted to grab him but he stepped past me fast and went to the stove. "Don't you use this thing? It's something below zero in here."

"Charley, remember I told you about that gypsy?"

He sighed heavily. "Yeah."

"See, I went looking for her, lots of times, and I finally found her yesterday. She's mean, Charley, and she's psychic or something. She called me a killer. She raped me."

He stuffed the fire, lit it and stood over it, staring down.

"Look!" I tore off my quilt. "See the cuts from her fingernails? See this green crap. And look—" I pointed between my legs. "Look real close and you'll see a hickey."

He threw me the quilt and tried to wrap me up but I broke away. "Fuck you, Charley! Leave me alone!" He didn't move, so I jumped for the door but he made it first and blocked me. "Damn, Charley! Why won't you love me?"

His eyes were sad and old and he stared at my filthy naked body. I could feel my gypsy's hands and the folds of her skin. There was horror in them, and horror in Charley's stare, the pain of some recognition he'd never had before and a monstrous grief, as if he'd go mad and break me in two or curse God for death and ugliness, as if he suddenly knew there was nothing without corruption.

"You want me to screw you?"

"Yeah," I muttered.

He led me to the cot and sat me down. I couldn't watch his eyes. Outside a pack of snow slipped from a tree. There were icicles like bars down the window and a gust blew in from a crack where a rag had blown out.

"Did you ever want it before? I never thought you were coming on to me."

"Sometimes."

"If I'd known that we could've left, you know, long ago."

"It doesn't matter now."

He seemed to shiver and blinked and rubbed his eyes. "In three weeks I go to court; I'm going to jail. I might be gone a year—shit, I don't know how I'll do, I might stomp a guard or something, I might be there forever. God, after all the times I've dreamed. In the army I hoped you could save me and make me forget all the screams, all the orders. But I thought I was only dreaming. I never had the balls to find out for sure."

I took his head, ran his hair down my front and laid his head in my lap; he spread out limp on the cot, staring at me. "Can't you stay, Charley? They'll never find you up here. They'll think we're both gone or dead and it'll be better that way. I'm scared, Charley, and my gypsy's for real."

"When I get out I can see my boy when I want. You don't want to hide forever. I'll find somebody else to come up; then you'll want him."

The kettle was whistling, so Charley made tea and heated rolls he'd brought. "It's hard up here," I told him. "You've never lived where the clouds come rolling down and scoop you inside them, so that you're living in the clouds, and all those people who look up and say how gorgeous—it's not so pretty from inside."

"Listen. Gypsies don't go where it's cold and the Washoes aren't crazy enough to come up here in the winter. Nobody's that crazy but you."

"Oh, yeah? You don't even know—there might be a whole town right over the ridge. You've never been there. Maybe she's an Eskimo."

"If you're afraid I'll take you back home."

"It's not my home. You're not taking me anyplace. Aren't you going to make love to me?"

He watched me for a long time, then filled his cup

with tea and gulped it straight down. *"So you need any-thing next week?"*

"Aren't you going to make love to me?"

He started to empty his pack. "No, Jodi, I can't just do it and leave. I know myself better than that. I'd end up staying here."

"You don't want to be a criminal, do you? You're a selfish prick, Charley."

"Yeah. So what do you want me to bring up?"

"Soap, and a little tub I can sit in."

He dumped out his pack and slipped on his snow-shoes. "I'll go. There's a storm coming anyway."

If I told him I was sorry, I'd just keep wanting him. I was better off angry. I watched him turn the bend in the road; then I picked through the pile he'd left by the door. There was food on top, vitamins, some novels I'd seen before but couldn't remember where, and on the bottom of the pile in a shopping bag and tied up with string were a stack of green notebooks, Phillip's.

I charged outside and down to the meadow. "Go to hell, Charley!" I screamed.

*　*　*　*

April 1, 1972

This weekend my grandma came up from Lodi to gamble again. She has pensions from my granddad and the post office, but whatever she saves she crams into the slots, sometimes a few hundred dollars a trip. It makes my dad furious, because slots are such lousy odds. He tried to teach her blackjack, but she won't play because the low-est bet is a dollar. He drew out a grid and tried to teach her craps, but she said she's too old to remember the rules. My dad kicked the table and threw the dice at the wall. He says she's always played dumb.

This evening they were waiting dinner for me. Grandma gave me a pair of knit gloves. Everybody gives me gloves. "I made them myself," she said. "A painter must take care of her hands. Keep them warm and you'll never get arthritis."

"They're tight," I said. "Good for packing snowballs."

"Arthritis makes it tough to play slots," my dad said, scowling.

"Ronald," grandma said, "you're so rigid. That's not from me or your father. Now that you're a reformed gambler—"

"Reformed?" my mom wheezed. "Where were you last Thursday, Ron?"

"Besides," grandma said, "what's money?"

"Christ!" my dad hissed. "What's money? Money's what those clubs have that used to be mine. You'd have a stroke if I told you how much I lost in ten years. What's money! Shit!"

"Wash your mouth out, Ronald."

"Money's what'll tell Jodi how she'll live her life," my dad said, "same as it told you and me and Abraham Lincoln."

"You think Abraham Lincoln was in it for the money?"

"I do."

"Well, I don't."

"Well, Jodi," my mom said, "how's school?"

"O.K."

"Why aren't you eating?"

"Fat butt," my dad said and reached to pinch me but I slapped his hand.

My mom raised her hand. "Your counselor called me." I froze in terror, imagined them moving home, my dad standing watch at my bedroom, picking me up from school, busting down Phillip's front door. I was ashamed, though I hadn't slept with him yet, angrily, unsensibly

94

ashamed, and I swore to myself momentarily that I'd forget Phillip after tonight.

"He said you've missed too many classes and you don't show up for detention."

"How are your grades?" my dad barked.

"You saw my report card."

"Grades aren't everything," grandma said.

Now I laughed at my guilty conscience, relieved, and I wanted to hurry to Phillip's. I lied that there was a party at Charley's, so they wouldn't expect me to stay home. My dad said he'd drop me on the way to King's Castle but that wouldn't be for an hour, so I changed and ran down to the highway. It was a beautiful night, crisp, with the tip of a full moon just clearing the hill. I walked the first mile, wondering what would happen at Phillip's, if this would be the night we'd make love. We always sat close while we talked and the radio played whatever he happened to find, jazz or classics or political preachers who made him laugh. But we hadn't kissed since that day in school. I was glad; my conscience felt right. Whatever happened I knew would be blessed because I had been patient and Phillip had, too.

After school we had driven to beaches and a meadow I knew on the west shore where wild flowers always come early, crimson columbine like sentries by the ponds and tiger lilies in bunches nearby. Phillip said it was too early but we looked anyway, sloshing in bare feet across the marshy places, running upstream to buds we thought we saw, but they were illusions, so we held hands and swung our arms in wide circles back across the meadow and sat on the car, rubbing each other's feet warm.

One day at Hidden Beach I tested the water. It was deep and freezing off the cove but I said I'd jump in first if he came too. He said we didn't have swimsuits. I grinned and he blushed. There was a little squall out on the lake and waves slapped the point hypnotically. We watched till it fell calm; then he lay back and rested his head on his arms. I watched a rowboat turn out of the cove, and when I looked back Phillip was sleeping. His cheeks were still pale, his forehead still furrowed. I rolled up my sweater and propped it beneath him. He seemed never able to forget what was on his mind. Even asleep, I believed, he was thinking, which told me that all he did was considered, weighed and chosen. How could I help but trust him?

Tonight he cooked dinner for me. I could smell it half-way down the block. I tripped where the porch step was missing, so he heard me and ran to the door.

"My dough's like rubber," he said.

"I just eat the stuff on top."

"You're lovely, Jodi. Have I seen you before in a dress?"

"Nope," I said. "I don't like my knees."

I wished he'd knock me down and kiss them, but he led me to the chair and ran off to cook. His living room has only the red stuffed chair, a floor lamp, an old maple desk, and his bookshelves made from scrapboards covering three walls, one wall only novels, alphabetized, Arnold, Dostoevski, Joyce, Proust, Stone, Wolfe, reaching down. The next wall has four shelves of poetry, travel books, history, philosophy, religion. Beside his desk are almanacs, dictionaries, school books and a half shelf of green spiral notebooks. I wanted to take one out and read, but I felt like a snoop, so I peeked into the kitchen. He was slashing like a buccaneer at pepperoni, sausage, green peppers, mushrooms, tomatoes, slaughtering the cutting board, tossing heaps on the cheese and dough. I took the card table out to the porch and set it up, threw on a bedsheet for a tablecloth and came back to ask him for candles.

There were no candles in the house, so I ran to the store. On the way back Pastor Sandoz called out from the door of the church. "Coming tonight, Jodi? We have a guest speaker, a missionary."

"I couldn't sit still," I told him. "The night's too pretty."

He smiled and nodded. I waved him goodbye, walked up the block toward Charley's till he stepped inside, then I cut back to Phillip's. On the porch in dim light we couldn't be seen from the church. There was just enough room for the table and us on the railings. The wind kept blowing out our candle and after I lit it five times I gave up. The only light came from the living room lamp and the full moon behind Phillip, pale golden through the treetops. For a moment as he smiled and stretched, it ringed his face like a halo.

"It makes me sad," I said, "that people don't love Jesus."

He frowned and turned away. "Please don't mention that fellow tonight."

"Why?"

"I feel spied upon. I had a letter from my mother. She threatened to come see me. I'm afraid she still runs my life. Everything's because of my mother. I read because when I was a child it was the only time she'd leave me alone. I teach because she convinced me my hands were useless and business was for bolder men. I moved up here because she was down there. I gamble to piss her off!" He laughed outrageously. "Not really. Not entirely." Across the street the last people filed into the church. Then Pastor Sandoz pulled the door, but before it closed I heard a scream.

"The spirit," Philip said, but there was more shouting and in a few minutes an ambulance squealed up the block and pulled in at the curb. I jumped from the porch and ran across the street. They were carrying out Mrs. Resor; her tongue was out and her face was green. Everybody was mumbling and some dropped to their knees.

When the ambulance sped off we all stood watching, awed and confused as if we'd just seen a miracle. A man pushed through the crowd and ran off holding his eyes; an elder started singing a hymn but stopped when no one joined him. Pastor Sandoz called for us all to come in. I stayed still and he waited at the door for me, but I shook my head and he turned inside. Phillip was watching from the lawn.

"She used to give me dresses when I was little," I said, "and roller skates once. She ran the thrift shop." I'd never seen anyone dying before. I thought I should cry but tears just didn't come. I sat on the porch steps thinking of grandma, who was older than Mrs. Resor, and imagining Charley in the war stepping on bodies of friends and the ones they'd killed or no one knew who killed; more than for Mrs. Resor I felt sorry for Charley. Phillip stood behind me, touching my hair and my shoulder. "Jesus didn't give her the creeps," I said. He stayed for a moment, then let go, cleared off the table and packed it back into the house.

I walked in and he sat on the chair arm beside me. "I won't belittle your faith. It suits you like a beautiful gown. It makes you glow in the dark."

I reached for his hand. "You probably won't ever believe."

He shrugged. "I may reconsider when my mother dies."

"You sound like you wish she was dead."

"I often do."

We sat staring in different directions. Then Phillip went to the kitchen. I remembered when Charley took me to fireworks after he came back home and at every bang his shoulders jerked. I always knew why but I never understood, really. But now the argument people use, that folks go to church because they're afraid to die, made sense for once, and I wondered about myself, what

I was afraid of when I turned to Jesus. For me it was madness. I yelled in to Phillip, "Just because people are afraid when they turn to Jesus doesn't mean God isn't true."

He poked around the corner and smiled. "That's the problem with Christianity. No one with a conscience can believe it, but no one with a conscience can ignore it."

"I believe it," I said, but he'd gone back in. Jesus would take Mrs. Resor if she died. I could see it almost with my eyes, Jesus in shadows, Jesus walking tall. I wondered if some Christians didn't fear death but felt it the path to the kingdom it was. Mrs. Resor might feel that way. She was old enough and had always believed, she told me once.

Outside two men crossed under the streetlamp; then I heard something rustle in the bushes. "Phillip! There's somebody outside!"

He came out wiping a plate. "Out where?"

I stepped to the window and pointed down. I followed him out to the porch and we leaned around the edge. The men were running to the corner already. Phillip shrugged. "If they're thieves they could get a nickel apiece for my books."

We locked up and cut through the back to miss parishioners coming from church. Music was loud from the tavern and down on the beach were boys running dogs, couples strolling slowly, a party of kids from our school around a bonfire by the park. Out on the pier was an old fellow drinking wine. We passed him and bounced on the creaking boards out to the end. The water was oily from leaking motors and there were no waves. I was still thinking about old folks, Walker in the rest home mute and drooling; Mrs. Resor limp and green or dead already—I shuddered, my pulse raced, death seemed so close, a phantom in the air, not just Mrs. Resor's death, but all deaths and mine. My grandma was down at

King's Castle right now, cussing the slots, and cussing my dad when he tried to bring her home. She might die soon. She's seventy-four.

"It must be awful to hate your mother," I said.

"She's unforgivable, Jodi. When my father wanted to leave she made it known that I was hers. She made him believe she couldn't work. Still he was determined, and I wished to God he'd go, so I could run away and find him; he and I could have been lumberjacks or tramp sailors out from Tahiti. Each day he came home bolder, less tolerant of her nagging, talking back more, cussing her more, until I thought he'd found the courage, because he'd look at me as if he missed me already. Then she got sick, migraines and ulcers; for three years she claimed she had a tumor on her spine. Reverend Albright worked a miracle; but by then my father was too tired to run."

There had never been hatred in my family. Each of us meant more to each other, it always had seemed, than anyone outside except Charley. There had been spats, but Phillip was speaking of wars. I turned him around, wound my arms beneath his jacket, pressed my breasts tight against him and kissed him long and breathlessly. His mouth was cold. His arms were limp at first; then they squeezed me hungrily.

We only kissed that once; then I asked him to drive me home before my folks started calling Charley's. It was a lie. They wouldn't have called for hours yet. On the road a wind came up, blew down the mountain and roughed foam on the lake. I was afraid, for everyone, as though Jesus was trying to talk to me—but I wouldn't listen. If Jesus wants to tell me what I'm doing is wrong he'll have to speak louder. That would only be fair. Otherwise I've made up my mind. Phillip is the man I want.

* * * *
April 2, 1972

This morning when I called the hospital they told me Mrs. Resor was dead. I told my mom and dad but they didn't even remember her; then I lay in the sun all morning wondering where was my grief.

Grandma said she wanted to go shopping at South Lake so I offered to drive. She talked all the way, told me I was just like my mom, so talented they should grub up the money to send me to art school in Paris, where my mom had wanted to go when my dad first met her, but he was so handsome, strong and loyal and his heart in the right place, with the workers and the union even while McCarthy raved about communists; my dad was steward in his local as soon as he came back from Korea. Grandma said my mom loved him for that, that real artists—not the snobs and academics but the ones who drew what they saw and had enough guts to see clearly—loved men like my dad who were loyal and brave, even if they weren't so smart. But she should've gone to Paris, and I shouldn't make the same mistake. Grandma said I owed it to us all, and they all owed it to me.

It was a goofy idea, me going to Paris, calling myself gifted and trying to be a part of all that history and civilization, eating crepes and learning another language, new ways, renting a dark flat by a dirty river and painting these mountains from memory. Or I might grow beyond the mountains, away from them, find passion and torment in painting explosions like Dali's illustrations for the Bible. Or I might buy a hunk of marble and chisel Phillip's head, fine lines and deep-set eyes, hair that never lay right and a jaw always locked up tensely. But it was a silly idea. There was too much here.

A car like Phillip's passed going the other way through Zepher Cove, but I only caught a glimpse because I was listening to grandma. She said she had won last night, a triple jackpot on an electric machine, a couple more jackpots with quarters, and cherries and plums were all on her side. She said she'd give me her winnings for the whole weekend to save for my schooling. There was truth in my drawings, she said, no dead or useless lines. I told her I hadn't been drawing but she wouldn't listen. In South Lake I took her to shops I knew but she only picked through the racks and found a corduroy pants suit she thought I should have. She only wanted to go to the clubs.

I imagined my dad there, imagined our argument, me shouting that it was her money and him shouting that it wasn't, as soon as she walked in it was theirs, they'd pay the flunkies and take the rest to buy up the shoreline and the government. I stopped to wonder if I was arguing with my dad or Charley. It could've been either. But I had to let grandma stop. I wasn't the one to be bossing her. She said she'd meet me out front in an hour, so I drove to Heavenly on the Nevada side, up Kingsbury to watch the skiers, wondering where I'd be next season when my leg was all healed, wondering if someday I'd love skiing again, wondering if there was any chance this talk about Paris might be something real or even what I needed, a new place and a new life just after I'd turn eighteen. I felt cruel and a tramp, guilty for not thinking of Phillip so soon after I made up my mind to let myself love him.

Back in town I thought I saw Mrs. Resor on the sidewalk. I was late back to Harry's but grandma wasn't outside. I waited for a while in the car, then slipped in to find her. She was on a stool in an empty aisle, cranking with both arms on two machines, nodding on drops and wagging her head when nothing came. Both trays were full and her purse was stuffed with rolls of dimes.

"Lord, Jodi, I'm winning again!"

"That's when you quit, grandma, when you're winning. Dad'll raise hell if I don't get you home."

"He'll raise hell anyway."

"You still have tonight."

She frowned and cranked out another dozen plays, then climbed off her stool. "I'll win enough for your plane flight. You must have a goal if you want to gamble passionately."

At dinner my mom wondered if there were still good schools in Paris. She said she'd check at the Reno library. Her eyes were sparkling and we all knew she could see more than we could, things she had dreamed of forever. I said schools in San Francisco were cheaper but she said I should find a place where I'd meet people who'd help me, that in Paris I'd find a whole new world of friends who weren't held down by housework and labor, people with culture and money. My dad winced, as he always did when mom hinted there might be higher culture than that of common people. I was amused that they could talk about what I should do as though the decision were theirs.

My dad asked me to ride along to King's Castle. Grandma said come back at midnight, he said ten, he cussed, she bawled him out and they settled on eleven fifteen. On the way back we stopped in Brockway for ice cream. My dad scratched his lip with his teeth and stirred his sundae to a muddy goo. "What do you think about Paris?"

"I don't know if I want to paint."

"Well, just what do you want to do?"

"Do I have to decide right now?"

"Soon. Jodi, before you know it you'll be twenty-one, then thirty and thirty-five, and you'll be trapped. You can't guess how many traps there are, especially for a girl as pretty as you. You better start thinking."

"I think all the time. Deciding is what's hard."

"I don't want you to end up miserable, like your mother."

"She's not miserable."

"She is. You know she thinks she could've done better. Damn it, Jodi, I don't need my daughter to tell me pretty lies."

"She does not!"

My dad shrugged and dipped at his sundae.

"I'm going to walk down to Charley's," I said. "I think a lot when I'm walking. Dad, mom's no genius. I don't think she could've been."

Charley and Pancho were out somewhere and Paul was gone to a Bible study. Maggie was cleaning, as always these days, though it looks as though she ought to just sit, as big as she is. She doesn't sleep much—she says it's uncomfortable and only her eyes and her legs get tired. I tailed her around while she vacuumed and dried all the dishes and stacked them. She told me about Charley, how she thinks he avoids her because of the baby, because he doesn't want to think; how he spends the mornings on the phone, borrowing money and selling the last of Pancho's psilocybin. Soon he'll run out of people to borrow from. I knew he'd even called my dad. Maggie said he tried to touch Paul but Paul didn't have anything to loan. Even the unemployment people had turned Charley down, he had fallen behind with Maria, and his share of the rent was a month late.

I thought about the money grandma said she'd give me for school, and I thought about Phillip. I had already asked Phillip, Mr. Lopez and my dad to find Charley a job and I'd told Charley that if he brushed up he might get on as a skiing instructor, but it was too late in the year. I wondered, if I did find some money, if Charley would take it to San Francisco for heroin, and how I'd feel if he did. But that didn't matter much now.

I decided to try Phillip first, scared to guess what he'd

think of me asking for money, but his lights were out and his car was gone, so I hitched over the hill and walked to King's Castle. It was still a half hour before my dad would come, so I stayed outside, watching some kids a few years younger than I am doing like Jill and me and some others a few years ago, smoking ourselves dingy and hanging out on the sidewalk at north Stateline, or in South Lake if we could find a ride, staring inside and up at the bending lights, thrilled by the shouts and the bells and the horns and stumbling like drunken gamblers. One of those nights Jill—after her folks had found a stash in her dresser and she'd been holing up in the woods for three days and none of us had any money to buy her food and no one would give her a dime when she panhandled, though some of those pigs must've had thousands—went back with a man to his hotel. In the morning the police came. The desk clerk had called them and he stopped Jill on her way to the police car. "I have a daughter your age," he said as his reason; then he tried to hug her but she bit his arm.

Finally I thought maybe I'd missed dad and grandma so I walked in. A guard chased me back out but left the door, and I slipped through to a crowd. Before I found grandma I saw my dad watching a blackjack table. I started for him but just in time, before he saw me, I saw Phillip playing at the same table. He was splitting tens, then stacking his blue chips in short piles while the dealer threw his cards. I backed behind a big man, hidden from my dad. This seemed to me a Phillip other than I knew, though he had told me he gambled, talked of it often, in fact, as though it were something he found exciting or important or something he needed to confess, but still to see him in action frightened me just a little—there were still things about him I hadn't realized. What shocked me most was his seeming so at home, so comfortable there, handling the cards deftly, sitting straight-backed and cool as he never had in his classroom. I slipped away, looking for grandma, but I couldn't find her, so I went back to wait at the curb.

My dad was pulling her by the sleeve when he brought her out. "They've tightened those machines, Ronald, and don't tell me differently. Now you can take me to another club and lend me twenty dollars. Oh, Jodi. I lost the money, playing those five-coin quarter machines. Take me to the club with the old kind of machines, Ronald."

Grandma begged and pouted but my dad took her home anyway. I made us tea and asked him why he couldn't loan Charley some money.

"I can't touch what he owes, Jodi, so there's no sense in putting off what's going to come anyway. I respect Charley, but he made this mess and he'll have to sweep it. There are two kinds of people: Some kick shit aside and some step in it."

*   *   *   *

April 6, 1972

When Charley was a boy Mrs. Resor set aside nice clothes or shoes in his size, and winter coats that might fit old Walker. Charley worked at the thrift shop fixing toys and bicycles and building shelves and racks to pay her and for meals at the church. He borrowed a suit for her funeral and took me. Of all the mourners there, over a hundred, praising Mrs. Resor and making their pause at the casket, Charley was the only one who looked comfortable, the only one not asking for more or less grief. I wanted more or none at all. I had never seen death so closely before.

I had told Phillip that Charley was desperate. I

couldn't ask him to help straighten him out and he didn't
say much but I was sure he'd do something. Leaving the
funeral I hinted to Charley that something was coming. I
felt proud that I'd done him a favor and excited as
though I'd bought him a special gift and could hardly
keep from telling him, but he thought I was just being
religious.

"Because God loves me, right? And the birds and the
lilies and stinkweed."

"Naw, he probably picks on you. It's better you think
that. It's a good excuse," I hissed.

"Excuse for what, mother?"

"For drinking and moping and self-pity."

"I wouldn't need an excuse if I didn't live with you
and the pontiff."

"You don't believe in God at all, do you?"

"I believe. I just don't respect him."

"What?"

"His world is a Cadillac, my dear, twenty years old
with an Earl Shieb paint job and Pep Boys parts."

"Stuff it, Charley!" We didn't talk anymore. I was
hurt and angry, because I hadn't been preaching at him
or saying what he did was wrong. I couldn't remember
even feeling it was, except when he talked about San
Francisco, because no matter what laws or codes Charley
broke, I had always believed he was right somehow.
Back home he went to his room. I could hear him
thumping around in his closet. When he left I looked in.
His backpack was out on the bed. He didn't come home
all night.

Phillip was all smiles the next morning. I guessed he'd
found Charley a job or figured a way Charley could beat
the casinos, but he took me into his office and handed
me a check for $2000, made out to Charley. Behind the
partition I kissed him and told him I felt like a louse, that
I worried he'd think I was a con artist. He said he didn't

know Charley, but he'd give me anything I asked for. Besides, once a dealer named Charley at Harry's had paid him off on a long count of twenty-three.

I was anxious to catch Charley, so I slipped away and across the field and ducked out through the fence. They can't keep me in school anymore. I'm learning to make my own laws. I stopped at my folks' house and called Charley but the phone just rang, so I ran up the highway till I caught a ride, thinking he might be out in the yard, but he wasn't and his pack was gone. I called a couple of Charley's friends and Paul at work but no one had seen him. Down at the tavern the bartender said he'd been in last night, showing card tricks, calling the top card and dealing seconds and off the bottom, but he hadn't mentioned leaving. On the way back I stopped at Maggie's mother's. Maggie was there and said that Charley had taken food and said he'd be panning for gold.

I changed to my boots and set out for a cabin Walker had built on the mountain below Marlette Lake.

One summer, six years ago now, Walker found a job carving signs for a man who sold them to rich folks to hang in their driveways. The man did good business, more than Walker ever did on his own, so Walker stayed a month on the job and talked about keeping it longer. Then one day he left and a week passed by. I was with Charley when he came back, grinning and sober with his pantlegs torn, his face caked muddy and a dog he had picked up somewhere tagging behind.

"I found gold," he said.

We just laughed and he laughed with us but the next day he took Charley back up the mountain, and in trips up and down they salvaged what they needed and built the cabin, squatting there in the Toiyabe Forest. He claimed the gold was nearby, but he didn't show Charley where, or the dust he said he had. They finished the cabin before Charley had to start school again; then Walker

108

went back up alone and didn't come down much till winter. Through winter he didn't work at all, hung out at the tavern instead; when spring came he went up to the cabin for weeks at a time. Charley stayed alone and ate with us. Sometimes Walker gave us money.

In the tavern the other men hassled him. "Where you keep all that gold, Walker?"

"Buy it."

"Where's it come from?"

"Comes from hell, I guess."

"Why ain't you buying drinks? Why are we buying yours?"

"'Cause I'm pleasant. When Charley's a man I'll bring that gold down; then I'll buy the drinks and he can buy the eastern shore. Charley can buy what oughta been free. There's buckets of gold dust and nuggets as big as your nose, which is damn big."

No one believed in the gold but Walker and Charley. When Walker had money my folks and everyone else said he stole it. Even Charley, no matter how he argued and begged, never saw a pinch of the gold. Walker was too proud to prove anything; he told Charley a man had to have secrets and days to look forward to. He promised that the day when Charley graduated he'd bring out the gold and they'd run it to England or someplace to sell it, so they'd never have to pay taxes and no one could steal it or claim it wasn't Walker's. Then Charley could piss on princes or gangsters. Walker made me promise I'd be Charley's bride. I'd giggle and Charley would blush. Walker would wink and hug me. He often smelled foul, but I was used to him.

Then one day in August before his senior year Charley went up the mountain and found his dad upstream from the cabin in a gulley behind the aspen grove, blood in a pool at his mouth, a cracked whiskey bottle and a gold pan just past his arms. Charley made a drag stretcher from his jacket and branches. An ambulance came to Sand Harbor. Now Walker can't move his legs or talk, write notes or stop drooling. Charley paid for the first year in the hospital by selling their lot. Till that was gone, government aid wouldn't pay.

My second ride took me to Sand Harbor. I searched the woods across the highway till I found the dirt road up the mountain. I hadn't been up there since once when Charley was home on leave. Trucks used to be able to make it up the first mile or so but can't anymore; there are washouts and fallen logs. At each fork in the road I stayed close to the stream; I remembered that much. In the shade were patches of snow but most had melted in the warm spell. The stream was full and fast, rumbling over wide spots and hissing through narrows. Wild mint and thistle were coming up already and smaller trees bent from the wind down the mountain. I wasn't used to climbing or doing much of anything so I stopped often to rest. I felt bad that I hadn't gone to see Walker in so long, but the place he lived was creepy, the way they locked you in the ward with all the goofs and poor sad men, the smell of sores and shit in their pants. I was afraid to go there without Charley, and if Charley had gone lately he hadn't told me.

On the first pass I missed the cabin but at the end of the meadow I saw a T-shirt hanging on a branch. I crossed the meadow to the hill and from there I could see the rear of the cabin. The pines were thicker and the vines had grown. The door was open and Charley's pack was inside. I climbed to the ridge trail and followed it till I saw Charley below at the stream, panning in a shallow. "Charley!"

He turned to watch me run down. He looked silly, loaded or just grinning in an old engineer's cap his dad used to wear. "Must be farther up," he said. "Nothing but granite and mica here, but I'll try a while more."

"I'm sorry about yesterday."

"Nobody's fault. You know I always thought I believed the old man, but I've been trying every trick for bucks except the gold."

"You really think he found it?"

"Yep." He bent back over and filled the pan.

I sat down to watch him work. The breeze had fallen and the air was hot like summer, old summers when I'd sit with my toes in the stream watching the hummingbirds and slapping the flies. On a day like that, up that high, anything is possible. I could believe in the gold. The air is lighter, seeps right into your ears to rinse out old worries and for that time you can understand words like "peace" and "forever," till the thunderclouds come. Those days can't last long enough.

"Why are you panning, Charley? Why don't you look for his stash?"

"Look where?"

"Around the cabin maybe?"

"Or by the stream, or by the road, maybe halfway up to Marlette or down along the highway. Maybe in Incline. Once he grabbed a pen from my shirt and drew something or wrote something but it looked like a kid's squiggles."

"Wouldn't there be dust in the stream, just a little, even?"

"Beats me. I don't even know what gold looks like for sure and it might not even be this stream. It forks a half dozen places from Marlette down to here. He might've found it in streams that are dry now, anywhere around here. It's a big mountain." He flopped down on his back, tired and discouraged.

"Charley?"

"Huh?"

"I brought you some money."

"What?"

"I handed him the check from my pocket. He stared for a long time as if he couldn't read. "What the fuck's he giving me money for?"

"He said you cheated for him at Harry's."

"I don't even know what he looks like. I never gave anybody that much."

He stared again at the check, then handed it back, threw down his cap, picked up his pan and stomped off upstream. I followed but he wouldn't talk. I watched while he stopped to sift water, his shoulders scrunched up to his neck and his eyes down close.

"When will you come home?"

"When I find the gold."

"If you come down we could go ask your dad again."

"What for? Are you psychic?"

It was rush hour by the time I made South Lake. I walked faster than the traffic through town. I had terrible visions going into the rest home, that Walker was dead, or his skin had turned gray or his eyes fallen out by now. In the main wing old folks were hobbling in pairs to the dining hall, ancient old couples with soft eyes and looks of patience because they no longer have anyplace to go. In the bedridden hall dull eyes stared from wrinkled skulls, and their moans were afraid. I had to ring and wait at the door to the locked ward.

Charley had fought against where they had put him, but doctors claimed he was unpredictable, that he threw food and upset the other patients. The nurse said I had only ten minutes till they'd shut down the day room and give evening medicine. Once on a Christmas field trip from school I talked to an old guy who said the best day of his life was when they put him away, because he used to have to fight for drinks and now they kept him stoned all the time on pills. No one would say that about this ward. It was segregated, just men, some of them fierce-looking and not so old, others just bones hung on the benches along the walls. There was a concrete patio outside but the doors were closed and there were twice as many men in the day room as should've been squeezed in there. I could hardly see through the bodies to the end of the room where the wheelchairs were. The nurse closed me in. Most of the men standing turned to stare at me. Orderlies leaned outside a viewing window. Some men paced in crowded circles and others stood still. None of them smiled or frowned. They were slow.

I started for the other end, searching each face for Walker. No telling how he'd look now. I was nearly to the wheelchairs when I felt a hand on my shoulder. I tried to keep walking but the grip tightened on my jacket. I had to turn and face him. He seemed seven feet tall, in a torn shirt, with brown teeth and black-rimmed glasses and stubble for hair. I knew he wasn't Walker; he looked mean. A shorter man with brown splotched skin stepped up. "Hello," he said.

"Tell this guy to let me—" The short man slapped his hand across my mouth. I tried to scream but his hand muffled it, so I kicked out and whipped with my arms; I could see through the window that no one was watching. I thought I'd be knocked down, expected hands under my shirt and down my jeans, but only the one hand held me and the other gagged me. Then came a scream so deep and threatening that the two men let go. I turned to the scream. His head seemed swollen, his hair was gone, his teeth were bared and snarling. I started toward him but a nurse and an orderly ran in and dragged me back through the door.

"I have to see Walker!"

"You did," the nurse said. "You upset him terribly."

I was too freaked to hitch home, as though there would be ghosts in the dark, so I called Phillip from a phone booth, then walked up to the stoplight at the state line and waited. The clubs were just filling with women in pants suits and gowns, with their chins high and their eyes shadowed green, men with tight pants that bulged

113

at the crotch and behind from their wallets. Cars were all waxed and glittered beneath the lights. I hoped to God Charley would find his gold.

* * * *

April 7, 1972

Walker's grandma was a Washoe woman of a German father who had strayed up from the Motherlode. Walker's granddad was a vagabond. For years he lived the summers with a camp of Washoes, bringing them traps and rifles, fishing the lake and the streams where trout ran to spawn. But in the fall, when they went down the mountain for pine nuts and tedious winters, he ditched for the coast and rode down to Mexico, then wandered back up in the spring, working cattle, picking carrots, shooting game. The Washoes ran him off when he told them it wasn't foxes and such that made the world, but a skunk spewed it out of his asshole. When he got word that his woman died, he brought his two sons to Virginia City, where he worked the Comstock Lode till he died.

When Walker was born his dad was a guard for the railroad in Truckee and a boss over Chinese gangs building new lines. He had married an orphaned girl of French parents and bought her a house near Chinatown where there were fires and disease, opium and sewage in the streets, and thousands of solemn children. When Walker's dad quit the railroad they moved up the mountain, first to a cabin on the Truckee River where they sold supplies to coaches, later to the lake where they tried to run a café, but it was dirty and the food was cheap and simple, Walker's mother frail and moody, so the tourists passed them by. His dad had a tumor which grew out from his rib cage under his arm; when the pain became too bad he rowed out on the lake and jumped in.

Then Walker's brother left for Alaska, his sister mar-

114

ried a sailor and moved to Monterey and his mother died of pneumonia. Walker joined the navy for World War I and when he came home he learned that his brother had died in Belgium.

Footloose and curious, morose from all those deaths, Walker set off to find his Uncle Chuck, whom his father had called a bold little moron, nervous and quick on the draw. When he was seventeen Chuck had run a pack train from Placerville, along the south shore and up over Kingsbury, hauling supplies to the Comstock silver mines and bringing back silver with just himself as guard. In that one year he made and saved enough cash to buy a thousand acres of rock and timber near Sonora in the mined-out Motherlode country.

Walker asked around Sonora but no one had heard of Uncle Chuck. It had been years since he moved there, but Walker persisted, wandering the hills, quizzing isolated Indians and camps of Chinese who had stayed to work the shut-down mines. Finally a Paiute told him of a deep cave where Chuck had been living for years. The Paiute said Chuck had deeded his land to a Swiss dairyman in exchange for food, wine and opium lowered down to the cave once a week.

Walker took a lantern, found steps gouged into the granite, makeshift ladders on the sheer drops, tunnels through which he couldn't see light ahead but could feel fresh air, and KEEP OUT signs every twenty feet or so.

He was yelling, "Hey, Chuck, it's your nephew," but nothing answered, no noise but trickling water and rocks that broke loose under Walker's feet. Then came a gunshot like the mountain exploding; the bullet smashed his lantern and ricocheted off the walls, off and back madly; then it was silent again.

"How in hell am I supposed to see?" Walker shouted.

After a while came an answer. "You ain't."

Walker inched his way down, blind in the cave, no light at all from the small entry back up around turns and slim passages. Deeper, he felt space around him, like a grotto, though he couldn't see it; there was some change in the air and the scent of a pool. A step broke off beneath him; Walker thought he was dead for sure, so he was screaming when his feet touched bottom, just a few feet down.

"Hush, boy! Do I have a nephew?"

Chuck prodded Walker ahead with a stick, then shoved him down on a sofa covered with burlap. "Chuck?" Walker said. "How'd you bring a sofa down here?"

"Dropped it. Kicked it. Chopped it in half. Took the best of a month to glue it back together, least it seemed so—hard to tell time when they ain't no sun. When were you born?"

"Twenty years ago."

"Hell, that's before I came underground. Nobody ever told me. Now you see, goddammit, how people are? Never thinking on anybody else, 'less they're out trying to poison you. Them damned Chinese tried to poison me, but they still don't know I'm down here."

"They do," Walker said.

"Well, shit. You see any hanging around on top?"

"Nope."

"Good."

Chuck fired up opium and Walker smoked with him, so he didn't remember much after that but the feeling of peaceful death, being buried and no time passing. He never did see Chuck—there was just no light and Chuck turned back down after helping him climb to the first of the ladders.

"Say, nephew, since you're here, there's something you could do for me. I could use a woman who don't mind living in caves. But make sure she ain't a big talker. I'm just damned tired of screwing my fist."

Walker said only two things are important: brain food

116

and exercise. I wonder if he might've stashed the gold in a cave, if there are caves near the cabin.

I told my dad Walker's story. I was thirteen. My dad ran over to Walker's right then and told him, "You old maggot, keep your filthy mouth away from my daughter!"

★   ★   ★   ★

April 15, 1972

Phillip said he'd go with me to the cabin for Spring break, but we had to wait till my folks went back down to Reno. We planned an early start Monday morning, but Pancho had found a barn to salvage in a pasture near Donner Lake. A restaurant in Incline said they'd buy the wood for paneling but they needed it right away, and he couldn't find any help that morning, so Maggie and I went along. Pancho pried off the boards, Maggie knocked out the nails and I loaded Charley's truck till the rear end dragged. By the time we delivered and reached home it was midafternoon.

From the highway the lake seemed choppy, all foam. Light clouds passed on a southerly wind, one of those thoughtless days when energy comes from all sides. We found a turnout behind a bank of trees where Phillip's car would be safe from the road. Treetops bent over the ridges and streams had cut new paths. The road was muddy and, with heavy packs, the climb was rugged. Phillip was in worse shape than I was, panting, his face flushed, but he kept up and wouldn't stop till I asked to. We spent too long lazing by the stream, tossing stones, lying back on the dry brush listening, so by dusk we had only made the halfway mark, a stump I remembered. Phillip took off his pack and climbed to the ridge. When

117

I caught my breath I followed him. "Faces in the clouds are proud and brave," he said.

The sun squatted north of Rubicon and carved a red gorge in the mountainside. The peaks were still snowbound. Sunset burned off the clouds. That night, I believed, Phillip and Charley would talk, if Charley was still there, become friends, because they're alike in some ways, both thoughtful, both wise, though in different fashions—Charley knows the world and Phillip knows ideas and they could tell each other things. I had cider in my pack, cookies from Maggie, and the sad news about Charley's dad, that nothing was better. We'd sit by the fire or out on the hill, all sleep in the loft for warmth like a family of beggars.

"We'll get lost in the dark," I said.

Back on the road we tried to walk faster, but before long we were tripping on ruts in the darkness. Clouds had rolled down and taken us in; our flashlight was weak and finally died. We couldn't gauge our distance climbing so slowly. The meadows were too much alike to recognize and too wide to see beyond, so we crossed over the stream and kept to the north side, stumbling through thistles and low manzanita, wading through washes and jumping from bushes where creatures rattled and croaked. I climbed the hillsides to look back. I was on my way up when Phillip stumbled on Charley's pickax.

"Who's that?" Charley shouted. He didn't come to the door. He was curled in his sleeping bag reading a book by candlelight. "Hey, Jodi! I found my dad's whiskey, a case of old skunk piss stashed under the floorboards. Who's that?"

"I brought Phillip."

"Oh."

"You don't mind, do you?"

"No," Charley growled. "We'll play cards." He stood up, dressed and filled the stove with logs. Phillip stayed back by the door. I took our packs to the corner and be-

118

gan to untie them, watching Charley half-crocked and
scowling, taking his cards from a shelf, spreading a blanket on the floor, ripping pages from a magazine and tear-
ing them into chips. I thought there'd be gold, or some
clue at least to make Charley happy or hopeful, but he
looked like a man about to be sentenced. There would be
no joy in the evening. I wished he'd just leave, and I felt
like a hangman.

"Sit down," he said. "Twenty-one all right?"

"C'mon, Charley. We just climbed for hours."

"Yeah," he said. "There's stew over there." He went
back to his candle and picked up his book, *Gold for Us
All.* Phillip dug out biscuits and I poured canned noodles
into Charley's stew. While the stuff heated I led Phillip
outside. "Charley's angry," I whispered.

Charley started whistling as if to say he could hear.
While we ate he stared at his book and glanced up now
and then till I caught his eye. Phillip was nervous; his lip
twitched and his eyes shot around. Finally he turned to
Charley. "Quite a challenge, to build this place."

"Nope," Charley muttered. "Just labor."

"The road was better then," I said. "You could drive
up halfway."

"Still, digging in this granite, all hand tools, fitting
these boards so smoothly. It's solid, a marvel."

"You ready to play?"

"Lay off, Charley. Phillip didn't do anything. Neither
did I."

"You said he's a player."

Phillip pulled his sleeping bag up to the blanket and
Charley rolled his like a stool and did the same. Charley
passed out chips and called them all green. I was tired of
forgiving Charley. It was easier when we both were troubled; then his moods were touching. This time they were
just in the way. He was a bully, pouting, sneering,
throwing the cards like a smartass pro, as cruel and callous as any, while Phillip sat meekly, beginning to smile,

119

as if at some hope or understanding, like a wise and good father. I was all flutters inside. My anger made me want Phillip even more. His frailness seemed loving, Charley's power seemed brutal, and I watched Phillip's hands fingering cards and wished they were on me. I made up my mind I'd have him that night. I thought, but didn't care, that it would torment Charley.

Charley dealt fast but his hands were sloppy from drinking. I watched him bend back the top cards and deal off seconds as I knew he could, but I wondered if Phillip could notice, Charley was that good. He was winning all the hands but a few; Phillip busted with tens whenever he drew so he stayed always on twelves, but Charley never busted. Phillip split a pair of aces. Charley dealt him a five and a four. Phillip doubled on ten to Charley's five. Charley dealt him a six, showed twelve and pulled an eight. Phillip kept taking more chips and Charley wrote them down. I didn't know how to tell him that Charley was cheating. When I went inside he wouldn't follow me and I was afraid of Charley's anger.

"You're some mechanic, Charley," I said, but Phillip didn't flinch. He was playing carelessly now, not watching the cards as they turned, betting three or four chips at a time. "You're going to hold him to the money, Charley? Why don't you just steal his checkbook?" Charley tried to scowl but his face had softened closer to human. "We could go climb the hill," I said, but he waved me away. I walked outside. Fog covered all but the meadow and there were no sounds but the whooshing of the stream. My head ached, squashed between my brain and my heart, between love for Charley and a wish to mash him with his pickax. I wanted to run down the mountain and leave them with their game. I couldn't stand to watch Phillip lose any more, though it was just pretend. "Damn it, Charley!" I shouted. "Tell him you're cheating!"

Charley slammed down the deck. "You think he

doesn't know that?" He stood up and threw out his bag, then dropped his pants and climbed in.

Phillip gathered the cards, then came outside with me. "How much did you lose?"

"Enough." There was a puzzling calm in his face and a touch of arrogance I'd never seen before. "I bought him off."

"Bought what?"

"Jodi," he whispered.

Charley had taught me to ski, to swim underwater, taught me to love poor folks and wasted tries. He'd told me the truth about his war, showed me how to work hard and let me advise him when I had nothing but stupid things to say. He was my hero, my symbol for hope in the wreck of our world; he had the guts and guile we needed to keep living honestly. Now Charley had sold me and Phillip had bought me. I was proud and lighthearted. Independence doesn't give freedom; what does is the rules you choose and the ruler who owns you. There is no escaping being owned by someone, if not Jesus then Satan, and if I respect someone more than I respect myself, there is no shame in belonging to that someone. Besides, what Charley had done meant that he had prized me after all, or else he wouldn't have thought me his own.

Back in the cabin I heated our cider. I offered some to Charley, but he was pretending to sleep. I was sore now and limp from the climb. Phillip was nervous, fidgiting. I figured he'd sit up all night if I didn't make a move. I stepped back from the candle, found my nightgown and stripped to my panties and socks, my face to the wall, my skin and my nipples tingling and tight. With my nightgown on I took off my panties, tossed them on the pile, came back to the fire and sat down beside Phillip. His hands darted from his chin to his knee and rubbed his tired shoulders while he watched Charley.

"I bought new pajamas," he said.

121

"My nightgown's new too. My mom bought it for Christmas, but I only wore it once."

I moved to behind him and rubbed his neck. Then I stepped out to pee. When I came back he was in his pajamas. I climbed the ladder to the loft, dangled my legs over the edge and waited. He went outside, then came back shivering, dropped the latch bar on the door and warmed his hands over the fire. Charley was still. I couldn't hear him breathing. Outside were noises like footsteps on the road. With Charley below I'd be listening all night, wondering if he thought we were cruel and cold to his troubles, loving while he was empty, together on the boards just above him. It wouldn't be right, it would anger Charley and embarrass him, but I wouldn't turn Phillip away. He was staring up my nightgown. He walked to the window and stood for a while, came over and squeezed my foot gently. He blew out the candle and dropped his sleeping bag on the mat opposite Charley.

I was more relieved than disappointed, and proud that Phillip seemed thoughtful of Charley. The loft was musty and I heard bugs skittering around. In my bag I rolled to the window and ripped off a corner of the cardboard, smelled for the mist and lay listening to the stream. I was limp and aching, drifting to sleep, but I crawled up to the edge and looked down at Charley. He was still as before. "Did you find any gold?"

"There ain't any fucking gold."

In the morning he was gone. He had packed at first light and tried to slip out. Phillip had told him he'd leave or we'd leave, but Charley said no. The sun came over the south ridge and streaked the floor with shadows of vines. I climbed down brazenly, tossing off my nightgown, but Phillip had turned away. We ate rolls and apples on the hill above the stream, then explored the cabin, found the whiskey beneath the floorboards, still a few bottles left, dusty and sticky with the last six years, old magazines—*True Adventure*, girlies, and *National Geographics*—a chromatic harmonica, khaki work pants, cans of food with the labels ripped off, and two engineer's caps. I bunched and pinned up my hair so one fit me. The other rode Phillip's ears. We took Charley's book about gold along, and his pans and shovel.

We sifted in the sand the way we'd seen it in movies and I'd watched Charley do, gently so the heavy gold would stay at the bottom. What I thought was gold Phillip said was mica and what he said was gold I thought was pyrite. Because we still thought about Charley we were quiet and serious, but sometimes we'd laugh because we were on the mountain alone, the closest person maybe hours away, in our hundred square miles of trees, meadows, ponds, peaks, arroyos and the pale sky marbled with brighter clouds. We worked the stream straight up past the first two forks, then followed a south branch back down the far side of the ridge. There were buds of early snapdragons, skinny robins squawking in the cedars, dark cuts in the earth to bare granite, and toads, skittish chipmunks, coyote tracks through the mushy patches of snow, but only two people, as if the earth were new.

We talked only about the gold and Charley, old Walker and whether he lied about the gold, nothing about the game or the prize, what we'd do that night or sooner. In the warm afternoon I took off my boots and my jeans and lay back to sun and excite him, waiting to peel off my shirt till he showed an interest, but he hardly looked, kept his head in the stream and only called out questions to me. But when I dressed again and worked alongside him I caught him staring lots of times, through my clothes and deeper.

On the way down we gathered sticks for kindling. At the cabin we steamed rice and potatoes and carrots and took them up on the ridge to eat. The sun dropped quickly and the sky went gray and starless, glowing at north and south state lines.

"Shall I bring up some whiskey?" I wondered.

"Can't be poison. Charley drank it."

"He might be immune," I said. "But it's a good way to die, Charley's dad used to say."

Phillip chuckled. "Bring up my jacket?"

"Nope. Find a stick and we'll spin it, make fire." I ran down the hill. I scrubbed down a bottle of Walker's old skunk piss. Back on the ridge stars came out in clusters while we sipped and gagged. I was scared for the night, that he'd sleep alone again—though I thought he had done it for Charley's sake, I wasn't sure. I wanted to force a move, force him to feel it was urgent. I hadn't told him before about my family's plans for my going to Paris, because he might think I wasn't serious about him. But it was the time to tell him.

"Next year I might go to Paris."

"For a trip?"

"For school. My folks want me to study painting and my mom says I'll meet rich folks there. She thinks I'm an artist. She thinks artists need money."

"Practical," he said, watching me roughly, as though I'd said something foul.

"She's O.K."

I expected him to be frantic, to tackle me there or shy away hurt. But he shook his head once, then stared past me distantly. "I should be going myself," he said. "I'm a flop at teaching."

"Who says?"

"For each student I help, a hundred think I'm a twerp. Who'll listen to a twerp? I think poor teachers should leave it for others to try; new ones at least can take it seriously and believe in themselves, and perhaps that leaves the school less fraudulent. Besides, I'd like to run farther away. I've saved some; these last months I've

124

been winning, and I'm confident. It could last years. What else, if not for—"

"For what?"

He was watching my feet now. His lip twitched and he took a long pull on the bottle. "For what?" he whispered.

"You'd come?"

"You'd ask me?"

My arms grew to squeeze him. I fell to his lap staring up at the stars, other worlds. We took turns at the whiskey, sips and big gulps till the quart was half gone; then we ran down the hill to the cabin. Phillip tripped and tumbled on a manzanita; I tried to pull him out, but my balance was drunk and I fell in beside him.

In the cabin I picked up my nightgown and climbed to the loft. While Phillip stoked the stove I tore off my clothes, started into my nightgown, then laid it beside me instead. "It's warmer up here." I watched him undress, anxiously first, then slower, methodically, stuffing his socks into his shoes, folding his jeans. He climbed the first rung, then jumped back down for his sleeping bag.

I arranged myself crosslegged on the mattress and threw my hair over the front of my shoulders. He tossed his bag ahead of him and climbed till he saw me. His eyes stopped blinking and his jaw fell limp. Slowly as waking he climbed the last steps and crawled to me, dug his head in my lap as if he were hiding from someone. He wrapped his arms around my back, held tight with hard fingers. I lifted his head and slipped his shirt over, loosened his arm and pulled the shirt away. He sat up and took a deep breath. "Shall we spread out the bags?"

"One underneath," I said. "One on top."

"Can I just watch you, Jodi? Would it seem perverse?"

"It's O.K."

He leaned back on the wall. I felt like posing, bending every way so he could see me all over, bringing each part of me close to his eyes, touching his eyes, closing his eyes, showing him all that I am outside. But I didn't move much and couldn't look him straight on. He came over and pressed me down slowly. His eyes were frantic and his lips were muttering. Between my breasts his cheeks were hot and moist. His stubble beard thrilled me with pain. His chest was bony between my thighs and I hung my knees over his shoulders. When he slid up to kiss me I fumbled for his penis, ran my thumbnail down the ridge of its underside, took his nuts in my hand. He brought his fingers between my legs from behind and lay a cold finger just inside me. The breeze curled around the cabin and moonlight cut through the boards while he lay still and moaning. A coyote howled, then another.

"You won't call this sin, Jodi?" I pressed his lips closed and he kissed my fingers, each one in a line. There were sharp bones on his hips and a sunken place between his ribs, soft hair all down his back. His tongue was long and dry, his penis scaly and wide. More than anything I noticed my peace, my comfort and the journey I knew we had started on, loving unselfishly, everyone, fearlessly, for the good they had and the death that would take them away. It was a weird time to think of Jesus, but I did, on the cross and burning. Jesus was salvation, and I felt saved.

Phillip rolled stiffly on me, spread my thighs, fumbled and missed, then missed again. I reached down and helped him inside. He eased in, though I was slick as butter, and he worked slowly, pulled back till he almost slipped out and drove in deeper each time. His hands were tight and damp on my butt, his breath tickling my ear; I slammed up to meet him. He came once, kept on till there was a tremble in me, a flutter like an infant's mouth pulling to yawn, then a stop and a rush of tiny muscles tensing singly, reaching, spreading, closing around.

Then he jumped up. "My God, Jodi! I'm sorry—could you get pregnant? I didn't think."

"Don't worry," I said, and pressed him down to me. "Don't think about it tonight."

Charley thinks tomorrow is Easter, though it was three weeks ago. I guess he missed the real day. He took the check from the envelop where I had left it on his desk. I haven't seen him since the cabin and Maggie says she thinks he's skipped out; guys he owes have been calling and he fought on the phone with Maria. There was a note in my bedroom. "It's your week of forgiveness so think on me kindly." I don't understand him forgetting like that. On Easter Pastor Sandoz talked so fervently about Christ bleeding and dying for our sins that I told Charley I nearly asked to be baptised right then. Charley laughed it off. He kidded me about wearing a new dress for the first time all year.

Yesterday I went to a clinic in Tahoe City. The doctor gave me a prescription for birth-control pills. I'll take them and try not to think. I'll believe in forgiveness.

★ ★ ★ ★

"Should a wise man answer with windy knowledge," Eliphaz said to Job, "and fill his belly with the east wind? Should he argue in unprofitable talk, or in words which can do no good? You are going away with the fear of God, and hindering meditation before Him. For your iniquity teaches your mouth and you choose the tongue of the crafty. Your own mouth condemns you and not I. Your own lips testify against you."

Eliphaz thinks Job is paying for secret sins, but Job keeps calling out for the reason his sons and daughters are dead and he has famine and boils. His fear of the Lord is displaced by his anger. The only sin he knows is birth to a fallen race. Why this karma that goes on for generations and turns a righteous man over to Satan? Why does the Lord need to be justified? Why do I have

127

this boil on my knee that roots deeper and spreads each time I lance it? I'm tempted to suck it dry.

"Shall a faultfinder contend with the Almighty?" says the Lord from His whirlwind. He silences Job with a list of His powers, but He never comes clean, never says, "No sweat, it was all for a bet, the death of your sons and daughters. Now I'll make your trees bloom again and bless you with all new children." The Lord is too proud to confess, and I think Job remembers his first children laughing at bedtime and waving to him from the trees they climbed. I want a sweet Lord, gentle and merciful.

It's dark outside. There hasn't been sun in a week. On Mount Rose, Incline and Heavenly, boys are schussing down to lift lines, balleting down to the ropes for the girls in new tight ski suits, butts pushed out. Fathers are watching their pink-cheeked daughters learn to parallel and stay on their toes and everyone smiles with their lips chapped and the wind up their noses. Later they'll take hot baths, whirlpools or saunas, and rub down their skin with oil till they're drunk with looseness and fall asleep smugly. But one day they'll wake up with boils on their knees and hardened arteries, remembering when they first loved, when their children had soft lips and curly hair, when there were dreams that made the bad days pass quickly, hopes to wake up with, and they'll curse God for pain if they still believe, and curse Him for not being, if they don't.

Charley says my dad hardly speaks to my mom anymore. He doesn't sell much, sleeps as long as he likes and leaves the phone off the hook. He'll lose his job and be back driving equipment, bitching about his hemorrhoids, and he'll blame it on me. I wish I could still hate him. It would be easier. Every week, after midnight, he calls Charley to ask if he's heard from me, though Charley swore to him that the minute I called or wrote he'd tell him. My dad checks newspaper stacks at the library for news of the Children of God, to find where their place is

128

in Mexico, where Charley told him I probably was. He calls Danny a lot lately, to try to talk Danny into dropping school at the quarter so they can drive to Mexico and bring me home. But Danny won't go. He tells my dad to give me time and freedom. My mom thinks I'm still in King's Beach, hiding out and reading the Bible for answers. Last week she tried to give Charley $500 to support me. She has threatened my dad with separation, Charley says.

Charley came up for the last time today. He seemed so tired from climbing the drifts or from drinking and going without sleep, or from practicing being in jail. I used to think that in his war all his fear turned to anger, but here he was watching the fire with wide eyes as if there were some terrible thing inside, and he stopped in the middle of sentences, forgetting what he was saying. He bought me a rifle.

"Look, Jodi," he said. "We'll stuff it down under the floorboards where my dad kept his whiskey. You shouldn't need it till spring at least. There's enough food and no one will come up this far. Christ, I can't even find the road anymore. It's a mean winter; a fine one you picked."

"I picked it, you think?"

"Yeah. You could've hid in the Bahamas. Now the way it's set up Pancho's supposed to come for a while at least, Saturdays, same as me; then he might go south and he might find somebody else or he might not, I don't know. Who can you trust?"

"Nobody. Not you. You won't stay."

"You're welcome."

"I'm scared, Charley. You're even scared. How am I supposed to feel? Somebody'll feed you at least and you'll have people to talk to, maybe a cell mate with a soft butt."

"You've got your gypsy."

"You don't believe she's here."

"What do I know?"

"I thought you knew everything, like what's good for me. You brought up Phillip's journals."

"So burn them. Why don't you let me take you down the mountain?"

"No!" Down the mountain I'd still have to hide. I couldn't face the patronizing smiles, the way they'd either treat me like a lunatic or tell me to get off it and rise above self-pity. I don't feel singled out; none of us has what he needs. Charley only wanted to grow up independent, as he was when a child, but no one would let him, and Phillip just wanted the same, to be on his own. My dad only wanted to save me, but, like me, he's a killer. I only wanted to love someone as much as I'd always been loved. If I went back down they'd pretend things were right. Why should I let them lie? I'd rest and bathe and doze in the sun when it came, watch myself turn pretty again, or slice my face with razors to look ugly as I am, hateful and cruel. With patience I guess they'd convince me that my time up here was for working out grief so I could go back to a pointless and godless life where rich folks rope off the beach and hire the others as guards, and everyone wants just to win. I'd have to live with that or be a burden on people I don't love anymore. I must not love them or I'd want to be with them. At least up here I don't cost them much.

"I'm not that scared," I told Charley.

"You think you can shoot a doe if you're hungry enough?"

"I'm not tender, Charley. I could shoot you."

"Good."

"That means I'm grown up?"

"Yeah. Grown up, wise, a shithead like everybody else, adjustable. Now listen. When hikers come in the summer, keep the rifle unloaded. Chances are they won't find the cabin, but if they do, they might come over. If

130

*you don't like their looks just point the rifle unloaded
and they'll run fast enough."*

"You think I'm trigger-happy?"

"You can be weird."

*"How many people did you kill in the war? You never
told me."*

"You're a bitch, Jodi."

*"I can't let anybody see me. I'll have to shoot them
and bury them or else they'll go back and tell somebody,
who'll come up to get me. Can't you see me standing off
a platoon of guys in white coats and a kind old lieuten-
ant or shrink with a bullhorn. 'Give yourself up, Jodi
McGee. We're not here to hurt you!' How do they know
what hurts me? I won't let them take me alive."*

"Damn it, I can't tell anymore if you're serious."

*"Neither can I. Hey, maybe when I'm digging graves
I'll find the gold."* They might commit me, if I went
down, send me to a place like where Walker lives, feed
me downers, zap me with live wires or carve my brain
and leave me sucking cream of wheat through a straw.
Or they'd decide I was redeemable, place me in groups to
talk about pain and escape so we could cry ourselves
blind, then go back to living with terror stuffed deep in
our bellies and believe it was all sickness rather than awful truth. Sometimes I want to run down, when I think
about the way Charley serves me as if I were a princess
and he a eunuch, but he'll be gone soon. I won't live on
downers or lies. I'd rather have pain than nothing; joy
needs innocence and that's all gone. At least up here I
can walk where I want to in snowshoes, spit on the floor
and break things, climb through drifts to the top of the
ridge and flip off the rest of the world. I can play with
myself or go to my gypsy, sail off to magical places like
old times without hearing other people scream, like
Walker has to hear.

"I brought something else, the pouch you had hidden

away. I finally got into your room again." He took it out by the cord and tossed it to me. It untied and some of the pine nuts fell on the floor. "They're petrified. I bit one—I think it knocked out a filling. Who carved the faces?"

"My gypsy," I said. I picked each one out, more than a dozen. Each face was different, scratched as if with a needle or sharp razor into the tiny shells, with hair, ears, noses, mouths, some with jagged teeth if I looked closely. I passed each one to Charley. "See their misery and how they're all so different; there are this many ways to suffer and maybe lots more. I found them up by Marlette, almost ten years ago."

"Probably Indian. That skin's a coyote or something. It's not cowhide."

"Did the Washoes or Paiutes use voodoo?"

"Who knows."

"Maybe they cast spells and things but didn't work at it hard enough. I'll try it out." I went out back to a snowless place beneath an overhanging boulder, where the winds in the fall had blown clumps of pine needles. I took up an armful and brought them back in. They were damp and flexible. First I wove a straight trunk, then thinner sticks for arms and legs while Charley sat watching. He gave me his gum to press on the trunk for a neck with a pine nut on top. While he stacked away the food he had brought—his pack was stuffed with dried beans, grains and dried fruit, a duffel bag crammed with canned goods—I tore up a towel and sewed a jump suit for the doll.

"He's ready, Charley. Anybody you want me to cremate?"

He shook his head gravely. "Don't work it for me."

I laughed to pretend I was possessed. "You're not afraid of devils, are you?"

"Just pick your own target."

I first thought of my dad. I saw him in his chair,

132

brooding darkly in confusion and blaming his life. I truly wished he could see me now. I wondered if the faces were carved for personal enemies, or hunters and loggers, or silver barons of the Comstock days who drained the mountain water, or ranchers who fenced up the plains. "How about Harry?" I wondered. "You ever see him?"

"I saw Harry Junior once. He's fat, with ruby rings and a toupee."

"I'll try his dad." I anchored the doll's legs beneath the burner on the woodstove and bent its ankles till it stood straight. "Pray for God's mercy, Charley, like they did at the inquisitions." Charley just stared at the doll.

I touched off a stick from the fire and let a big flame rise, then dropped the flame between the legs of the doll. It sputtered for a moment on the damp needles, burned off the jumpsuit first, then caught the needles at once, flickering blue and yellow. I felt a strange peace and solitude, watching the fire. The gum melted to droplets on the stove and the head fell off, charred black but still tough. I wiped it and put it in the pouch with the others.

Pastor Sandoz said the unpardonable sin is blasphemy against the Holy Spirit. He said it was impossible unless the Spirit was in you or you'd seen the face of the lord, as Judas and Satan and Job had, but there is no Spirit in me, and whirlwinds don't answer my prayers.

Charley made ready to leave. I couldn't believe he'd let them take him to jail. "Why do you trust me with that gun, Charley? How do you know I won't shoot myself?"

"How do I know you won't hang yourself or light your jeans on fire?"

"Wouldn't the gun be quicker?"

"Maybe not. You might shoot the wrong part of your head and lie there twitching for half a day. I'll write. Whether you'll get the letter I don't know. Damn, Jodi, I wish—"

"What?"

"I wish we'd come up here five years ago and never gone down."

I dropped the sack I was holding and squeezed him till I thought I heard bones crack and hard muscles tear. "Stay with me, Charley."

He stood for what seemed like minutes with his eyes closed; then he said no, shouldered his pack with a desperate smile, kissed my forehead, then turned out the door. I watched him walk on his snowshoes on top of the drifts and into the evergreens.

"Have you an arm like Jehovah," says Himself to Job, "and can you thunder with a voice like His?" No, but I could spit on His boots if He stood here and call Him a coward and bully. I'm delivered from righteous fear through anger and I'll shout whatever I please. There is no Jesus to step in and make peace between us. I believed the Lord was merciful, but His mercy is infinite, so I can't see it. Job's children might be skipping through daisies in Heaven, or sleeping to wait for the rapture, but I'm locked in this cabin, 150 square feet, in a snow-white hell, with a boil on my knee that I can hear squeak when I walk.

I've tried to repent a hundred times, but my heart is dry. Who is Jesus, if only the righteous can repent? I've lost the fear of pain and death and hell. Pain sets my mind turning tricks and sends me to my gypsy; death is just a movement in space; hell the divorce from God and goodness. That's already done.

Our Lord sets the odds against us, makes the rules so the only way you can win is not to play, the same as at Harry's. He gives us away to temptation. Our Lord admits to Job, "His heart is hard as a stone." I'll weave another doll and burn Him; I'll dream a God of my own.

"Whatever is under the Heaven is mine," says Jehovah. Nothing is mine, says Jodi. I'm sick of this mountain

134

and the sound of my voice, sick of the boil on my knee.
And Charley is gone.

★ ★ ★ ★

April 22, 1972

Monday at school, the day after spring break, the beginning of the last stretch toward summer, when kids are already speaking of trips and moving away, yawning dreamily as if it were already here, teachers good-humored and lazy with assignments and discipline, Miss Waterman came into our room after last period to give Phillip her resignation.

He told her to take it to Mr. Furby, unless she'd consider waiting till the end of the year in case she felt different by then. But she said that the school board had finalized the elective proposal, that she'd made her stand and wasn't speaking to Mr. Furby because he had several times failed to show her professional courtesy. She eyed me suspiciously and left the room wiping her cheeks with her sleeve.

"Shall I give him mine, too?" Phillip sighed. "Damn responsibility!" He walked to the door and stared down the hall past Miss Waterman's classroom.

I told him it wasn't his fault. "But I judge myself harshly, Jodi. Mother would be proud. I find guilt very interesting. Are we born with it? I wonder. Shall I find a therapist? Manipulation might do me good but I'd feel like a hockey puck. About gambling they'd say I want to lose. I'd deny it. Stalemate. Most often I do believe guilt is hereditary. See, I am a Christian. Another stalemate. So much for therapy."

At the gate to the parking lot Aaron and Jerry were waiting. I saw Jill out in Jerry's car with a girl named Suzette. Aaron blocked the gate. "Hi, Jodi, wanted to tell

135

you I found a book in the library, a Catholic *Kama Sutra*, tells you how to—"

"Excuse us," Phillip said, but Aaron wouldn't budge.

"Mr. Oswald," Jerry said, "what was the homework today? Or was it yesterday? Or in math? All that brain work you give has got me befuddled. How about we go down to your house for some tutoring?"

Phillip's face had gone pale, and he was biting his lips, panting through his nose, "Come in tomorrow," he muttered, then twitched from his neck as though cussing himself for talking stupidly.

"Hey, Mr. Oswald, you look faint. How's your old heart?"

When I grabbed for Aaron to pull him away he took my wrist and bent it. I tried to yank loose but his fingers were tight. "Let go, sucker! I'll—"

"What?"

I leaned back to kick him but he caught my leg and nearly threw me down. "Come on to the car, Jodi. We'll give you a lift."

"A ride," Jerry said. "I'll give her a ride."

"Shut up, Jerry!" Aaron snapped. "Jerry can drop us at my place; my dad's gone. You know you've treated me badly."

"I haven't treated you at all. I haven't done anything to you." Behind I could see Jill trying to jump from the car, but Suzette was holding her back. Phillip was standing with his arms spread and his knees bent, but it seemed he couldn't move. Aaron let go of me, I jumped back to Phillip and we turned toward the office and the front gate.

"Wait up," Aaron said. His hair was mussed and his face sincere. For a moment I was confounded, drawn toward him. He stepped up shyly as though he'd say he was sorry. He ran his arm down my back. "I didn't mean we should fight. Look, I'll take you both out for dinner tonight." He slid his hand down the rear of my jeans.

136

I cocked and slapped his face before he could stop me. Phillip howled like a black belt and swung toward Aaron, but he missed by a foot when Aaron jerked back and pushed him down from behind.

"Hands off, professor. You know there is a law against fucking a kid, not for me, but for you. I know where to go to start the law moving, and Jodi's old man's a big dude. He doesn't like guys fucking his daughter, take my word." Phillip stood up, trembling with his fists in the air. Jill was screaming from the car. Suzette could hardly hold her, and Jerry was walking that way. I wished to Christ Charley was around so I could take him to Aaron's to smash his face ugly and kick his brain goofy, spoil his future. I was disgusted at Phillip, beaten and cowardly, but the next moment I thought him a saint, his pants torn and his knee bleeding, his eyes suddenly bloodshot, raging. He wasn't a coward. He just wasn't a bully. I watched Jerry's car spin up the gravel and slide out the gate.

In the car Phillip wouldn't look at me. He seemed ashamed; he wanted to take me home but I told him I wouldn't go, so he drove, straight-backed on the seat and his arms straight out on the wheel as if he needed all his strength to turn it, up Mount Rose to the crest, where he stared past the grasslands and over the eastern mountains. "I could kill that boy," he said. "If I had a gun I could shoot him again and again. If I saw him on the street I'd run him down." I tried to tell him I understood how he felt, but I didn't. He was the one who was beaten. His face was still pale and furious and his shoulders still quivered tightly. I wished I could have fought Aaron, but I was thankful I wasn't a man; I had a choice.

At the beach rowboats were tied to the pier, bobbing gently in the rough small waves. The sun was gone behind thick clouds and the beach was deserted. Phillip stared down at the water. With dusk the sky covered darkly; tamarack, birch, and cedar seemed stubble up the black mountains high into the clouds, far above the fire-fly lights spaced and humble on the western shore. There was majesty, heavenly power and energy from the sky, and a dark and fierce challenge, what I guess pioneers called America. Charley fits this land, but Phillip is a foreigner.

"We could borrow a boat," I said. "I'll row, or you can, whatever. Aaron's a bully. He knows he can intimidate most everybody so he does it. You're not the first or the worst."

He ripped the button off the collar of his shirt and tossed it, watched a wave take it down. "I think I'll go home, Jodi, if you don't mind." Before I could answer he was up and gone.

I watched him cross the highway and then I walked up the beach to the park, took off my sandals, rolled up my pant legs and waded past the new condos and up to the hot springs at the base of the hill by the state line and left as ruins now. Once it was a fine resort of healing water and horse trails; a minister who ran it a hundred years ago preached Christ at the springs. Now only a few of us came. Charley had first shown it to me. Dark had come so I stripped and jumped in where the hot water cooled away from the source. I felt exposed, though trees and a wall blocked my view of the houses above and I was under the water. I wanted to feel exposed, for penance or something, something to do with Aaron which I couldn't quite understand. Maybe I'd left him and despised him from jealousy, or I didn't despise him at all; for me, no matter how I denied it, he was the hero today. I scooted back toward the source of the spring till it burned me.

Jill called just as I walked into the house. "Jodi," she said, "Jerry told me Aaron only wanted to ask you out and he hadn't been able to talk to you at school or at home because you were always with Mr. Oswald. He's really pissed, Jodi. He might do something weird. He still likes you. I don't think he's been dumped before. I guess all this time he thought you'd come crawling back when you unloaded that—"

"What?"

"That Christian jive."

"Isn't he going with Suzette?"

"She'll do anything he says. His cousin gave him some cocaine which he didn't want because he said he was in training, so Aaron had her sell it for him and she brought him all the money. She's a slut. I think she goes down for Jerry, too. I told him to split today." She said all our friends knew about Phillip and me, that it made some of them angry though she didn't know why. I'd hardly seen them all year. She asked to come over but I said I was going to Phillip's, so she said she'd call again.

Maggie was alone, knitting a tiny sweater and baking bread. "I'm glad you're home," she said. "I'm so sick of reading baby books. Somebody called you from the principal's office this morning. They said you didn't come to school."

"I was just late."

"Don't they ever bust you for ditching? They caught me every time, almost. I had to do fifty-four hours of detention in the last six weeks, else they wouldn't let me graduate. Maybe because your boyfriend's a teacher? You don't think that's funny? Charley called, too, from south shore, and he said he found a job, but he wouldn't tell me about it. Charley's getting stranger. This house is a real freak show. You and Pancho are never around."

"When will Charley be home?"

"This week he said. He met a girl down there but he isn't in love."

"What did he say?"

"Just that she had big boobs and a hysterectomy and she gave him free drinks where she worked. He likes that best. Jodi, I've got to tell you, sometimes I get real afraid. Today I went to Mrs. Bostwick's, you know, across the street. Have you talked to her? She showed me pictures of her grandchildren. They had on the cutest little dresses. If only Paul had a better job. You know he just quit the hardware for a job at the church? He's a counselor for youth groups or something. Who could he counsel? I heard him on the phone say he was a heroin addict once, so he'd sound more reformed. There's a new pastor, real young. Paul makes only sixty dollars a week; how can we buy anything for our baby? Mrs. Bostwick says she's a girl. She put a key on a string and hung it over my belly. It spun clockwise so that means she's a girl. Mrs. Bostwick's a psychic; she studies Edgar Cayce—he's another psychic with a pretty good record—and she talks to dead guys who are in limbo. Don't tell Paul; he'd burn her house down for sure. Did you know I won a contest once, for being the cutest baby in Anamoose, North Dakota. There were only six babies. Jodi, do you think I'll ever be pretty again, you know, lose all this weight and these pimples and stuff?"

"Sure, Maggie, in the sun and swimming a lot. You can take the baby down to the beach."

"I will. I'll wear my old two-piece. I stashed it away at my mom's. I'll have to get skinny to wear it. Maybe I just won't eat for a month after she's born. Just drink milk with protein powder. I might look good with big boobs if I did a lot of sit-ups and stuff. I don't care what Paul says. If I found somebody else I'd probably leave him. Do you think guys are scared off by girls with kids? I worry about everything. Do you think Paul's crazy?"

"Sure."

"I mean really crazy, like he might kill somebody?"

"Not that crazy. You think he might?"

"Oh, I don't know. I just think about dying and things. My mom says everybody does when they're eighteen. Some ladies die in childbirth, not many I guess, but this morning Mrs. Bostwick said she smelled death when the wind came from the lake, and last night Paul said I should make my peace with God like there was a rush and all."

"Doesn't he say that a lot?"

"This time was different. I almost thought he was loaded. Oh, God! I burned the bread!" She jumped for the oven. There was a tap on the counter behind me.

Paul was there, glaring. He snapped, "I don't like to be talked about!" Maggie threw the bread in the sink and started to cry. Paul took her shoulders and led her away. I could hear him yelling in their bedroom. There was nothing I could do. It seemed just a desperate day, so I walked down to Phillip's.

He was on the porch rail, staring up at the trees. "Guess what I came home and did? Push-ups. Then I shadowboxed the wall till I couldn't hold my arms up. Do you know what it means to believe you're a coward? There's always some need to stand up coolly and fight. I tried to think back. Whenever I fought, whenever I competed, I lost. So what's the sense."

"Today you just weren't ready for it."

"I won't let it happen again. I swear."

"I want to take you to a place I know. It's a healing place."

We walked up through Brockway and down the Hotel road. The trees were spooky with dew and crickets, and people were out on their balconies. I didn't know who owned the springs, the beaches were private on both sides; no matter where you go, unless you own it or it's paved you have to assume you're trespassing. Phillip kept looking over his shoulder, not used to being a criminal as most of my other friends were, always with a joint or out too late or driving somewhere they shouldn't. I nearly had to pull his pants off at the springs. "What if we have to run?" he said. "I don't want to run naked," but he laughed at himself while he said it and his nervousness was part of the game, like kids shoplifting or throwing rocks at windows. In the pool he shivered though it was lukewarm where we started. I rubbed down his neck and shoulders, squeezed him hard from behind, tugged his arms to pop his back and dove down to tease him and pinch, to let him shove me away and help him feel strong.

There were still clouds, dark water, and we climbed to the wall beneath the houses where we could see in the windows. A fat woman flicked the T.V. dial, a man stared at us but we knew he couldn't see. Phillip was standing tall and grinning like a schoolboy, tossing stones in the air and catching them behind his back, picking me up on his shoulders, showing off. I reached between his legs and wouldn't let go though he tried to run. Back in the spring we slid up toward the source, a yard at a time so we could stand the heat, till we were limp and dry inside. Then I dared Phillip to jump into the lake and he did, on the run and howling. I was so proud, as if I had made him new.

While we walked home barefoot he told me he used to run cross-country, the only sport he tried for long. "I could run till I thought I was bleeding inside, then run faster to keep from thinking. I ran barefoot on the hill behind our school, leading them all in practice, the only one who didn't wear shoes even in meets. I didn't care about rocks or stickers; my feet were tough, calloused like a hard sole, but not much bounce. I never could win a meet. Maybe if I'd worn shoes." He laughed and hugged me to his side. We strutted through town leaning together.

At home he was quiet. He stood in the doorway and watched me all the time I cooked our dinner, studied me dreamily, admiringly, as if I were in a gallery. He only spoke to answer my questions, where were the salt and the knives, just leaned against the wall and now and then smiled thoughtfully. We drank wine with dinner and afterward till I was dizzy and he was thinking about something he wouldn't tell. He propped a pillow against a bookshelf and sat on the floor yawning. I laid my head in his lap and closed my eyes while he toyed with my hair and ran his fingers across my lips, and I knew peace and confidence so still and sure that if I'd recalled a troubled or restless time, I would've doubted it had really happened.

Still dizzy with the wine I stumbled while I pulled off my jeans; then naked, I stopped to watch him stare. He was enchanted. Shadows from the kerosene heater danced on the ceiling. I reeled into bed and held out my arms. When he undressed, a knife, a switchblade like ones I'd seen kids bring back from Mexico, dropped from his hip pocket.

I slept there three nights this week. Phillip is different at home. He leaves school tense and talking too fast, but over the evening I watch him mellow, till finally he's calm and talked out. Then I ask him questions and he only smiles. It doesn't bother me. There's always tomorrow. He hardly eats at all. I wonder what it means, to take care of someone.

★   ★   ★   ★

May 1, 1972

School has been tense; kids grinning and making remarks so we'll know that they know about us; teachers tapping each other to point and stare at me when I come into the faculty lounge. Jerry makes some crack every day, which Phillip lets pass; Aaron waits at the end of the hall after third period just to watch me smugly, as though he has a plan for revenge. I've gone back to gym third period and I eat lunch by myself some days, out on the benches past the high-jump pits. In class Phillip tries to treat me like anyone else. After school we don't talk about school but drive places where we won't be recognized. We try to ignore these changes, believe everyone will soon lose interest, and hope the rumors don't reach my folks.

Phillip's teaching suffers. He forgets his lectures and neglects to make lesson plans; often he just tells us to read or gives us a worksheet, while he leaves the room to stand in the sunlight. Today he seemed particularly vulnerable, looking anxious, fidgeting, impatient when kids asked questions. I asked him what was wrong; he motioned around meaning just everything. When I asked him what was really wrong he just stared at me coldly.

Today from Mount Rose we could see clearly the high lakes of ice blue, white pine and aspen over chalets and A-frames, the sun dropping golden streaks from Tahoe's shores to its depth, thinning out as they neared the center, like highways to a place from where we could dive to the middle of the earth. "With the surface of the mountains brilliantly photographed on its still surface," Mark Twain said, "I thought it must surely be the fairest picture the earth affords."

Though the trees have been cut and are only half grown back and thinned, though highways cut the passes and casino hotels teeter on the south shore like dominoes, though sailboats and neon give the illusion of civilization and most of the fish are gone, still the water seems virgin out deep and a squall at any moment can beach a sailor forever. In reflection, Mt. Tallac hangs like a cone suspended from Emerald Bay, the snow melted enough to show the white cross on its slope, once above and once on the water, as though there are two gates to heaven.

We stopped next at Burton's Creek, where Pancho used to stay in the summers. The road was torn up from washouts but we drove it anyway, a mile past the NO TRESPASSING signs. There were flowering sage and dandelion in the meadow and more kinds of buds than we could count along the shore of the creek, but few had begun to bloom. The frame Pancho built for his tent was still upright and the dugouts he had used for fires were pools now. I had come up here often, even after they ran Pancho off. It was kind of a shrine to me, a place to think about freedom, like Charley's cabin, because Pancho and Walker had both just set down where they pleased. But Walker had been more shrewd, hidden better. Pancho didn't see the need to hide. Before he came here he worked himself straight through college, but he hasn't held a regular job that I know of since. Four years he split between Mexico and Tahoe, and he never seems to plan like other people, or wonder what he should do. If you ask him why, he turns it to a joke, or shrugs it off— people think he's loaded most of the time, but he only smokes in the evening, not like Charley, and he doesn't drink at all. He just doesn't seem to need to defend himself. I wanted to take Phillip to ask Pancho about traveling, how to live cheaply, and what kinds of thoughts a vagabond thinks.

We browsed in the bookstore in Tahoe City, then drove to Truckee and past, pulling off to let hurried cars pass, dragging a dead dog from the road and tossing her into a gulley. We turned back in Mohawk and stopped in a grocery by the Truckee rail yards, from which they had once shipped silver, and the lumber and fish from Tahoe, over Donner Pass and out to the coast. There was no sign left of the old town, of the Chinese huts where Charley's granddad smoked opium and Walker was born.

The Truckee River was high up its banks, covering the shrubs which had grown up or come back to life since winter. A tourist carried a sack to the trash bin, picked up a stone and flung it at a squirrel. The squirrel scampered furiously, then spun on its haunches as if to stand and fight, but the man was already back in his Winnebago, cranking on the generator, which chugged like a steam locomotive. I shouted that he should turn it off but he didn't hear. We took our apples and cheese and a blanket and slid down the bank to the side of the river, close enough to hear it and catch the spray. Once I had slept here with Charley and Walker before fishing for brown trout at dawn. Today the grass was flooded, but there was a drift log for us to sit on. Phillip stared off downstream. I covered his hand on my knee. "Tell me," I said.

"Sanctuary," he whispered. "Islands and mountaintops. It seems this year will never end."

"Seven weeks after this one. I wish we could drive to New York. I've never been east of Las Vagas, but I'm scared my dad will find out you're going. My grandma's buying the ticket and she wants me to fly from L.A. I guess she thinks I might get lost. My dad says he can send me a few hundred a month, now that he's selling all right. My mom's been writing to schools, but she'd decided you can't find out anything that way so I should just go hang out till I can see for myself. My dad got mad when she said 'hang out.' I guess we should just meet on the plane, huh? Later I'll write, 'Guess what. My English teacher's here.' "

"Set the date, so I can book the same flight."

We're really going, I thought, wondering, though I knew it already. Since the cabin it had been decided, or even before, like a plan already laid but not recognized till the time we needed a plan, a future. Phillip tossed cheese on the bank for birds and I threw an apple at the Winnebago. We turned back down the mountain, then east, fast around Reno and slow by the pinion trees on the warm brown hills where the Washoes used to winter. In Virginia City we stopped in souvenir shops, which had just opened for summer tourists. Phillip bought a gold dollar for luck and a silver cross for me. From a hill we stared down on Victorian mansions, which still stood by street lamps from Comstock days when hookers turned into fine ladies pranced down the boardwalk with silver barons who used to be tramps; the ladies, laced in corsets because they were fat, wore diamonds in their

146

hair to make up for the beauty they'd lost. I asked around for the Farragut mine where Charley's great-granddad died, but no one had heard of the name.

South past Carson we turned up a dirt road that led to a ranch and pulled off where an old tractor sat rusting. The air smelled of alfalfa, and cows bent over a water trough in the closest pasture. An irrigation ditch ran straight as a level toward the low eastern range and straight to the west, under the highway to the base of the mountains below Kingsbury. The only trees in the valley were planted windbreaks along the ditches and around the white ranch houses. They swayed in the wind like creeping shadows, and apart from their rustle and the rattle of trucks on the highway, the evening was silent.

The tractor blocked the wind and we sat on the running board. Phillip was watching up the valley toward the cloud of vaporous light above Carson City. There was strain in his face again and his shoulders were hunched.

"Are those beef cattle?" I wondered.

"I don't know of any dairies."

"How old are they when they sell them for meat?"

"Don't know."

"When I was twelve, I think, there was a steer in the meadow up the hill from our house. My dog Sherlock used to chase him and he'd run for a while just for fun. Once he dropped his butt down and whopped Sherlock with his tail, so Sherlock wouldn't play anymore. I never knew who he belonged to, and then one day he was gone, and I've always wondered whether they ate him or the zoning guys kicked him out. Phillip, it's creepy here. I've been around here a hundred times, but it's never been creepy before. I used to come down with Danny on his dirtbike. He'd come straight down the wash over there and straight back up. But tonight it's musty, like cemeteries or taverns, like two-headed cows or devils. I don't know what's the matter with me."

"I'm the matter, Jodi. My mother's gone mad, madder. Last night she called me, today she called the school. She told Furby I was depraved, psychopathic, that I used to beat dogs. She wants me to come home. She'll do anything. She can be convincing. Furby sent an aide to cover fourth period and called me to his office. He's heard about us, though he didn't say it. I should've told him right then I was leaving, but he had me defensive. I wish he'd fire me."

"What did he say? You didn't beat dogs, did you?"

He jumped up and kicked the tractor; then he paced in front of me, kicking up dirt and rolling his eyes. "Damn her! Damn her to deepest hell! She's like a hook, like a wooden leg. In high school I decided to be a Marxist because I wanted children to live in group homes. I'd die this minute for the chance to be born again fairly. God, I can't even lose the jargon."

He came to me slowly and covered his eyes. "Feel me now, how loose I am. I'm purged. I'll buy a punching bag or a tape recorder to scream at." But his arms were trembling.

We were slowed by a mudslide on Kingsbury grade, and we stopped for coffee in Incline. Phillip said he'd have his phone number changed tomorrow. He was nervous again, worse after two cups of coffee. He asked if I wanted to go to King's Castle; maybe they wouldn't check my ID. I said no, that if gambling was what he wanted to do he could drop me at Charley's. I was a little angry, but I had no right to question or moralize—he hadn't tried to change me.

Charley was gone, Maggie and Paul were sleeping and the lights were out in Pancho's shed. Strangely, I felt like calling my mom, though I didn't know what I'd say; it was too late, anyway. I couldn't sit still or get my mind off Phillip. I hitched up the highway to Incline and walked down to King's Castle, snooping through the framework of houses and a shopping mall under con-

148

struction, finding electrical cords to spin like a whip and nails to zing up at the trees, and thinking.

When we come back to Incline after Paris, if we do, there might be a city here with freeways and medical centers, sports domes, and hydroplanes down on the wharf. No slums. No slums ever in Incline. They'll be over in Carson Valley, where there's cheap land and musty air.

There were no guards at the casino doors. I slipped up to the lounge area and sat by the fireplace, looking out over the gamblers for Phillip. People yelled at the craps table and floor men converged. A western band was playing too loudly from the bar and stopped in the middle of verses to tell dirty jokes. Finally Phillip came down the aisle from the slots or the rest room. I lay back so he couldn't see me but he didn't look up and sat at the second table below me, between a lady in furs and a boy in blue jeans and a Stetson. The dealer was long-faced and wide-eyed, cranking on speed, I guessed. Through a gap in the players I could see Phillip's chips, lots of chips, maybe $200 in fives, which he fingered between each hand. He watched all the cards as they turned, and sometimes, low in the deck, he played two hands. Though cruel thoughts occurred to me, like wondering if he used to beat dogs and if he still carried his knife, I was proud of him there, betting $50 on one card, though in a year we might be jobless and scrounging for money. He had some kind of faith, at least in his luck, something to build on.

Now I'm back in his house. I love his house. The north wall leans, the roof leaks in the kitchen, the faucets just trickle water, and in the bedroom the floor dips so things slide across it. It's a fine old house, even more of a dump than Charley's. I wonder who will live there when we're gone. They'll probably tear it down and build a triplex. There won't be houses like this in Paris with the smell of evergreens, or the mountains on all sides, or the lake so deep that as far as I know they've only hit bottom by sounding. But Phillip will be with me. We'll have peace, excitement and a new life.

★　★　★　★

May 9, 1972

I miss studying on Sunday afternoons with Pastor Sandoz. There's something about him—maybe his confidence in me—that gives me faith in my faith and judgment. But it's too weird, talking about God across the street from Phillip's house. In services I don't feel uneasy because I'm alone and invisible, but if I have to answer questions or ask them myself, I feel a hypocrite. I compare my devotion to Pastor's and the others' and think that they sacrifice so, living by the laws. I'd tell Pastor about Phillip if I thought he'd give us his blessing, but he wouldn't, he couldn't—it just doesn't fit with literal scripture, at least none I can find. No matter how certain I feel, I can't justify myself to other people, I won't even try. I guess I could argue that God unites two people in marriage, but it's not that simple and I don't feel married. I don't even know what married means to me. I try to read the Bible receptively, for truth, but I find myself looking for excuses instead. So I don't read the Bible much lately.

I stay at Phillip's most every night now. We correct papers and tests that have piled up because Phillip has been giving assignments just to keep the kids busy and out of his way. Every evening we walk down to the beach—we've given up trying to avoid people we know; it seems useless—and sometimes we barbecue there, or eat from the taco stand. Usually there's a bonfire on the beach and Saturday there was a dance on the pier. One guy fell into the lake. Cops checked IDs and told kids to leave, but they didn't take anyone away.

About ten we go to bed and talk for a while. Mostly Phillip tells me things he has read about Europe. Or we read, on top of the covers to feel the breeze through the window. The evenings are warm and couples walk outside till late, old folks and children, and people often stop to talk beneath the streetlamp just outside our window. I try to listen but no one speaks loudly, except children, this time of year. After we make love I go to sleep easily now and often wake up before dawn; even then the birds are singing. In the mornings the world seems like heaven to me, as though the Tribulation, Armageddon and the Judgment all passed in the night, and here we are, everyone forgiven, me for my sins, Paul for his harshness, Phillip for not believing, and all the rest of the world, and Jesus will meet us for breakfast. I haven't heard an ambulance in days.

In Phillip's class we're preparing to put on a play. The kids are excited, agreeable, not much boredom or grumbling now, and most of them even treat Phillip politely and me as a friend. He assigned the *Canterbury Tales* and asked us to write a tale of our own. We voted on which to use and chose José's—he's an exchange student from Brazil. He calls his play *The Serving Girl's Tale of the Princess's Tail*, but it's not lewd, only suggestive. The jester seduces the serving girl; she wants revenge because the jester is hot for the princess, so the serving girl convinces the jester that she can work a spell on the princess if he'll give her a pouch of gold, which is all he owns. The jester agrees and gives over the gold. The serving girl claims she'll work a spell so the princess will love the first man to touch her privates. I'm a lady in waiting. I don't have any lines. I just smile a lot.

Because the year is almost over, I guess, and because Phillip and I have become old news to the kids, and Mr. Lopez found someone else to go for his coffee so I don't have the teachers staring, school has been almost fun this week. Even a boy named Turley who was burned in a fire last year, whose arms and face were covered with red scars, who always scowled since the fire and argued with everyone, smiled at me in the hall one morning and said hello. It seems his scars are healing and I suspect a miracle. Jerry leaves us alone when he comes to class, which isn't often, and I haven't seen Aaron in days.

Jill came to visit at my folks' last Saturday. She has a new boyfriend already, who goes to college in Reno. He studies philosophy and she says he sometimes even talks Christian. She laughed that she might turn to Jesus, which ex-hookers sometimes do. I think she feels tainted forever.

★   ★   ★   ★

May 10, 1972

Today some kids asked Phillip to stay late so they could rehearse. I had things to pick up at my folks' house, so I told him I'd meet him at his house, walked part way, then hitched and stopped to talk to Maggie. She told me that Charley had a job, but he wouldn't say what kind.

When I came up the street Phillip was sitting on his porch steps. "Look inside, Jodi."

The living room floor was smeared with black oil; books and notebooks were strewed across the floor; the desk and chair were flipped over and everything spilled; records were out of their cases and broken. In the kitchen the cupboards were open and dishes thrown down; the garbage can was dumped on its side and dish soap dripped from the sinkboard. In the bedroom our clothes were piled in a heap and seasoned with catsup, chili sauce and honey. The bed was slashed to the springs with a kitchen knife.

Phillip was walking behind me. "In daylight," he said, expressionless, cold. "Who do you think?"

"Not Aaron. He'd do something clever. Maybe Jerry. He might blame me that Jill dumped him."

Phillip shook his head and bent over a pile of books. Pages were ripped out of some and others were face down in oil. "Maggie's got stuff to clean anything," I said. He didn't even look up.

Maggie said she'd come help and Paul volunteered, but when we had bundled all the gear, she had pains, so she went in to lie down instead, and Paul stayed to watch her. I came back with my arms full of mops, cleansers, a duffel bag for packing clothes to the Laundromat. Phillip had righted the chair and was sitting with his feet in a puddle of oil reading a book. "Can I read you something, Jodi? It's from *Crime and Punishment*. Raskolnikov, the murderer, before he murders, is talking in a saloon to Marmeladov, a derelict whose daughter Sonia is a prostitute so she can support his family. Marmeladov tells of his vision:

" 'And He will say, "Come to me! I have already forgiven thee once. . . . Thy sins which are many are forgiven thee for thou hast loved much. . . ." And He will forgive my Sonia. He will forgive, I know it . . . I felt it in my heart when I was with her just now! And He will judge and will forgive all, the wise and the meek. . . . And when He has done with all of them, then He will summon us. "You too come forth," He will say. "Come forth, ye drunkards, come forth, ye weak ones, come forth, ye children of shame!" And we shall all come forth, without shame, and shall stand before Him. And He will say unto us, "Ye are swine, made in the Image of the Beast and with his mark; but come ye also." And the wise ones and those of understanding will say, "Oh Lord, why dost thou receive these men?" And He will say: "This is why I receive them, oh ye wise, this is why I receive them, oh ye of understanding, that not one of them believed himself worthy of this." ' "

"I've never read that before," was all I could think to say.

"Remember, Raskolnikov didn't kill till after he heard this. Though he was an atheist he needed the hope of forgiveness, just in case, before he could kill."

"Does it have anything to do with this mess in the house?"

"I'm considering murder." I watched for him to laugh but he didn't, didn't scowl or clench his teeth. He didn't do anything or show any expression.

"Most of this stuff we couldn't take with us anyway."

"But sometimes I think about justice," he said.

Phillip couldn't kill Jerry, even if he knew for sure. It nearly broke his heart to squirt oil on Jerry's letterman's jacket, back before we were lovers.

* * * *

May 14, 1972

Thursday night, while I was in the bathtub Phillip fell asleep reading. I was restless, so I dressed again and walked down to Charley's.

Charley was in bed, tossing and grumbling as though in a nightmare. I stood over him for a while, then took a handkerchief from his drawer and wiped sweat from his forehead. He woke up, shook his head and rubbed his eyes.

"I guess you were dreaming."

"Yeah. Thanks. I'm a daddy, Jodi."

"Oh, Charley! Today?"

"Yesterday. He's a little guy, six pounds. No hair. He looks like Maria before she makes up."

"Is it wonderful, Charley?"

"Sure. Only reason I knew was she called me to come down and set up the payment. She's got spies or something. She paged me in a bar. She had him in the room

154

and told them not to let me in. You believe that vindictive bitch? Because I missed a few payments. They told me to come back and look through the glass in the nursery. He's slow, Jodi, he doesn't move much like some of them."

"Can I go see him? When can we go?"

"You go. Just gives me nightmares. I want to help the little shit grow up, Jodi. I want to teach him some things, like how to pick women. If I live long enough I think I'll be smart."

"Can't you sue her or something?"

"I don't like courts. I don't like to pay lawyers. What I need's amnesia." There was such a long silence I wondered if he had his wish, staring the way he did around my eyes but never quite at them, the rest of him still. There was something between us I couldn't reach through; my hand just fell in the air. Finally he stretched his back. "What time is it?"

"Almost midnight."

"Shit."

"What's your job, Charley?"

"Driving."

"Parking lot?"

"Nope."

"Tell me."

"Like a rental agency. Good bucks. I drive down to Reno mostly, sometimes from there to Vegas, maybe San Francisco and L.A. later on."

"Is it Hertz?"

"Nope."

"Avis? How come you drive so late at night?"

"That's the job, Jodi. Look, I have to go."

Charley tugged on his jeans and shirt on the way to his truck and tossed his shoes in the cab. After he pulled out I walked the neighborhood, sat on the walls in front of dark houses, thinking. I tried to imagine how much I'd miss Charley, how much he'd be on my mind after I leave. If I had the money I'd ask him to come along—his baby, too. We could start a family; I could have a child to play with Charley's, to teach each other things by some lake far away. But Charley wouldn't use my money, and he wouldn't live with Phillip and me. He could kidnap the baby, though, and live somewhere near, close enough so we could see each other when we needed to. It didn't seem fair that you had to give up one friend for another, that you couldn't hold on to them all. But I was just thinking myself into trouble. Charley wouldn't go.

Saturday morning I went with my mom to Tahoe City. We shopped for summer outfits and a swimsuit she said I could wear to the Riviera. We picked through baskets of first-of-the-season strawberries till we found the best one, took it down to the beach to nibble, watched a volleyball game and kids throwing Frisbees, sailboats tacking against the wind. My mom said she hoped Mark would move home when he left the army, next year, and she hoped Danny might practice law up here. She said if I didn't marry some rich lawyer from Wall Street or French novelist, I might even move back and paint here when I finished school. She worried about housing for me in France and the devaluation of the dollar. She said it was good that dad had given us practice in living cheaply. He has nearly convinced his company to let him work from home because they sell so much equipment up here, snowplows, bulldozers, backhoes for digging new sewer lines. He's selling more than he thought he could, though he hates to be congenial; he dislikes himself because of it, but she hopes he'll keep selling, because she's restless to move back home—there's not much to do in Reno but fight with Aunt Rosie, no room to leave her paints and brushes out, and Rosie watches over her shoulder when she tries to work. She wants to plant new flowers here at home, start new sketches and try selling in the summer street bazaars.

My dad went fishing that morning at Fallen Leaf, for

the last lake-stocking before the tourists come. At home he was waiting with brown trout gutted and ready to fry. He was in a playful mood. He said the jeans mom bought me were too tight, that Frenchmen would be grabbing my butt, because I had the cutest butt in Nevada—he'd seen one cuter in California, he said. He told me to stay away from dukes and counts and jet-setters and made me promise I wouldn't let my armpit hair grow or the hair on my legs, because it looked crummy under nylons, and he made me promise that I'd go see Mark first thing. Mark's last letter said he could take leave most of the month of July. After the rates went down we called Danny. There was music in the background and voices, like a party. He said Charley had called a few weeks ago saying he might move there, but I told him that was off, that Charley had a job. Danny promised to come to see me before I leave.

This morning I walked up the street and cut through the banker's yard where Walker's house used to be. I climbed the hill behind the kennel where the banker keeps his pit bulls when he comes up, and I started down toward the fifteenth hole, where the meadow used to be, the shortest way to the grocery.

"Hi, Jodi." Charley jumped from a low cedar branch. "You remember this tree? Look." A piece of bark was chipped away and our initials were carved in a heart on the trunk. "You said Jill made you do it, remember?"

"Did you believe me?"

"Sure. I stopped this morning to see my dad."

"Is he better?"

"Better than what? He ain't even better than dead, except they keep him loaded on downers all the time so he stays in bed a lot—then they don't have to pick him up off the floor. A nurse told me a welfare worker came by to get him to sign some papers. That's a gag, huh? He kicked her in the knee. First time they've seen his leg move in months."

"You want to come down to the house for lunch?"

"No. You want to go see my baby?"

His truck was parked on the next street. "I've been thinking about economics," he said. "Not school kind, simple economics, like how to get what they've got from them that got it. Long as I have to be a capitalist I might as well go all out, don't you think, or are there degrees of sinning?"

"I don't think much about sins anymore. Just sometimes about sex. If we didn't know about sex, or if sex was O.K., things would be simple, wouldn't they?"

"For you maybe, for now. Listen to a poem I learned. It's by Black Bart, the stagecoach robber. He was a skinny accountant during the week, then kind of like superman or Zorro on weekends. It's a poem about economics. 'I've labored long and hard for bread, / for honor and for riches, / but on my corns too long you've tread, / you fair-haired sonsabitches.' "

The baby was home now with Maria. She called him Errol after Errol Flynn and her granddad, and she used her own last name. Charley said we were lucky to find her home, he thought she'd be packing the baby around town already. Now she was out by her apartment pool, in a two-piece with the baby in an infant seat beside her. She hadn't changed much from pregnancy, just a little stretched around the middle. She played happy to see Charley, tried to sit on his lap, but he shoved her away. She must've thought I was his girl friend.

"Here's five hundred dollars cash," and he counted it out. "So you want it to stop or will you stay home sometimes and not hang up when I call?"

"Don't make me sound like a monster, Charley. I don't stop you from seeing him."

"Not when I'm bringing money. I want to take him home today till tomorrow."

"You try it and I'll call the heat. You got no rights, Charley. Anyway, you plan to nurse him?"

"Squirt me some in a bottle, bitch. I want him to see me when he wakes up and when he goes to sleep. I want him to know I'm his dad."

"He's only four days old, Charley. you could move in with us." She grinned up at me.

"Fuck you, Maria!" Charley said.

"Anytime, darling. I'm horny."

"Yeah. I bet you are."

Errol looked like a runt in Charley's arms. He was pretty, with Charley's little ears, Charley's cleft chin, and brown, like Charley. Maria came to take him but Charley kept holding on, moved over to the shade and rocked him, but Errol cried frantically till Charley gave him back and we walked out. "Take the truck home," he said. "I'll get it tomorrow," and he shuffled off. I called after him but he waved me away.

I was two hours late with the groceries for lunch. My dad had been out looking for me and came back in a rage. "We talk about sending you halfway across the world, busting our ass for the money, and you can't even get to the grocery and back!" I tried to tell him that I had needed to go with Charley but he wouldn't hear it. "You, Charley, all you damn kids, take on jobs—I'm not just talking about these groceries, I'm talking about the way you live—but you go off on your whims, like they're nature's law!"

He would've kept yelling but I stomped up to my room. I heard him bust something downstairs, and when they left for Reno, only my mom said goodbye.

★ ★ ★ ★

May 20, 1972

Several times Phillip has asked me, "What would your folks say, Jodi?" I've only been able to guess. My mom has never been strict about my dating. She liked most of my boyfriends, Aaron particularly, but she might think Phillip threatened my going to Paris, or doing what I should there. My dad judges people so quickly, likes them so well or dislikes them so roughly, I can't imagine what he might do. When he makes up his mind he believes very strongly, so arguments or evidence don't matter much—like me, he's often confused; nuances and subtleties drive him wild, because he's smart enough not to deny they exist but not smart enough to use them. I wonder if any of us are. No matter that he treats me like an adult, he still thinks I'm innocent and that I can be fooled. If he doesn't trust Phillip, or thinks he's a twerp, he'll fight us for sure.

Phillip said he could quit early, so we could leave right away, and could probably arrange to have my diploma sent, since classes were only a few weeks more and my grades were O.K. But my folks would be proud at graduation. And grandma wouldn't buy the flight tickets if she knew I was going with Phillip; she's just not that modern. My dad probably wouldn't send money, and then I'd have to use Phillip's. Besides, they are my family and they've done right by me. I don't want Phillip to have to keep me, and I need the time to say goodbye.

"You could go ahead," I told him.

He thought for a very long time. "No. For a month we can stall."

One day Mr. Beavers came to our classroom for lunch. "Carrots!" he griped. "Carrots, celery, cottage cheese! No dip even. Eva thinks I'm a bunny—Phil, now kick my ass if I'm out of line—I heard a persistant rumor that you two are . . ."

We both nodded.

"Good. I suspected you were an anarchist. They'll put you through hell. Any particular battle plans?"

"Disappear," Phillip said. "I might be too young for a last chance, or too old, but I believe this is it."

"I'd hate to see you quit teaching."

160

"Why?"

"Well, there are too many tweaks in this profession, too many egomaniacs, too many lackadaisical dingalings. I know you're not an orator, you're not charismatic. I know you detest forcing the kids to compete, and giving grades tears your guts. You're not a devious guy, Phil, you don't follow a pattern, you're transparent, you won't disguise your feelings. That's an important example. You're sensitive, Phil, and you have courage. Damn it, have you ever met another teacher who would sit here coolly eating peanut butter with his schoolgirl sweetheart, not denying a damned thing, while the tweaks are tittering in their coffee klatch and Waterman's baring her teeth for the kill? You've got balls, Phil. What else can I say?"

Phillip grinned sheepishly. "Thanks. Now I can leave proudly."

"If you have to leave. They can't run you out if you use tenure. They won't have the nerve to take you to court."

Another day Miss Waterman came in during a break. "Mr. Oswald, is there any substance to these rumors?"

"Which rumors?"

"Of yourself and Miss McGee?"

"Specifically?"

"That you're having an affair."

"I'm pleased that you bother to ask, Miss Waterman, but it's not your business."

"It is everyone's business, Mr. Oswald. It is the most despicable conduct I've known in thirty years of teaching. She was a fine young lady. To turn her into a tramp! If it is true I'll see you punished!" She stumbled on a desk leg and ran from the room.

"Dear lady," Phillip said. "Are you a tramp?"

"I don't know what that means," I said. "Tell me."

"That you give yourself to the world and call no place your home."

"Then no. I'm selfish."

When I came home yesterday my mom was waiting. "Hi, mom. You're home early. Didn't dad work today?"

"I found a ride, Jodi. I wanted to see you alone."

"Why? You in trouble?"

"Come inside."

"I cook tonight or you?"

She fell on the couch and stared at me like a trespasser, with mixed fear and anger. "Mr. Furby's secretary called."

"Mrs. Bodine."

"I know her name. Damn you, Jodi! I always thought if something like this happened you'd tell me at least."

I knew when to keep quiet and let her talk on. Now I felt like a tramp, not in Phillip's sense but like a thoughtless sensual bitch with no loyalty, a bitch cornered.

"We trusted you up here alone, we thought you had standards, we thought you'd grown up, so you have an affair—with a teacher!"

"What's wrong with a teacher?"

"It's a scandal at the school!"

"I didn't make the scandal, mom. They did."

"You're living with him?"

"Sometimes. Sometimes I stay with Phillip and sometimes I stay at Charley's. Sometimes I stay here, remember?"

"Do you sleep with him?"

"Of course I sleep with him! You think I should sleep on the floor? I give him blow jobs, too!" God, I was sorry for that. I hate to argue with my mom. She cringes too easily and makes me feel powerful, as though I could crush her with the wrong words. But this time I was powerfully mad. "I slept with Aaron, too, but you didn't want to know that. Was it O.K. with Aaron? How do you know Phillip isn't a rich kid?"

"He's thirty years old."

"So what? What's different? It's different because

162

Phillip is different from Aaron. Aaron's a prick, mom; he just cares about pussy and being on top and he'll say anything or do anything to get him there. Phillip wants to win but he won't cheat and won't fight back because he might hurt somebody. He lets himself be punished because he thinks he deserves it. When he's angry it shows like hurt; he can't be a phony, so I can't ever hate him. He lets everybody kick him around, and he's weak from it. I make him feel good, and that's what makes me feel good. Besides me all he wants is the rest to leave him alone. That's a safe way to live, mom, there's no greed in that. And he doesn't hold me. If I want to go, I just go; if I want to be alone he walks out. See, he doesn't think he deserves me. He doesn't have pride. I want to be like Phillip, mom."

"People without pride are ruthless, Jodi."

"No. People without pride are honest. People without humility are ruthless. Aaron's ruthless. You just loved his money. He could buy anything from you."

"Jodi, I think you can do great things, but you can't be free without money. This is the real world."

"That's bullshit, mother. God's dream is the real world. And nobody can give me freedom, they can just not take it away."

She didn't know how to fight me. I believed she had more strength than she'd admit, but she didn't know how to use it. She was tame, compared to my dad and me. She began to sob, then sucked it in, walked to the kitchen, then came back timidly. "You might be right, Jodi. I don't think deeply anymore. It's a hell of a way to live, smiling though nothing makes you very happy, not like it did once. It's almost a physical change, growing tired. But I can tell you something about lovers. They never let you go. Jodi, in a few months this will be over but you'll be hurt deeply. And you'll never live down the trouble you've caused."

"What trouble?"

"For this man. For us. Whenever there's a scandal there's trouble. Remember your friend Jill."

"Why does somebody always bring up Jill?"

"Because what's in that space between your legs is golden. Everyone wants to own it."

That stopped me cold. I felt a swelling down there and something told me it was hateful. Inside me was a conscience, I believed, and a spirit, and a sludge pot of crap I had learned. How could I tell the difference, without the Holy Spirit, and the Spirit had left me on my own. "Mom, I think about things before I do them; then I try to do what's right. Everybody makes mistakes, but if I've done something wrong, I believe I'll be forgiven. That's what Jesus is for."

"You have a habit of believing what you want to believe."

The pulse in my neck throbbed, my eyes swelled with blood and I wanted to hit her. "Everybody believes what they want to believe."

"Oh, Jodi." She reached for my hand; there was that strength that I'd guessed. She'd always keep loving me.

"Does dad know?"

"I haven't told him yet."

"Will you?"

"I don't know. Should I?"

"If you do we'll all be miserable, he'll make sure."

"I know."

"Don't tell him yet."

"You won't consider leaving that man?"

"No." I started for the door.

"Jodi."

"Yes?"

"Will you come home tonight?"

I said I would; then I walked all the way to King's Beach, remembering sorrowfully my childhood, before adolescence, before I knew in my blood why people would want to stab themselves into each other and onto each other, before I knew how deeply guilt could penetrate. I felt as if I had done something brutal. At north Stateline the sidewalks were loud, as in the summer; bells rang every second in the casinos and kids stared in. A man in a green-flecked leisure suit stepped from a club and onto the highway, holding his eyes. Brakes screeched and drivers screamed at him, but he just walked on, still holding his eyes. When I reached Phillip's door it was open and he was reading in the bathtub. "They told my mom," I said. "Mrs. Bodine called her."

He slammed the book and sailed it out the door. "You'd think they'd have the courtesy to talk to me first! What did she say? Your mother?"

I slipped out of my clothes and stepped one foot in. "She said I should leave you." There was no room with his legs pressed together and his arms out stiff on the sides. "But she won't tell my dad. We're as good as gone."

He rolled from the tub, on to his knees, as though I had pushed him out. "I feel like a pervert," he said. I asked him to wash me.

★   ★   ★   ★

May 2, 1972

I set my alarm early for time to get ready for church; I wanted to wash my hair and set it, make up and do everything to brighten Phillip's morning, since I had to leave early the last two nights, to keep my mother from talking. I borrowed my dad's car. It was warm early and Pancho was on Charley's front porch playing his guitar, so I stopped.

"Damn me!" Pancho said. "You're gorgeous, Miss Nebraska, scrubbed and ready to recite Rudyard Kipling. Hey, I got a job playing Thursdays at Gimpy's. Come up and kiss me congrats. I won't drool on your lipstick." I did. Then Paul came out in his striped suit and his hair slicked down. "Calls for a serenade in context," Pancho said.

Paul shrugged and rolled his eyes. "Indulge yourself."

"Always." Pancho tossed me a kazoo. "Back me up.

"I know Jesus loves me best.
He don't hardly like the rest.
Guess you prob'ly wonder why
I am such a holy guy.
'Cause I'm a Baptist!
'Cause I'm a Baptist!"

Phillip was still in bed. I'd never asked him to go to church with me before and I didn't hope to convert him so soon, but Pastor Sandoz was smart, gentle and slow to condemn. His ways had caused Paul to switch from his Community Church to the Baptist church and take his study group with him. Pastor Sandoz might lighten Phillip's ideas of churches, I thought, and bringing Phillip with me seemed an honesty I needed.

"Jodi, the way you dress I've come to love Sundays."

"Come with me to church?"

"Is this a nightmare? Lie here with me instead."

"Please, Phillip. Pastor Sandoz is mild; he won't try to drag you up front or stare you down while he's talking. Afterward we can go for a drive, or rent a boat, if you need to recover."

"All right, I slept well, so I can survive it." I waited outside while he dressed. Children in ties and frilly dresses jumped cracks in the sidewalk. Pastor Sandoz waved across to me and I blushed, being at Phillip's house. When Phillip came out I took his arm and we crossed the street and climbed the steps quickly past the people I knew who stopped to watch us as though we were famous or strange.

Pastor gave his hand to Phillip. "You're welcome here,

Mr. Oswald. I haven't seen you fishing yet this year." He
didn't seem to question when he looked at me, as though
I were above suspicion.

Inside Phillip asked, "How did he know my name?" I
said I hadn't told him. I saw some seats up front and was
headed there but Phillip pulled me into a back row and
slid to the middle behind Mrs. Pruett and her fat husband. They were whispering, arguing it seemed. Phillip
sat straight and stared forward. Elders closed the doors,
then came around front to lead us in hymns. Phillip fid-
geted with his tie, his hair, his chin, his belt. His lips
moved as if by reflex but he wasn't singing or reading
the hymnal.

Pastor was soothing at the altar, large and soft-spoken,
just hesitant enough in his speaking to make him seem
one of us all.

"There are many new faces here today, some from
Donner Camp. I'll be brief on such a glorious day. Christ
is with us to witness my words. I can't speak more than
the truth.

"John 3:16: 'For God so loved the world that He gave
his only son, that whoever believes in Him shall not per-
ish but have eternal life.' Nothing could be more simple
and clear. Who in here does not believe?" No one, not
even Phillip, made any sign, and I wondered how many
were lying. I believed. Though He hadn't been the bulk
of my thoughts lately, I believed as much as ever in the
living God; it was His rules I questioned, the justice in
His world, the nearness of His mercy. I thought about
last night with Phillip, about my mother the day before,
and I was ashamed.

"Then you all shall live! If you drink, gamble, murder,
fornicate, blaspheme, envy, never see this room again,
you cannot die, so long as you keep believing. Blessed
promise.

"What is this belief? If you were to ask where my
brother lives and I were to say, only guessing, 'I believe

167

he still lives in Montana,' my language would be at fault. But a daughter, sick and confined to her room, knowing that her father has never broken a promise, asks him for a coloring book, and because he agrees, all the while he's gone she looks happily forward to coloring, so certain that when he comes home she says 'Thank you, father, for the coloring book,' even before she sees it. This daughter believes, not from a mystical leap or blind decision, but from promise and fulfillment. Jehovah has not once gone back on a promise.

"Is promise from scripture alone, and are we then to believe everything we read? No. I'm speaking first of testimony, for we all have seen miracles if we have looked, and we must speak aloud the gifts we have known, the miracles, our daily blessings of and from faith. You who know me, if I were to say that yesterday I hooked a three-pound trout in Carnelian Bay, would you be skeptical or would you believe in my trout, and if its size amazed you, wouldn't you tell family and friends? And if a hundred more were to tell you of similar fish, would you have any doubt, wouldn't you know the trout were there though you hadn't yet seen one? Then why do so many reject the Lord and contend that He must show His face or a personal sign, though He has given the world, the heavens and the testimony of millions? I suspect because we all wish to know we're special to Him, among the very blessed. That day will come.

"Many refuse to take the word of any but righteous persons. But men are not righteous, neither are women; rather our nature is tainted with sin and its consequences. Even witnesses too often turn away, usually when temptation meets impatience, the curse of our age. A man wants a television; he shows a charge card and takes it home. He asks for grace once, twice, three times, then turns away bitterly. Our Lord deals with believers, keeps His promise in the time He chooses, and those of

168

us who have not yet been blessed with new life need only hold on to our belief and wait for the day.

"Christ said to Nicodemus, 'Except a man be born again he cannot see the kingdom of God.' The birth is contained in the promise, but we cannot choose the moment any more than that of our first birth. We can only live justly, pray faithfully, and be assured our time will come. Blessed faith! Then our joy will be multiplied by the days we have anguished.

"Believing faithfully is believing constantly, turning by choice from doubt. If you would have peace, only look up. Up is where the heart looks for relief; up is where the child looks for love; up is above us as hope is above despair and love above censure. Up is where Christ rose to and from where He will descend. When you are troubled, look at Christ; when you wish to give thanks, look at Christ; when you are bored or restless, look at Christ. Never doubt you are less than blessed."

I tried not to look at Phillip. It was better to ignore him squirming beside me. Unbelief is a sickness, I thought. Belief is a natural condition, a chamber of our hearts, and denial like a rusted valve, rusted from cruel handling, carelessness, from neglect and sin. Phillip seemed pitiful beside me, a palsied cripple. But Pastor said love was above censure.

"We believe what we see, what we hear and touch. Watch for the shadow of the Lord, listen for His whispers, reach out to feel Him moving. Faith heightens our senses. Faith is the eye of the soul, not a leap in the dark—that would still leave us in darkness. Faith is the woman who touched the hem of the garment of Jesus, so that she should be cured. Faith is the penitent thief crying 'Lord, remember me!' Faith is Peter's desperate cry, 'Lord, save me!' They had heard; they believed; so they witnessed.

"Now, the ways of this world are Satan's ways. Most

success implies corruption; lust is praised as the golden thrill; skepticism is congratulated; innocence is called stupidity. If we live by these values and still call ourselves Christians we either live a lie or accept both sides of a paradox—and that is madness."

Pastor stopped, looked out over us all, at me in particular, I was sure. I fumbled for Phillip's hand.

"Beware of madness. Madness is the soul split in two. Better, perhaps, it were whole and given to demons."

Madness was why I pounced on Jesus rather than tracked Him slowly. Madness to me was poisoned thoughts and hatred, drowning in cold dark water. Phillip might lead me to madness. Leaving him might lead us both there.

"If we thrive on this world we haven't the time or the need to ask for salvation. Will and should our Lord forgive one who breaks His laws and then doesn't ask for forgiveness? Perhaps—He sees the depths of that person's heart and perhaps there are reasons—but surely it's clear that sin hardens hearts and brings some men to a state where they could not find joy in the kingdom. If I wrestled a gambler from his table, dropped him beside a brook with his feet in cool water and his face in the warmth of the sun, wouldn't he ask for a game? Look for yourself in any casino on the most lovely day of the year. We go where we choose to go. We must all be free. Blessed freedom.

"Watch this world, see its errors, its cruelty, the horrors that sin breeds, and turn away, to Christ. Some may turn like Levi when Jesus said, 'Follow me.' And he arose and followed Him. Jesus told Zaccheus, 'Make haste and come down.' 'Behold, Lord,' said Zaccheus, 'the half of my goods I give to the poor.' The whole of Cornelius's household was converted suddenly and on Pentecost three thousand were baptised. But others who saw the body of Christ and heard His human words did not know their day until late, Paul the Apostle for one. The

170

Lord decides when to send His spirit, and whether it is best for us to receive the gift full grown or as a seed to be tended and nurtured. If you fall to temptation, turn again to Christ, if you fall again, turn again and again, being harsh on yourself before the sin, but gentle, forgiving, when the sin is done. Be merciful as our Lord, to yourself, to your brethren.

"The gift will be given, and once done, is ours forever. We cannot lose it through negligence and it shall not be taken away. The Lord will hold us, as the shepherd holds the sheep. 'If the son shall make you free, you shall be free indeed.' Psalm 121:

> " 'The Lord is your keeper;
> The Lord is your shade
> upon your right hand.
> The sun shall not smite you by day,
> nor the moon by night.'

> " 'The Lord will keep you from evil;
> He will keep your life.
> The Lord will keep
> your going out and coming in
> from this time forth and for evermore.'

"Storms may come and hurricane winds, fog may blind your road, fires may fall from the heavens and the weight of the world press upon you as the mountain upon the root at its base. But the root reaches deep into springs which shall not dry and the tree grows tall, in the rock at the right hand of God.

"Once forgiven, shall we fear sin? Though our pardon will hold, our sins thereafter will dog our tracks, nightmares of the evil we cause will allow us no rest. Cynicism and ignorance will no longer excuse our crimes. From Jeremiah, 'Your wickedness will chasten you and your apostasy reprove you. Know that it is an evil thing and bitter to forsake the Lord your God.'

"We forsake the Lord, He does not forsake us. 'I am married to you,' says the Lord, and He will not break His vow. Even Judas when he sold Christ was not beyond His mercy. Had Judas asked for mercy it would've been given. But he could not live with the knowledge of his crime. The backslider consciously casts off the gift. It is not lost or stolen away. Peter denied Jesus three times, was forgiven and remained the rock on this earth. There is no spite in our Lord. There is no damnation for the believer, except they return the gift and quit the belief by choice; but the believer can suffer like no other, for the law he breaks is the law of his own heart; 'In the roll of the book it is written of me ... O my God thy law is within my heart.' "

Pastor stepped back from the altar. Phillip shook off my hand and broke away, squeezed out past the others and ran for the door. I stayed to pray and after prayer I stayed for another hymn and a baptism. Mrs. Pruett shoved her fat husband forward and knelt behind him while an elder brought the vase to the altar. Pastor Sandoz touched the water, then Mr. Pruett's head, and spoke too softly to hear. Someday I'll be baptized in the lake, though it might be a long, long time.

Phillip was waiting on the curb where the parishioners passed, leaning forward as though he were stooping for penance. His face was brooding but there was no softness, only the beginning of anger. I tried to think of an excuse for staying behind when he might've needed me, but it seemed that would be like denying my God.

"Why did you leave?"

He looked puzzled, a little amused. "Why did I stay so long?"

"Wasn't it different?"

"Not enough, Jodi.' He opened the front of his shirt. There was a rash on his chest, like hives. "Sometimes I overreact."

Part Three

SNOW IS UP TO THE WINDOWS and icicles are bars from the eaves to the snow. Each morning I shovel a path to the woodpile and bring back enough logs for the rest of the day. Charley left me plenty. There is new powder most every night but the days are clear, though the sky is gray and icy and the wind curls along the hill from over the mountain. It should be warm from the east but it's not and it never seems to shift. I can't keep the cracks in that side of the wall plugged anymore; the wind finds its way and the rags just freeze and slip; when the fire burns out at night I bury my head in the covers. The smell is musty and rank.

My gypsy says there's a place where it's always warm, where no one could see me, where smoke is mist and fires make steam and children stare blindly up, waiting. Eternity turns back upon itself, rolls in endless loops around tunnel walls, in and out so one point passes itself going both ways and at the end of the tunnel is a rainbow which never comes closer no matter how far you walk but everyone keeps walking and there is brotherhood because no one is sure there is anyone else because everyone is blind and how do you know what you touch is real if you can't see it? You need all you've got to tell what is a dream and what is not.

Charley called my gypsy a dream. I don't think it matters. Once when I was little I asked my mom about God and Jesus and she said it was a story of which we don't know the truth. But we can believe in any story because one is as good as another, even what they call fiction— the writer doesn't know but that it might be true, that somebody might be living those things she's making up or she might live them herself someday. Everything is a story because you can't take anyone's word; all you have is what happens to you and what you've heard or read in a book or newspaper or the Bible, and you'd go nuts trying to test what is true and what isn't if you really had to verify it. Even then you'd only be working on evidence and evidence is full of lies; sometimes I don't know when I'm awake now and when I'm asleep, there are so many stops in between. So how do I know which was real and which were dreams back down the mountain?

Charley said that some days when Walker was mad enough he could crack logs on his knees, and I saw him do it once but I don't know if it was a dream. When I was little there was a lion in a mural on my wall who jumped off every night and slept with me. When I was cold he kept me warm and when I was hot he breathed cool on me. My mom and dad couldn't see him and I couldn't either, but I felt him sure as anything, with my hands, and his fur beside me, so we called him pretend, and that was just madness and too easy because pretend doesn't mean anything; pretend is in the mind and sight is in the mind just the same. If they took out my mind I couldn't see a thing.

It's all the same—my gypsy and the mornings, or fairylands where tin men are rusting and hawks perch on Mexican cactus, hugging my pillow and pretending it's someone, climbing down the ladder and waiting by the window for Charley, riding out storms at sea and trying to crack coconut shells, staring at pages of solid black in the Bible and straining to focus to pick out the words when the lines don't make any sense, trying to pray, dancing in crowds, screaming, puking in alleys, the sound of the creek which I can't see beneath the ice and snow, my gypsy's wrinkles and scabs, her filthy, matted hair. Or the night I heard my dad calling from down the road. I watched through the window and saw him stumble; then I woke up and ran outside. Snow in the meadow was up to my neck but I made it all the way to the road and waited till my bare feet were warm and then ran back through my tracks, rubbed my skin with a brush to make the blood rise, then pulled on my jeans and jacket and boots and waited beside the door. My legs throbbed from bruises from rocks beneath the snow. I listened but all I could hear was the fire popping and the wind through cracks in the walls; he called once from above, again from below, again from the south ridge. I walked back out but I couldn't see him. I hoped he was there. If it weren't for my dreams I'd go crazy.

Charley is in road camp. Pancho has come up twice so far, but I wonder if he can make it now because the snow keeps getting higher. He doesn't worry about me the way Charley did; I think he likes me being up here. He likes anything that is weird, calls them alternatives, as if I had a choice. I should tell him there aren't any, not one thing that isn't inevitable; it's all predestination, only destiny assumes a source and a purpose and I don't believe in those.

They must keep Charley in chains or always guarded. When he was in the army I thought he'd walk away. Charley and Walker used to steal NO TRESPASSING signs and bring them up here. That's what the outhouse is— just a frame and NO TRESPASSING signs. It's illegal to shit in a national forest, honestly, a ranger told me so.

If I were brave I'd kill myself just to see where I'd go. Optimists call suicide escape. They're nuts to think death is nothing. Nothing would be too easy. If not hell, there could be molecular consciousness and who's to say that

177

molecules can't suffer even more alone than in mass. Pancho said that once when he was loaded on mushrooms in Oaxaca he saw an angel playing basketball. Staying alive is cowardly. Sometimes I see death waiting for me like a meadow of pink flowers and I think Jesus will be there after all, kicking up dirt so the wind can catch it, but suicide is a deadly sin. I don't believe that. What if I killed myself because I feared I might kill somebody else? There has to be judgment. Faith is too stupid. I think my heart is petrified.

Today is Christmas, such a lonely time in a season of fancy; legends say that Christ was born in winter, but there was no winter in the desert and grass was always brown. People say it wasn't Christ's birthday at all but winter solstice and pagan feasts. With the solstice the days will be longer now, and if the sun comes out the snow will melt someday.

I've never climbed to the snow cross on Mt. Tallac, because the closer you get to a mystery or a person the less they seem to be holy. This morning the cross didn't show through the snow. I needed a miracle.

All that stood out in the basin were the red lights at the state line in South Lake, lit even in daylight now, maybe for Christmas. I'm above it all; I try to be. Maybe I always was, a spirit when they built the casinos because the mines ran out in Virginia City, the trout were too fished out to make them money, they'd logged all the big trees and shipped the cattle north or down to the valley where they could graze more months. The bears were gone and the wolves were gone, and the Washoes and Paiutes ate leftovers and drank a lot so they wouldn't have to move from the land where they thought they'd lived since the wind and water cracked the rock and turned it to dirt, since the trees grew up and fish came from the sea and the birds flew in from nowhere. Some Washoes still think that the coyotes and weasels made *them and made the mountains. Or they pretend that they think all that, because those are the stories they tell, and stories are all sacred to the Washoes and everyone, all true and all lies just the same. And they used to be afraid of the snow because they didn't have the food Charley brought or down quilts, so they picked nuts on the way down, in the foothills, and ate them in the winter, waiting for the snow to melt and turn the mud thick to hold their feet and cake on their skin, waiting for heat to thaw them from winter and make them love the coolness of the mountains again. Then they wove fiber nets and broiled trout, danced in the evening moon along the lake shore while the children wouldn't sleep and ran to the dark woods to look in, every summer just the same, forever.*

Every day is the same, every Christmas can happen today. My dad can find a perfect tree and bring me a gift; Jesus can be born in Bethlehem or here, because the earth shifts, so this spot might be where that spot was then. Every place is dry.

Who cares when Jesus was born? Once there was the lake at the south of the basin and the glacier at the north mouth, a great block against the shore; it rose, leaning with the push of the water and the fires in the earth, then broke free, slashed the Truckee gorge in granite, shoved hills aside, launched missiles to pit craters in the Carson Valley. Who cared about Jesus back then?

Before all that the glaciers had to melt, first chunks in the summers, then all year long as the sun came closer. The lake always rose, always and always, after years of nothing but ice, after the volcanoes and the pull from below, where vacuums couldn't be for long and there was no air. In the basin were fires, and sparks leaped high from the white dry snow. And before that was stillness, after the earth sank and sediment slid down from the banks and high places to level the ground, because ground wants to be level. Where the earth sank it rose again against gravity, which is just a story and can't keep anything down, so all that sediment fired to stone from heat, like an infection, and arched a mile high into thin air, a ridge of great pimples—the Sierra Nevada. Before all that they were silt beneath a shallow sea. I can be there, up on my ridge on Christmas morning, kicking my toes in the ooze, a spirit walking out in great circles, building a world fit for me, as Jehovah built His to fit Him.

I climbed a cedar, the oldest on the ridge and the tallest, left at the first logging and nearly as thick at the base as the width of my cabin. I took a star I had carved out of tamarack with Charley's buck knife and painted with oils, silver and golden flecks to make it luminescent if the sun came out, but it was still too early to tell, still all gray. To use both hands for climbing I had to tuck the star into my coat. The trunk was brittle with cold, and bark broke off when I grabbed for a hold. Branches were thick and close together, so the first half was no problem, like climbing a ladder. But as I climbed higher I could feel the sway from my weight, though I don't weigh much now, and from the wind, though it was gentle. The branches were thinner every rung and cracked if I stepped out too far, and the trunk thinned down till I could hold it around with my arms, though the top was still twenty feet away. I guessed I'd meet Jesus today, one way or another, or find he was just another story. Neither Charley nor I had ever reached the top of a cedar; the top of any tree is always a twig, way up from even where loggers top them, and instinct tells you when to stop. But the star had to be where it had to be or else it needn't be up there at all. The tree held out, though it whipped down low above a boulder higher than snow. I tied the star on with string, then held the trunk with my arms and folded my hands, but I was too anxious to pray, waiting for baby Jesus. When Jesus grew up he be-

180

came a God, but as a baby he was still a man, without words or wrath, or favorites.

I knew he was around, somewhere; like a leaf in the wind he was skimming the treetops and watching. I made a rock ring beneath the tree and built a fire to warm my hands. For a long time I waited patiently, till I saw there would be no sun, faithfully, muttering the Lord's Prayer like a rosary, not for Jesus the God, or God in a whirlwind, just for Jesus the baby, before he could make up sermons. Words were lies and they could mean anything. I just wanted him to smile at me.

But he never came. I ran to the cabin and took Charley's rifle from under the boards, checked the clip, and ran back out and up the ridge. I drew a sight on the star and squeezed till the star exploded. There were echoes off all the mountains.

At least I knew there was nothing, no spirit, no Jesus, no time. I knew I could go on living. Skepticism, anger was a religion. And Phillip was just a weakling. I picked up one of his notebooks from where they had sat unopened since Charley left them, because every time I moved toward them something had pulled me away, fear or worries that he might not be a saint or that he wrote things about me in anger.

The one on top was only half filled. I stopped at a page carelessly scrawled in red, "From Dostoevski, *Diary of a Writer*—'Following the loss of the idea of immortality, suicide appears a complete necessity for every man who is in the slightest degree above the beast of the field.' "

There's a cathouse in the valley where Charley went once, not far from Carson. Charley said no one would recognize me, I'm so skinny and pale, unless my dad came. But he'd have to be drunk to go there, and I'd be hard to recognize, even for him, made up, with my hair pinned high, and screwing all day must make some change. If my dad picked me out of the line, I'd take him on; then I'd kill myself. Or they might let the guys from

181

road camp come there once a month, or if I got word to
Charley he could break out at nights. At least he'd be
closer.

★　★　★　★

May 28, 1972

Wednesday in sixth period we dress-rehearsed our play.
The third scene was the banquet, the princess's birthday,
where the jester plans to grab her so she'll fall for him, as
the serving girl had promised. Melinda was the princess
and all week she'd been warning José to not really try it
or she'd kick him sterile. But you can't tell about José;
he's been after Melinda all year and he did the casting.

José, as the jester, wore a cat costume, mewed around
the banquet hall, reciting Spanish poems and nuzzling
the legs of us ladies, making his way toward the princess.
We'd pet him and pinch him and the knights tripped him
down and yanked his tail. He bit their ankles and tickled
our feet and ran out from under the table once with a
garter in this mouth; then he ducked back under and
kept still while the dancers spun and the jugglers
dropped their balls and we were all supposed to forget
about the cat. José mewed and nuzzled my legs—I was
next to Melinda. Then he moved over to her, and just as
he yowled and poked at her skirts the serving girl ran in
with a tray, tripped and grabbed the table for balance, to
pull it down so the king could see the jester under the
princess's skirts—but at the same second Mrs. Bodine
came through the door.

The room hushed, which startled José. He jumped up,
his hand beneath Melinda's hoop skirts, flinging them
up high, and with a shriek she fell over backward, grabbing José and pulling him down between her bare legs.

Mrs. Bodine dropped her package of announcements
and charged out the door. Kids fell down laughing and

182

Phillip pounded the wall. "Mr. Oswald," José wailed, "I'll be expelled! I'll be deported! They'll cut off my fingers!" There were hysterics and kids in the hall came to the windows. "This is my debut, Mr. Oswald. What if my sister the nun finds out?" The bell rang but everyone stayed, kicking the chairs and the table aside, sliding in spilled water, crashing into the piled desks till they tumbled down. Kids outside were shoving for a view through the windows.

Phillip and I stayed to straighten the room and Mr. Beavers came in to help. He said we should have given an open performance. "Guerrilla theatre, goofs and gut punches, time to get in your licks."

Phillip said the play was innocent comedy, today was a fluke. "What you call innocent," Mr. Beavers said, "and what they call innocent, is obviously not the same."

On Thursday, Phillip told me, Mr. Furby had called him to his office. "Oswald! First your mother calls. Next these rumors of you and McGee. Now Bodine tells me you're holding Camelot orgies. What is it, Oswald? Syphillis? Organic schizophrenia? If I hold back your contract you don't work until you win in court."

"No court. I'm gone with the end of the year. You keep the contract and I'll remember better times. But don't try to intimidate me. No more."

"You keep McGee out of sight, don't flaunt it, and the play just closed for bad reviews. Deal?"

"No orders. Didn't I make that clear?"

"Suggestion, then?"

"I don't flaunt Jodi and I don't keep her out of sight, and the play is the students' affair, none of mine."

"Three more weeks, Phil. You're nervous, and I have a ringer of a substitute starving on sixty bucks a week, with two kids and a skipped-out husband. Are you that generous?"

"No."

"Sonofabitch!"

Phillip stepped forward and glared. Mr. Furby flinched. They must think Phillip's mad. "All right, let's be calm. Are there extenuating circumstances? Did McGee ask for special help? Did she throw herself on you? Do her parents beat her?"

"None."

"Give me something. I may have to answer the school board—oh, hell, get out of here!"

Friday, Phillip and I were in bed after a movie in Tahoe City when the phone startled me. It was Maggie. "Jodi, Charley got busted for something. He's in jail. I don't know what to do. I'm here alone. Paul's still at the church. I don't want to call him. I'm scared, Jodi."

I dressed and ran down to Charley's and Phillip followed with the car. Maggie was pacing with her hands on her head as if holding it on.

"Why's he busted, Maggie?"

"I'm scared, Jodi. I'm having contractions and they don't feel right, not like they told me at all. I'll rip, my baby will die. It's not my fault. I can't let it die, Jodi! Take me to the doctor."

"Where's Charley?" What jail's he in? What did he do?"

"What about me?"

"It's just a baby, Maggie. They just come out, don't they? I mean you're not sick, you're not even in trouble. Charley's in jail."

"Just a baby? You don't know. You never had to do it. You're not my friend. You're just Charley's friend. I don't have any friends now that Paul . . ."

I tried to hold her but she pushed me off. "I'll call him, Maggie, or I'll take you soon as you tell me about Charley."

"Charley's a thief. We should've never had anything to do with him. Remember his dad? Once my grandma caught him stealing groceries out of the trunk of her car."

"That's a lie!"

"I won't let Charley around my baby!"

"Where is he?"

"South Lake. He wouldn't tell me anything. He's not my friend. Jodi, I'm scared."

I led her out to the car, where Phillip was waiting, but Paul came through the gate. Phillip came to help, but Paul turned on him. "You're Oswald. I know you. You can't find a woman your own age, but you're a big shot at school, right? You're a liberal, right? Or a free thinker. It's a mirage, buddy!"

Phillip stared dumbly.

"She's having contractions!" I said.

Paul wheeled to Maggie, reached for her arm, but she yanked it away. "I don't want you there! I don't want him there, Jodi! He won't let me cry. He'll watch me!"

Paul slapped her. I kicked him; Maggie took off running down the street toward her mother's house. Paul caught her halfway down the block. We watched till they turned the corner; then we drove down and saw that her mother's car was home, so we started for South Lake.

"Is that Paul fellow crazy?"

"I don't know." I didn't care. Charley was in jail, for something bad or he would've told Maggie. I could see him snapping Maria's neck, stealing his baby, shooting somebody in a dope deal, or flying loose with a hatchet or just his hands, breaking mirrors and chairs and tables and smashing whoever came near, if he finally lost his temper. "Can't you drive faster?"

He took turns at sixty and ran the slowdown zones too fast to talk; we could only hold on and I could only think about Charley. Whatever happened was my fault, because he took care of me and I took care of him, as sure

185

as though we had a pact in blood. I almost told Phillip I couldn't leave the lake without Charley. It was guilt working on me again, I knew; I felt responsible for Charley. But the last thing he needed was to feel responsible for my not leaving. And we weren't each other's keeper anymore, because our childhood was over, long ago it seemed. I almost told Phillip to turn back around, to leave Charley to watch out for himself, but that was too cruel.

At Stateline were a billion early summer gamblers, show bands pounding when the doors opened, and shouts of excitement. Teenagers, loaded and restless, pitched pennies at the walls; Corvettes and Jaguars crouched at the stoplight; taxis blocked traffic and backpackers leaned on lamp posts. An old guy with a waist-length gray beard and a fox-hunting cap stood on the curb by the Sahara, bending to touch his toes, then reaching full length, wild-eyed and shouting, "Balls! Balls and cunts and cocksuckers!"

"He lost," Phillip said. Phillip had to swerve to miss him.

At the jail a dozen people were ahead of us, and only one desk cop was on duty. A woman kept beating her hands on her sides, and the man beside her kept nudging her. Those in the line who weren't frantic slept standing up, and the ones behind them shoved them along. A radio played easy-listening music and commercials from Reno, and a switchboard kept buzzing somewhere behind a wall. The clock had a cracked crystal, and the second hand was turning too slowly. Charley might die in there or drop into catatonia. He needed air and a place to wave his arms.

At the desk I told the man I was Charley's sister.

"Miss Walker, then?"

"Yeah."

"First name?"

"Jodi. Where is he?"

"Address?"

"612 Fox, King's Beach. What did he do?"

"Age?"

"Eighteen."

"Occupation?"

"Nothing. Come on—"

"Unemployed or student?"

"Both."

"All right then, Miss Walker. Your brother was apprehended leaving the Sahara parking lot at eight twelve P.M., May 26, driving a 1972 Ford L.T.D. The registered owner was found, and your brother was booked on one count of grand theft auto. He had no outstanding warrents, though a civil action is pending against him in California. This may not have been his first auto theft and he may not have been working alone. Night court has set bail at five thousand dollars. Bondsmen you can find in the phone book."

By 2:00 A.M. Charley was free. They opened a side door and he came out shuffling his hands and feet and staring at the ground.

"Charley!" I ran up and hugged him but he stayed limp. When I backed off he stared at me and brushed his hair from his eyes.

"You could've let them keep me, Jodi. I've got no reason to be outside."

"You could say thanks, Charley. Don't try to be hard. Why did you call if you didn't want out?"

"Because they've got a machine in there, subliminal tapes or something that spurts out symbolism, like when you go by a hamburger stand they blow sauce smell at you. This one makes you feel guilty, no matter how pissed off you are, even I bet if you didn't do anything. Try to sleep, it makes you dream of roller skates and hopscotch, Kool Aid, telling lies to your dad—then you wake up and feel like crying, because you're bad, always wrong."

I hugged him again but now he was stiff. "He pay the bondsman?"

"Uh-huh."

"How much do I owe?"

Phillip stepped up. "We'll play cards again."

"Nope," Charley said. "Cheat all I want, I'd still probably lose."

All along the highway the lake was calm and glassy. The moon was behind the mountains and the night seemed open to anything, the kind of night to leave home. I stared at the white line with my head on Charley's shoulder.

"It's not your fault."

He didn't answer.

"You had to do something."

"Did they tell you about it?"

"A little."

"Sometimes we stole cars in Reno, sometimes up here, took them to a body shop in Carson, or over to Oakland. Next week I was going to L.A. They took orders; every night this guy had a list for us. His name is Roy Rodgers, can you beat that? We look for the cars, and if we find them he sends the locksmith, magic. See, punks like me and the guys I work for, we've got to do this petty kind of shit because there's nothing else left, and we've got to have money, like we've got to have sex, like a junkey's got to have a jam. You can't beat the big fuckers, Jodi; it's tied up. The money—we just get leftovers. The guys who own these casinos—one was a butcher at Stateline, now he owns half the world; and the old guy who leases all the land, fifty, eighty years ago somebody bought it, now it's his. Private enterprise, right? There ain't enough left, Jodi, and every pimp's trying to hustle you for the scraps you get. Sometimes I feel like going to my old man and screaming 'Bastard, didn't you ever think about me!' I could make something, Jodi, I could take something

from them, I could be shrewd, if I got out of debt. . . . I'll
pay you back some way, Mr. Oswald."

"You can't, Charley," I said.

"Yeah. Thanks for reminding me."

"We're going to Paris. We won't need it for a long
time." My stomach turned. I felt my words were cruel.

Charley's glare was cold and strange. "For sure now,
huh?"

"Uh-huh."

He wouldn't say any more all the way home. Phillip
dropped me at my folks'. In bed I started thinking about
Maggie. I hadn't even told Charley; I hadn't remembered. On the phone to the hospital I couldn't find out
anything, just a runaround, and it made me think Maggie
was in danger or something had happened already. I
called Charley's but he was the only one home. He didn't
need my worries. I dressed and decided to drive to the
hospital. My dad usually left the keys in the car but this
time he hadn't, and if I woke them and they started talking about me my mom might say too much. So I watched
a movie and a morning sermon till seven, when my dad
woke up and I could drive to the hospital.

I tried to slip down the hall to find Maggie's room but
an orderly turned me back and I couldn't find a friendly
nurse. They only told me she'd had a daughter. Finally,
about 8:30, they let me in. Maggie was sitting up with a
glass of juice. She looked hung over, clammy-skinned
and cross-eyed.

"Hi, Jodi. Did I say some mean things last night?"

"No. Where is she? When was she born?"

"About five, Paul said. She only weighs six pounds
but her skin's not very red. They shot me up with something. I didn't want them to."

"You feel O.K.?"

"It didn't hurt much except at first, or else it hurt so
much I can't remember. I had a shot but it didn't knock

189

me out—I only buzzed. They said it was fast but I don't know; I couldn't tell time. I'm supposed to be sleeping but Paul wouldn't let them give me a sedative. He's gone now. I want to call her Bambi, but Paul wants to call her Judith. That's such a stiff name. Who gets to fill in the birth certificate? Jodi, I wish she was Charley's baby."

"Why Charley's?"

" 'Cause at least Charley's my friend. I hate Paul, Jodi. I won't go back there."

In the nursery Bambi was pale like Maggie, with a stone face that seemed unable to cry and eyes stuck shut. Someday I'll have a baby, a boy smart as Phillip, generous as Phillip, with my eyes and my long fingers and a heart blessed with love. When you're loved you want to give love away, but it's not that easy.

* * * *

June 3, 1972

Since yesterday my folks are home for good. For the three weeks left I have to try to forget everything, faith, loyalties, home. I stay in my room to keep out of fights and hold back all the things I wish I could say, because they're dangerous. If I were a Catholic, confession would take hours—all the bad things I've done and the hatred. I don't want advice, only penance, a million Hail Marys or whatever they do. Pastor Sandoz would want to counsel me that life with an unbeliever would discourage my spiritual growth. I don't want to grow. I'm frightened to grow. I just want to leave. There's no one to talk to, not even Charley anymore. When I see him I want to preach, tell him—I don't know what. What do I know? All he could do is run, but how do you run from your own child? And if I try to tell Charley my feelings, if I mention Phillip, he shifts his eyes and turns off. If I told him about what Paul did to me, Charley would kill him in a flash, or Aaron, if it was Aaron—either one of them.

Maggie didn't come home from the hospital, she went to her mother's instead, so the last days at Charley's were horrid. When I went back for clothes and things Paul met me at the door, followed me through the house, called me a bitch and a slut, threatened that I'd better bring Maggie back home—hatefully, as if he'd punish me terribly somehow. Once Charley came out of his room and stepped up like Goliath. Paul shrank back and went out, I guess down to Maggie's, where he goes about ten times a day, but Maggie just tells him no. She won't argue, because he has all the answers and he can yell louder. He won't hit her with her mother there.

I don't know what Charley is doing in his room, may-be snorting dope or just thinking too hard. He keeps a note pad by his bed, with numbers scribbled on it, and he practices cards a lot, dealing so fast to no one, with the deck hidden under his big hands. Pancho calls the house Gehenna. He won't come inside anymore.

I won't tell Phillip what happened till we're gone, safe away from here so we can talk truly. Then I can confess that for these days his anxieties about his mother and what he calls his cowardice—questioning every move and doubting his decisions, asking me every day if I'm sure I want to go to Paris and want him to go—all seemed trivial and self-indulgent. And I can tell him, when we're ten thousand miles gone and safely together, that these days I thought I'd just rather go off on my own, because of anger, which can't exclude anyone.

Grandma bought my ticket already, and Phillip booked the same flight, June 24 in the afternoon, L.A. through to New York, one stop in Iceland, then to Paris, such a rush. I've never been on a plane before, or any-where they speak another language, except Chinatown and east L.A. I'll leave from L.A. because grandma wants to ride down with us to visit my cousins. It'll be a long drive. I can't talk civilly to my dad anymore and grandma will expect me to be tender and grateful. My dad expects honesty, he wants me to confide in him and he's always promised he could live with whatever I'd do if I was sure and I could justify it. But when he gets mad he doesn't want to hear me out, like with Aaron, though he was too god-awful right about Aaron, I know since last night. Or I think I do. God, I just don't know anything for sure. And when dad found out I smoked grass and tried to lock me in for a month till he thought I'd quit, he might've been wrong in his reasons but his warning was right. When you break the law you're a criminal, you only obey the laws you agree with, sometimes not even those. If my dad said cruel things about Phillip I'd pay them more mind than I want to, more than I can stand to. If I left Phillip because of it I'd hate my dad, but I couldn't turn mom against him. I wouldn't have any family then. Without a family I'd be on the run.

Out of habit my mom and I whisper at home now, whether he's there or not, no matter what we're talking about. I've told her the kind things Phillip has done, lending Charley money, the way he treats kids at school, considering their feelings and showing respect. So she speaks his name kindly, sorrowfully, as though she knows how much I'll hurt him when I leave him behind, which she thinks I'm planning to do. I hate this lying. Only last year I thought I'd never look back in guilt on anything.

Last evening my dad was high with coming home after his first day back. He spent all morning on the phone making appointments, and all afternoon driving around. He sold a grader in Homewood and said he broke a monopoly by selling Nevada a snowplow. He was raving, excited, I guessed because he felt successful.

"Salesmen are pigs. You want to buy a car, you should order from a Detroit catalogue. You don't need middle-

192

men. Or advertising. Cut out the ads and you'd get quality. The workers would learn craft and pride; the best ones stay and the ones who can't learn it find something they can. Bad artists don't make money, unless they have salesmen, or are salesmen."

"Bad artists," my mom said coldly, "are housewives for pig salesmen."

"I didn't mean you."

Mom stared away.

"I was telling Jodi to work hard over there. You plan to paint or take up with socialites?"

I just shook my head.

"You can't answer? Think you're a hotshot already?"

"What did I do?"

"Nothing. You don't speak to me. Why bother with children? Last fall you live at church, you won't go with us to Reno, now you clam up. What are you hiding, Jodi?"

"It's a hard time for her, Ronald, can't you understand that? Imagine if you were leaving home—alone." The doorbell rang and my mom went for it.

"Without you, Jodi," my dad said, "there won't be a family."

I watched him suspiciously, wondering if this was a trick, if selling had turned him deceitful. Paul came in ahead of my mom, passed my dad without saying hello and stepped up to me.

"You done eating?"

"Why?"

"Come with me then."

"Jodi doesn't take orders," my dad said.

"What's the matter, Paul?"

"I'll tell you on the way."

"I'm not going anywhere with you."

"You are!"

My dad jumped and grabbed the scruff of his neck. "Adios, sucker."

Paul broke loose and crouched, clenched his fists and hissed. "It's about your boyfriend, Jodi."

"What boyfriend?" my dad asked, but I ran around to the door and Paul followed me out. He had a van from the Baptist church.

"You would've told him, wouldn't you?"

"Sure. Listen, Jodi, if I was the bastard you think I am, I'd tell your dad and I'd show Pastor Sandoz the film."

"What film?"

"You think I want to be heavy, get my kicks as a tyrant, but you don't know my mind, you don't know what it means to take the Lord seriously, you just think He's there to get high on."

"What film?"

He stared at me, first suspiciously, then puzzled. "Honest?"

"Tell me!"

"He's a devil."

"Who?"

"Your boyfriend."

"What is this?"

"You'll see." Now he looked troubled, quiet and even embarrassed. I tried to think of a clue, something to guess from, films that Phillip had shown in class or if we'd ever gone to see an R-rated movie, but all I could recall was Miss Waterman raging in the faculty lounge about film classes.

Paul pulled into the lot at the Baptist church. It was the evening of his Bible study but still early. He led me through the hall to the nursery school. There were Bible scenes on the walls—the woman at the well, the resurrection, Christ reaching down to the children. Paul set up a screen, wound the projector, flipped off the lights and stayed just to focus, then walked out and shut the door.

The film was gray in dim light and streaked as though shot through a dirty lens; it focused on Phillip's bedroom, from the window side. I came in just in panties and a T-shirt, looking back over my shoulder, then slipped off my shirt, pulled down my panties and tossed them toward the camera to the chair. I bent down and touched my toes then jumped on the bed and bounced, curled up toward the pillows and threw back the covers. When Phillip came in I was stretching and rolling my shoulders so my breasts shimmied, and Phillip was drying his hair. Forgetting where I was, because it seemed so innocent, and weird to be seeing, I almost laughed, till I thought of the someone behind the camera, someone who hated us, watching. Phillip slid in beside me, pulled up the covers, leaned over to kiss me, but I rolled back away and jumped off the bed, ran around and dove on top of him. He grabbed my waist, pulled me beneath him and buried his face in my belly. I kicked off the covers. His butt was up high and his legs spread, his penis hard, bent down against me; then he dropped and all you could see was his backside, my hair and one leg rising between his. Then I switched on top, my butt high and my legs spread like Phillip's before and his hands crawled up my hips, squeezed and pulled tight, spreading my cheeks; then the camera zoomed in to a closeup, my asshole.

"Paul!" I screamed, and I kicked over the projector, kicked it again so glass broke and gears sprang. Paul pulled me off.

"Did you watch it? I'll bet you watched the whole thing! You wanted to see me like that, why didn't you just say so? Let me go. You want to stare up my ass?"

He dragged me out to the hall and set me down on a bench by the Ping-Pong table. I was too horrified even to cry or fight anymore. "Why'd they do that? Why'd they make it dirty?"

"They didn't make it anything, Jodi. You just watched yourself in action. That's how Jesus sees you."

195

"Where'd you get it?"

"From a guy. I guess they took it through the window and they're selling them around."

It had to be Aaron. He owned the equipment and nobody else would hate me so much. A torrent of rage swept through me. I'd find him, and if I could I'd slash his face, tear out his heart.

"Jodi, it doesn't matter."

"What?"

"Who did it."

"What matters, then?"

"The church."

"What about the church?"

"You're committed."

I couldn't argue. In shame I let go of my rage. I just sat with my face in my hands, wondering how they could hate us so much. It was hatred that made it filthy. There was always a person behind any camera making a scene what it is; it wasn't me in the film, but that other eye telling my story.

Paul arranged chairs for his Bible study and kids started coming in, going to the Coke machine and playing Ping-Pong beside me, silly voices and giggly hellos, the good kids I'd always thought of as lame, the ones who believed everything they were taught or were too timid to admit they didn't, the Christian kids in bonnets skipping to church in Western movies, the virgins who didn't get loaded or stay out after curfew. I knew what Charley meant by the guilt projector in jail, which made you dream whatever might make you feel most foul.

Paul called them. A Ping-Pong player griped and hit one last shot, footsteps seemed all coming toward me, then chairs squeaked and silence.

"Jodi!"

I didn't look up.

Paul's voice was practiced, gentle, stern. "Come over here, Jodi!" I squeezed my arms over my chest and curled down to my knees. I thought I could run if he tried to take me, but then he had my arm and I was following, trying to shake loose but too weakly. A boy held a chair for me across the circle from Paul's. It was a different group from the old Bible studies; only a girl was the same, Debbie, but there were other kids I knew, Zack from math class and Toni from gym.

"Join hands."

An Oriental girl took my left—her hand was cold—and a boy with pimples my right—his was sweating.

Paul was fatherly here, serene and controlled, even now with Maggie gone. " 'Blessed is he who fears Jehovah, who greatly delights in His commandments! His descendants will be mighty in the land; the generation of the upright will be blessed. The wicked man sees and is angry; he gnashes his teeth and melts away; the desire of the wicked man comes to nought!' Joining the flock we are of the flock and if we wander from the hill the shepherd and the sheep will call us back home. Our guest is Jodi McGee, my friend. She lived in our home. Say your names so Jodi can know you."

"Jonathon." "Deirdre." "Carl." "Pete." "Laura." "Toni." "Margie." "Zack." "Debbie." "Bruce." "Carol."

"Tell us what brought you here, Jodi."

"You did," I muttered.

"You have a special burden tonight?"

"Yeah."

Toni smiled. She was clean, always happy. She had always been sweet to me. "Tell us about it?"

"No."

"We won't judge you."

I tried to stare back at them all but every eye turned me away. They weren't lame, but children of light and wisdom, and I was old, dirty and ashamed. Hands lifted mine again for prayer and everyone bowed but me. Then Paul took up his Bible and passed another to me. In Genesis we read about Abraham and Isaac; Paul said Abra-

197

ham was not a callous man but would've killed his son only because he believed absolutely, and strict obedience came with belief, naturally, logically, because punishment was sure and swift, for Abraham. Though Isaac was innocent he was like the arm of his father, who would've been guilty, and the Lord could show him worse things than simple death. Paul said that Job's bitterness and determination to argue and know the reasons were signs of how far men had come from simple belief in the years between Abraham and Job; though Job was the most righteous man of his time, he contended with the Lord. Christ had not come yet to return us as children. There was perfume and dust in the air and no one asked questions. After the study they prayed again.

"Aren't we your brothers and sisters, Jodi?" Deirdre asked.

"My brothers are angry," I said, "and my sisters are whores."

Paul stepped across. "Take my hands."

"You want to dance?"

He just waited.

"Go away! I'm not on your Little League team!"

He still waited. He'd never go away.

"Are you Oral Roberts now? You Kathryn Kuhlman, Charlie Manson? Back off, fuckhead, I'll tell Charley!"

"Why violence, Jodi? Why do you threaten me?"

"Violence? I was the one kidnapped."

"You came on your own."

"Show the film! I don't care if they see it. I don't mind being exposed. Humiliation's great—you should try it!"

But he had the power. He called the right moment and showed the right tenderness, knew when my bluff was gone. "Be on your knees, Jodi." Bruce and Carol took my hands lovingly. The night was so warm, heavy like water. I dropped to my knees and crawled.

"Where we gather together in Christ's name He is with us. Precious Lord, cast this curse from our sister

198

who is before You now in fear and trembling, asking for Your love and ours."

There were spasms all through my shoulders and up my spine. "You go to hell, Paul!" I tried to jump up but arms were all over me, each one so terribly strong. "You go to hell!" I screamed over and over till my strength was gone, then fell forward, nauseated and whimpering. Paul laid his hands on the sides of my head. I tossed to shake him off, but he pressed me low, my lips to the floor.

"Beg! Beg, Jodi! Beg!"

Around me they all prayed aloud and they all laid on their hands. Their prayers turned to frantic shouts. The floor was green, swirling with white foam. Jesus was rising beneath the water. I cried and begged, but He drowned in the cold, hard waves.

★ ★ ★ ★

June 11, 1972

Now I know how Jill feels; almost three years ago they busted her for a hooker, but she can't throw it out of her mind. She believes she was framed, as I was, as Charley was, that it wasn't something she set out to do. Still I didn't go to school for two days and now that I do I duck down the halls and only look at my feet so I won't see anyone leer; in classes I keep my nose in a book, singing songs to myself so I won't hear anyone snicker. I'm afraid of them all, thinking they've all seen the film and when they look at me they see it again. Jerry checked out of Phillip's class on some special deal with a counselor. I've only seen Aaron from a distance and I'm trying my best not to hate him, not because I think he deserves forgiveness, at least not from me, but because hatred poisons everything I do. I suppose I should confront Aaron, kick his balls or scratch scars in his pretty face; then maybe I'd be soothed enough to truly forgive. But Phillip

199

would hear and I'd have to tell him about the film, so all I can do is suppress the hatred. I can't be kind to anyone, even Phillip.

The day after Paul showed me the film I told Phillip I had a cold so I wouldn't come over; the next day I told him I'd stay home and lie in the sun to drain my head. Monday, the first evening I saw him, he talked about a trip we'd take to Pompeii, near Naples, where rooms had been left whole beneath lava and people had turned to stone while they ran. He read to me of hotels in Nice which aren't too expensive and showed me photographs of Monte Carlo casinos where gamblers dress like royalty. With me for luck, dolled up like a princess, he said he knew he could win. It was the first time I could remember him saying "luck." Before, he had used words more cosmic, like "fortune," or talked about systems which turned the mathematical odds.

All evening he kept looking toward the bedroom but I pretended not to notice. Finally he asked me straight out if I wanted to go in. I lied that my period had started early and said anyway I had to leave because my dad was waiting up to talk about how much money we thought I'd need in Paris. Phillip looked puzzled, then troubled, because it was only 9:30 and I hadn't mentioned any of this before, but he said O.K. I wished I could tell him about the film, to explain my coldness that night and however long it lasts, tell him it had made sex seem filthy to me, that I'd hate myself and him the whole time—maybe in a few days I'd be back to normal. But I couldn't tell him because of his pride, because he'd have to go after Aaron this time, else feel like a coward forever.

Thursday evening we drove to Truckee for tamales, then pulled off by the river on the way home. There were several campers, the river was lower already, below the shrub line, and the banks were dry. Some men were night fishing, so we walked downriver beyond them, to a grassy spot without beer cans or toilet paper, and Phillip opened the book he had brought, rubbed the seam so it lay flat on the grass, and shined down our flashlight. In the photograph the sun ricocheted off red mountains, the sky was turquoise; in a village of white houses and dirt streets was a plaza with fountains; above the village olive trees made a checkerboard with red soil and a stream zigzagged down to a black-earthed valley where an ox pulled a plow. "We can visit there, Jodi. No one will know our language."

A boy came running. "Let me use that flashlight! Jamie's got a monster on the line." We followed and watched as the other boy reeled in a cutthroat, held it up by the line and clubbed it with a hatchet. Then he threw it back into the river.

Farther downriver where we walked was a wide crossing only waist deep. We were alone. Phillip wanted to undress and swim, but in the water my period would be no excuse so I said I worried about getting my cold back. He started at me angrily.

"I don't believe that, Jodi."

"Then what do you believe?"

He shook his head.

"You want to screw in there, don't you?"

"Not necessarily."

"Don't lie to me! I know what you want."

I felt both sorry and foolish; I threw myself on him and buried my face. I told him I was just upset with the thought of leaving home so soon, but he didn't believe me. On the way home I asked him to tell me more about Nice. He said he had told me all he knew. If he'd have asked me that night what was really wrong, I'd have told him about the film, but he doesn't push me for answers.

This morning Charley came to see me. I was up late last night; after my folks were asleep I went out onto the roof from my window, where I can see the lake all across to Rubicon and feel surrounded by holiness, so I have to be touched by it and cleansed. I stayed out there till I couldn't keep my eyes open, then set my alarm to get up in time for church. But when it rang I fell back to sleep, so it was already late when Charley came. I opened my eyes to find him sitting over me, smiling and brushing back his hair.

"Morning, Jodi."

"A real smile, Charley?"

"Yep."

I sat up and leaned back. "Tell me why?"

"Because your buttons are loose."

I yanked my pajama top together. "Don't stare at me."

"Why not? You're pretty."

"Just don't."

"All right. Private property. So you're going away for sure?"

"Let's go downstairs, O.K.?"

"Sure."

"You go while I get dressed."

"Yes ma'am. Shall I leave?"

"No."

He nodded and went on down. When I came into the kitchen he was drinking coffee with my mom and all of a sudden I remembered I hadn't told him not to tell her that Phillip planned to leave with me. "Mom?"

She wheeled around, startled. "Oh. Good morning, Jodi. Charley was telling me he's working again. Can you picture him as a grumbling dealer in black slacks? I never could."

Charley grinned. "You don't know my darker side."

"I hope I never do."

"Charley's fast," I said. "He cheats good, too. At Harry's?"

"Yeah."

"How come they hired you back?"

Turned my way so my mom couldn't see, Charley touched his finger to his lips. "Summer help," he said.

202

My dad had gone off somewhere already. Mom made us waffles and Texas grapefruit. "So, Charley, what do you think about Jodi leaving for Paris?"

I kicked him under the table and he looked at me confounded. "Can't say I'm happy about it. Who's going to tie my shoes?"

"But I think it's best for her future, don't you?"

He squinted strangely at her, puzzled again. "I guess."

Out in the truck I told him, "She doesn't know about Phillip's going."

"She thinks he'll let you go alone?"

"Yeah. She's never met him."

"Jodi, what kind of guy is he? I mean, you've told me he's sweet and this and that and he keeps giving me money but that's not so hard if you've got it. What else?"

I had to think hard, to try to make it simple, because I knew I could go on forever and not say what I meant. "Maybe he's just older, or whatever makes you have more reverence for little things, know what I mean, like smiles and weeks as much as love words and lifetimes. And he stands back when I need it; you can feel most guys tugging like they have hold of your hair."

"O.K."

"So how come they took you back at Harry's?"

"Well, there's a pit boss, I'll call him Zed—he's got names all the way from Alfred—who has sidelines, like a certain paint and body shop. He worked it out. They want me to say what they want me to say when I go to court, so I'll say it. Lucky part was they didn't take my gambling card at the jail."

"Do you want to go back?"

"Yeah. Really. I've got plans. Born to cheat. Fast hands now, and when I get my photogray glasses next week, upstairs won't even know what I'm doing. All I need is a partner with a thousand disguises."

"You said you can't beat them." ·

"Did I say that? I don't know, but you've got to go where they keep the prize. You go to Paris, I go to hell." He chuckled.

"Be careful, Charley."

"Why?"

"I don't know." I couldn't think of a reason to be careful; it never seemed to matter. "Where are we going?"

"To see my dad."

It was the first time I'd been there with Charley since right after he came home from the army. We found Walker in the day room with the goony giants, the spacemen who bobbed and rolled their eyes and the old men who couldn't stand up long or at all and seemed only to wonder where they were and why. Walker was by the television, up too close to see and staring over it, anyway. There were lines a half inch deep across his face and scabs on his cheeks and his hands. His head was shaved and blotched with white stuff and oil. From behind Charley shook his shoulders. "Dad, you're looking fit and ready to rumble."

Walker turned slowly and looked at me, not at Charley. His eyes were doped up, for sure. His arms tried to lift, then fell back down, and he hissed a sound of disgust. Charley bent down closer. "Staying sober?"

Walker crooked his neck and spit sideways all down his chin. Charley sat beside him on a stool.

"Walker, I'm going to Paris," I said, but nothing showed that he heard or cared to. He just looked away and back like an old fool not wanting to be bothered.

"Listen, dad," Charley said. "Things have gotten rough, you know. Can't do much without money these days and I've got a son now, remember?" He waited a minute; then he took out a paper and pen and slammed them down on a lunch tray and set it between the arms of Walker's wheelchair.

Walker didn't move.

"Come on, you old bastard, do it! Where's the gold?"

"He can't, Charley!"

"Hell he can't! Write it, you fucking old liar!"

"Leave him alone!"

"Not this time. All my life he's been bluffing, made me think that deep down he's a good guy and honest. Write it, drunk! Do it, bum! I'll snap your fucking neck off!"

Walker's eyes pinched shut and he breathed hard through his nose like a bull snorting. Charley walked away. I begged him to say he was sorry, to kiss Walker or hug him or just say goodbye, but he wouldn't, so I did instead. Charley went on out and I found him on the sidewalk staring across at the lake. "He was crying," I said. "You should've felt his cheek."

"That was spit, Jodi. Now drop it."

There was nothing to say on the way home, nothing to think but everything miserable, till Charley pulled off at Sand Harbor and walked me down to the dock. He kicked at the sand and threw a stone out as far as he could, a long way. "He's not really a liar, Jodi."

* * * *

June 14, 1972

Monday we put on our play, on a platform beside the football field, where the cheerleaders held pep rallies. Mr. Beavers had tried to get us the auditorium but they turned him down. About a hundred people showed—not bad for after school—with lots of teachers and Mr. Furby, Aaron and Jerry and more of their friends standing in front. Mr. Beavers cheered us on while Phillip just watched from the side, down below, looking around coolly and seeming to stare at the other teachers as if in a challenge. Jerry leaned on the stage and shouted at the dancers, waved at me and bent down pretending to look up my dress, and the rest of the boys with Aaron, but

205

not Aaron, hollered and threw things on stage till Coach Fabriano had to come over and stand beside them. Mr. Beavers yanked Jerry from leaning on the stage and ran him down the row and out.

I couldn't play my part, pretending to drink and laugh; I just sat still and watched, thinking the play corrupt and impious, particularly feeling it penance to be exposed in front of all those people, and irreverent, because the tale began on a pilgrimage. Miss Waterman must've thought it lewd, because I saw her leave half way through. But no one else seemed to mind. The play went smoothly; most of the audience snickered when they were supposed to and kept quiet enough so they could hear the dialogue. The king caught the jester beneath the princess's hoop skirts, threatened to behead the jester but decided on banishment instead. The serving girl went on her pilgrimage, told her story to the others, and went off with a horny knight just back from the holy wars. Mr. Furby even came up afterward, thanked us and nodded to Phillip in a friendly way.

After we'd stored away the props and everybody had changed and picked up their things in the classroom, Mr. Beavers invited us to his house for dinner. Phillip brought me home to change and said he'd meet me at seven at the stoplight by the highway. But at 6:30 I was still in the tub when I heard a car screech up to the curb. When I got to the window Phillip was running up the steps with a bundle of my things. I threw on a towel and charged down the stairs.

"Jodi!" my mom said. "Put on your clothes. What if your father comes home?"

When I came back down they were both on the couch. "Well, Mr. Oswald. You don't look like your pictures in the annuals."

"Why did you bring my clothes?"

Trying to look at both of us at once, he appeared to be twitching back and forth.

206

"Are you O.K.? You're pale, like yellow."

"Tomorrow I'll be worse, and the next day and so on. My mother is here."

"In person?"

"Yes. She was waiting. Your things were piled on the porch."

"What did she say?"

"I didn't stay. I just grabbed these and ran. I needed time to compose myself. You can't hipshoot my mother; you have to take aim and fire coolly."

He called Mr. Beavers to tell him we wouldn't come. My mom watched him studiously, then squeezed my hand. "Would you like a cup of Sleepytime tea, Mr. Oswald? It's good for the nerves."

"When's dad supposed to be home?"

"Don't worry," my mom said. "We'll lie."

He gulped the first cup, so she brought him another. I had him sit on the floor and rubbed his neck. None of us talked much, Phillip too ponderous and I guessed my mom afraid of being caught in my lies, the same as I. He left before dad came.

"I thought he'd be older," my mom said.

"Sometimes he is older."

"I can't picture you with him. Bulls like Charley and your father seem more your type. He's so fragile. When will you tell him you're leaving?"

I just couldn't lie anymore. It was hard enough to live with myself, and now that his mother was here we'd surely be caught anyway, or that's what I thought for the moment. "He's going with me, mom."

She stopped still and batted her eyes, her jaw open wide and her tea cup spilling.

"Please, mom, just shut up. Just leave me be." I ran up the stairs, put on my sandals and left before I saw her again or my dad came home.

Lights were on at Phillip's, but his car wasn't there. I stationed myself by the gate to the church and watched what I could through the window, which was nothing but the lamp and sometimes a shadow crossing past it, slowly, powerfully. Just her silhouette gave me chills.

Pastor Sandoz came around the path. "Jodi. Did you come to see me, or . . . ?"

"No. Not tonight."

"Is there a meeting I've forgotten?"

"No. I'm just thinking."

"We missed you Sunday."

"Pastor, I'll tell you now; I couldn't tell you before. I just couldn't. I have a boyfriend."

"Yes."

"I have sex with my boyfriend."

He looked around to check that we were alone. "Yes."

"Tell me about it. It's got to be sin, doesn't it, after I've promised myself to Jesus?"

He sighed deeply. "Jodi . . ."

"What?"

"I find it so tender, young people turning to Christ, aware of what you're giving away, the thrills, restlessness and the passion you turn inward. You give your beauty to Christ. It must be precious to Him." His eyes misted and he wiped them with his arm. "Please be kind."

I wanted to ask, Kind to whom? but he was choked up, as though I had just added to some tragedy or deep meditation of his own. I couldn't quite figure what his answer had been, but I touched his arm and let him walk away. He looked back over his shoulder and I waved, wondering if Jesus ever cried and if there could be better men than I knew, Charley and Phillip and Pastor Sandoz, even old Walker, no matter what Charley called him. Everyone hurt everyone, but hurt swelled the heart so it could hold more joy, I was certain.

Phillip turned the corner and I ran across the street to meet him.

208

"What are you doing here? You didn't go in?"

"I was waiting. Can't I meet her? I could say I'm a neighbor."

"No."

"Where did you go?"

"King's Castle. I won a hundred and fifty dollars. I feel lucky, justified. I'll take her on now. You go home."

Before I could answer he jumped away and went up the steps. She was waiting in the door, tall, heavy, steel-gray hair in tight curls, an old German mama in a black gestapo coat though the night was warm even outside.

"I saw her, Phillip!" she said shrilly. "I still see her. She's behind your car!"

He shoved her inside and I ran up to the window, open a crack, so I could hear.

"Here's her brassiere, a box of Tampax and a shameful nightgown."

"What do you want, mother?"

"I want to save your life, Phillip. I want you in my hand because that's the only way you'll keep from destroying yourself. I'd turn you out, if it were just up to me, but your father, you know how dear you are to your father."

"How is he?"

"Sick, Phillip. Very sick."

Phillip walked to the wall and leaned. "What's the matter?"

"Kidney stones, continuously. He can't afford the operations. Our health insurance is criminal."

"You need money?"

"Certainly he does. He'll have to retire this year."

"There'll be a pension, and you have the house paid."

"That's nothing, Phillip. We're to live on half what you make, for the two of us, our responsibilities to the church, and paying on medical bills?"

He pushed himself off the wall and jumped in front of

her. "I don't want to hear about the church, mother. I swear to God the next time you mention the church I'll . . ."

"What?"

He just kept glaring.

"You won't do anything, Phillip, because you're afraid of me. I don't know what I've done to make you so, but you are. You're a coward."

"I'm afraid of you because you're stupid, hateful, blind, because you'd take me when I was down and grind your heel in my eyes!" He stormed past her and into the bedroom.

"I won't stand for you walking away from me!"

"You won't stand?" he shouted. "You leave now, mother! This once I'm telling you!"

"Not until you come with me. I've found you a job at a Christian school, where you'll be watched over. You'll live at home and help us. There won't be a chance of you finding another slut! . . . She's there! She's at the window."

She charged and I ran, up past Charley's, where the lights were out, down to the highway to hitchhike. He was right—that woman deserves to die, as Aaron deserves to die. She's another one who bends what people do and breaks them with it, and feels no remorse herself because she's convinced of her infallible righteousness. She can justify anything. That's how I see her.

The next day Phillip was nervous and today even more so. He picks at the hairs his razor missed and he rubs his eyes so they're red and swollen as though he hadn't slept, though he says he has, and he won't look at the same spot for more than a second at once. I tell him we should go for rides after school or anywhere to keep him away from home, but he won't listen to me; he goes on home. I hope by this weekend he'll have the nerve to leave and go up to the cabin. I'll tell my dad Charley's

210

taking me; Charley will back me and my dad won't mind, unless my mom tells him first. She hasn't talked to me for the last two days and I think she's not sleeping, because I hear her up in the middle of nights.

I hope by this weekend I can believe in myself as Pastor Sandoz believes in me. I don't know if he meant I should be kind to him, which would mean not to do things which harm my soul, because they hurt him because he cares for his brothers and sisters; or if he meant to be kind to myself, and if so, does that mean to do what I choose and forgive myself or to guard myself against any sin? I have to think he wants me to make up my own mind, or he would've said it more clearly.

I still can't imagine sex without eyes all around, drilling inside me, without my looking for parts of my body and Phillip's that smell rank or feeling those hands pressing me down. Paul called tonight to ask me to come again to Bible study. I told him to go to hell.

★   ★   ★   ★

June 18, 1972

Friday afternoon was hot. In just shorts and boots Phillip was silly looking, all white and bony as though he'd fall on his face after the first half mile. But he was determined, marching up the road ahead of me, testing himself, I thought, his pride and endurance. I worried because the mountain was hard, he hadn't slept much, and I could hear him panting so far ahead. When I caught up I coaxed him down to the stream, to a shallow where hot rocks warmed the water. While I splashed and wet my clothes, on my back with my feet up to keep my boots dry, Phillip stayed standing, watching upstream and rolling his neck and shoulders. Then he sat down in mud where the stream had lately overflowed. I wrung out his shirt and took out two of my panties for sweat bands, tied one on him and one on me while he drew circles in the mud.

"Why's your mother like she is?"

He stabbed his finger in the middle of his circles. "Now that she's here I wake to yellow eyes staring at me. All she knows, all she speaks about is doom. If she's said a hopeful word in all her life, it wasn't to me; I've heard only complaints—too much work, not enough money, always people imposing and no one to give her a hand. You should hear her version of hell, a snake pit where the saints will laugh at our horror. Her parents were German farmers, stern, I suppose, but not like her. At least they could smile for photographs. My dad met her when she was sixteen. He said she was beautiful, stately, smart; she learned English in six months. I swear I've never seen her smile. She'll bare her teeth, curl her lips, not smile. She only knows crime and punishment, duty, burdens, furious faith. Draw me a picture of her God someday, with red eyes and fangs, hair like cables and a bomb in his hands, cradling it and waiting for the day. She thinks she'll be his right-hand man. She thinks Jesus is a pushover.

"I don't know why. Some people are born with harelips or water on the brain. Perhaps she's a mutant, or once killed a child and can't forgive herself, how should I know? A scorpion crawls into your bed and you knock it away, then it crawls up again and you knock it away again, but one time you'll kill it, just so you can sleep. With her here I've remembered everyone who ever scoffed at me, everything I've ever feared. I wake up nights pounding my bed, with scars in my palms from my fingernails; my teeth hurt from gritting and grinding. For whatever reason, or for no reason, she's contagious. Many times I'd have killed her, if I wasn't afraid. I swear to God, Jodi, it would be a righteous act—listen to me. I'm her son after all, aren't I?"

212

"No!" I pushed back his head and stared into his eyes; shame there—I knew what it looked like. "You're my man."

"Man," he muttered. "Man." He stood up. "Man!" he shouted so echoes came back. "What in this world is a man?"

He climbed to the road and I ran after him, dragging my bag. Farther along and down to a wash, the sun dipped and the creek and the road fell into shade. Phillip was gone, over the next rise, I thought, so I tried running, winded and dizzy by now, but at the crest I couldn't see him, so I looked up the hills and back down the road till I heard a clack on wood and I climbed toward the sound, up to the sunshine. He was on a stump with a long stick, smacking it down. The lake was golden with the last full sun before it touched the Rubicons. "See the sailboats, Jodi. See how they glide."

From there on we held hands walking. It was quiet near dusk, just a few crickets down by the stream and rustles of creatures above us in the trees. It was time for deer to come down to the water, but today there were none—like a city holiday with families out of town and the streets left for lovers. From miles back at Sand Harbor or the marinas farther north we heard speedboats gearing down and sputtering and sometimes a high-pitched scream like a happy child's. I thought about walking along the Seine at dusk while the shops were closing and old fishermen yawned, and painters, I imagined, packed up their easels and turned to watch light fade from the city. I couldn't believe it was only a week away.

At the cabin Phillip sat quietly, dealing out twenty-one hands and betting against himself. I started to sweep but there was too much dust, so I let it settle, lit up the fire and heated up soup and sliced our bread. We ate in the dark, limp from the climb and both of us too thoughtful for much talk, with just the firelight and coyotes howling up the hills. Afterward, while I made our bed in the loft, Phillip took the dishes down to the stream to wash. I dreaded him coming back, naked, horny, violent perhaps in his fury at his mother, or maybe at me. Since the film I had kept him off me with all the tricks I could find. I undressed and dressed and climbed under the bags to wait. He came up in his shorts and hung them neatly on the ladder rail, threw back the top bag.

"Pajamas?"

"It might get cold later," I said.

He lay down and turned into my arms.

"Can I rub you, Phillip, so you won't be sore in the morning?"

I started with the top of his head, his temples and ears, down to his neck, slowly, working his shoulders and all over his back, down his legs then up again and back to his shoulders, feeling tightness give way and his breaths go longer, determined to keep on till he loosened and finally slept; when he did I lay back, listened to the last of the fire and wished for simpler times and easier answers to easier questions.

In the morning we packed a lunch, crossed to the road and started our climb, still early and cold. I told Phillip we could make Marlette by noon, spend the day starting a summer tan so we'd look good on French beaches. In the first sunlit spot I took off my jacket and flopped down on the dewy grass. Phillip stood over me fidgeting. I gave him my hand, meaning for him to sit down, but he pulled me up instead, asked if I was tired already, then turned back up the road when I said no. I wanted to stop and look at wild flowers, feed squirrels our bread and stop to splash in the stream, but I had to keep running, trying to catch up with his long strides, tripping on ruts and branches blown down on the road. Above the hill past lightning-split stumps to the south end of Marlette's valley, my legs were aching and my heels were blistered

214

and swollen, so I took off my boots and socks, caught my breath, then ran barefoot. Near the valley he turned southeast, away from Marlette. I yelled and he stopped to wait, bent over with hands on his knees and his cheeks sucked in.

"You can't go so fast up here in thin air. It'll kill your brain. Can't we eat lunch now?" He was panting too hard to talk. He staggered backward till he hit a stump, then slid down it. I gave him a sandwich, which he set on his knee, and an apple he rubbed between his hands.

"Can't you eat?"

"Sure," he said, but he didn't.

"Can't we go to the lake? I'll show you the water flumes they built to Virginia City."

"I want to climb that peak." Where he pointed was sand-white and high, a thousand feet above timber.

"I can't rest, Jodi, I can't sit still. I see sparkles and blowups, things like when you close your eyes or pinch them against the sun. I'm dizzier sitting than running, for now."

"I'll wait for you then, by this end of Marlette. Turn back about three, O.K., so we can get down by dark."

He stuffed his lunch into his day pack, kissed my forehead and walked off across the valley. But he was no mountaineer; I didn't trust him up there alone, so after a few minutes I changed my mind, tied on my boots and followed across, started up, through gulleys and brush, past the fir and cedar and stumps at the timberline, to the bare slopes and crumbling granite. Pain shot up from my heels, my toes throbbed and I fell and scraped my knee. I was slick with sweat, thirsty, and Phillip had our canteen. I turned back down toward Marlette.

I was naked and sleeping when he found me, my hips and neck already burned. His eyes were glazed and clouded, two layers, one like a mirror with the sun refracted, and beneath it a soapy pool.

"I dreamed you walked off the edge."

"It was lovely up there, Jodi, hard winds, Carson and Gardnerville and thunderheads across the plain, the whole north end of the lake and south to Emerald Bay. There was a small eagle, or hawk or buzzard—I couldn't tell because she was flipping loops and diving. Can birds go mad? Do you remember in Revelation, my mother's favorite verse, 'Then I looked and I heard an eagle crying with a loud voice as it flew in Midheaven, Woe, woe, to those who dwell on the earth.' "

"There used to be a man up here," I said, "a flume-keeper, who spent years, building a ship, a sailboat. Then he trucked it down to Tahoe, tested it, shipped it out to the coast and sailed away. I think he never came back." I dressed and took him around to where I had found the pine-nut faces, down in the mud where my dad was fishing.

"Voodoo," he said, then chewed up gum and stuck a few rocks together in a shape like a snowman and heaved them far out into Marlette. Smiling and tender, close beside me, he rubbed my feet while the shade crept over.

The run down was easy and fast and we made the cabin long before dark and crawled up to the loft for a nap. I just dozed, but he was hard to wake up. I brought in firewood, swept up the cabin till the dust was thick and Phillip came down from the loft, choking. He found the loose floorboard, Charley's whiskey, and we drank on a rock beneath the ridge all through sunset and dusk, talking about what we thought of each other before we turned lovers, before we first kissed or even held hands. The night came happily. I was high and Phillip was more so. He drank fast, which I hadn't seen him do since the last time at the cabin.

"I decided today"—he held up his arms—"that I don't have to think anymore, or feel sorry or strange." He opened his hands, turned up his palms as if something were in them. "I've given up thinking. I'll work on impulse and be a natural man. Haah!" He took a long pull from the bottle. "I just have to distinguish between thought and impulse. There's the rub, huh? I won't depend on a system; I'll play hunches when they're strong. Killing off logic, Jodi, that's the peace of your saints."

Back inside I cooked our soup, but we didn't eat any; the night was such magic, a last going-away gift from Charley and Walker. For once their drinking seemed only reasonable to me. I laughed at myself, thinking my worst problem was that I was always sober. For a long time we sat in a trance, an aching and wonderful time, pulled between joy and exhaustion, batting our eyes just to keep them open, sipping and drifting off. There was no guilt or anxiousness about this last week; our spirits had flown away and we were just bodies again.

"But the money!"

I jumped, startled. "What money? What happened?"

"I gave too much away. I sent my father five thousand."

"Don't talk about that kind of stuff, Phillip. My dad will send money and Charley will pay you back. You can be a foreign correspondent and I'll dance in cafés. I just have to learn how to dance. Or I'll be the correspondent. Can you dance?"

"Sure," he said. "Now I can believe in what never happens, in obvious fictions and kiddies' rhymes. And I can be anything, a thief, a boxer, even a saint. You hear me, Jodi? Christians are manic. I could believe in God. Do you want me to?"

"O.K.," I said. He was very drunk. So was I. We walked out into the meadow, weaving and stumbling, pulling each other down. By the creek he popped my button and yanked down my jeans. I laughed loudly and screamed. "Nasty! Nasty old man!"

He tackled me and pinned me down. "I'll get the money," he said. He was heavy on me till I pulled off his shirt and shorts and he gagged and bent off me; then he

217

caught his breath and puffed up bigger than life. I rubbed him with grass and dew, licked his sore arms and everywhere, and he did me so all my muscles ached and stretched and I knew I could spring loose and fly, drift with the moonbeams and fall with the stars. Touching the water we shivered with tiny fingers, hummed and moaned loudly in love. Only the moon was watching and only the summer lay ahead, water and meadows and jets through the sky, all in the plan so our joy, now and forever, was written on the very first day.

This morning I don't feel so good—not so much hangover or even ashamed, more empty, as though I've given too much away and I'm not sure what's left or what's mine anymore. Phillip is still sleeping, not moving at all, though I've been up a couple of hours and set a bouquet of wild flowers beside him, for the first thing he'll see when he wakes up. We'll have to leave soon to go back down the mountain.

★   ★   ★   ★

Most of the snow is gone, magically, out of the wash and the meadow, gone from around the cabin except behind, where the sun never hits. The stream is a flood of white water and foam to the top of the north bank and gouging beneath the road, so rocks tear loose and slide down. The hills are eroding with culverts; chunks of ice slide down carrying twigs from beneath the snow. It is too early for the final thaw; there'll be another storm soon, but for now I can spend my days outside. I like to lie in the mud after it warms about noon, watching the insects and waiting for flower buds, planting seeds Charley brought me last summer, carrots and greens, though they'll die beneath the next storm. I can get more seeds. Hawks like to perch in the cedars, thumping their wings and cawing as though they have something to say; some days there are three or four at once, never close to each other. If they don't leave soon I'll shoot them down.

When Pancho came up I was sitting in front of the mirror Walker brought, with a blanket draped over my shoulders and nothing else on, thinking of brushing my hair. It was matted with dirt on top and frizzing all down the sides, dull and dead and tangled. I hadn't combed it in a week at least. I was picking the dirt and hair from my brush and staring at my body; there's not much left, only burned skin and ribs and bones so prominent they seem popped out of joint, no fat anymore, nothing that grows or ripples, no muscles to flex, only a skeleton covered. But still I feel stronger and I don't sleep so much. I love my spectral eyes. I was laughing at myself, thinking I could be a cover girl, when Pancho burst in. I dove for the rifle; then I saw it was him and sat back up. "I could've shot you."

"What for? I brought you good stuff, even ice cream, strawberry crunch, but I ate it on the way up. Say, Jodi, I'm not used to, uh, talking to naked ladies—platonically."

"You want me to dress?"

"Not really," he said.

"O.K."

"O.K.? No fire anymore? You're a eunuch for Christ, maybe. Hey, that'd make a good name for a cult."

"I don't need it."

"Yeah." He emptied his pack: lentils and peas, a bag of gumdrops, dried fruit and cans of V-8 juice, teas and a jar of aspirins and vitamins, cold pills. "Stays pretty warm in here, right?"

"When there's no wind."

"Listen, you don't need it. Do you want it?"

"Do you?"

"Always."

"Then let's do it," I sneered.

"Jodi. I take people at their word. I'm no therapist."

"I don't lie."

"Come on, then." He picked me up easily.

I started to smile but I laughed instead, loud in his ear so he pulled away. *"Weird,"* he muttered. *"Too weird."* Then he carried me up the ladder. In the loft he threw off his coat and kicked his boots downstairs. His jeans were dirty as mine but he smelled clean like showers and bubble baths. His hands were soft, so light I could hardly feel them.

"Is this rape?"

"No," I said.

"What about Charley? Are you Charley's girl? He says no but he might just not know it."

"Where is he?"

"Road camp, still, working mostly down by Fallon. I brought a letter."

"I'm not Charley's girl," I said, but it hurt me to say it, like a lie, but I didn't think it was and I would've lied anyway to keep his hands on me. Though I couldn't get hot or feel any juices or hardly respond, there was pain where I needed pain and softness where I needed softness, and a voice above me. That was enough, but too fast; then he was off and downstairs.

"Hey, Jodi. You sure know how to make a man feel fucked!" Then he went outside, laughing. I climbed down the ladder and picked up the rifle. When he came back I aimed at his head.

"What did I do?" he said. *"I gave it all I had, man. It's hard to get off on fucking a sponge. Put that thing down."*

"Where's Charley's letter?"

He found it in his pack.

"Read it to me."

"Look, you can play crazy, just put that gun down."

I flipped off the safety. *"Read it."*

"Yeah. 'Jodi, I met a guy in here, Lucky, who says he knows you from the snapshot in my wallet, but he calls

you Gwendolyn. Maybe it's somebody else. These green shirts think they're the law, a pain, and I could get loose when we're out. There's just a guy who sleeps in the bus most of the time. But then I'd be on my own, tired blood, you know what I mean? Lucky takes care of my veins.' "

There was more, about hot tar on the highways and what some were in for, and that he hadn't heard from Maria. I set down the rifle, wrapped in my blanket and shivered.

Pancho came over and held my shoulders. "You said you weren't Charley's girl."

"I'm not."

"Yeah."

"I'm Phillip's girl, or nobody's."

"Burn it, Jodi! Times pass. Hey, I'll cook you something." He carried in logs, went to the creek for water, fed me lunch and crackers the way Charley used to do. Afterward I took him back to bed, though he argued he shouldn't and said he thought he couldn't. I told him I had to pay him something and I'd try harder this time. That made him mad so he came to me angrily, but I tried very hard and soon he was gentle again. It wasn't so bad, being a whore; Charley would never come home.

I walked a half mile down the mountain with Pancho, my first time that far back. It was too late to go out more that day so back inside I finished washing my hair and combed it out straight, then went to bed early to wait for morning.

At dawn I filled the clip in my rifle and brought along extra rounds. It was muddy going, mud sticking to my boots, and my feet slipping, hard climbing on my skinny legs and the wind was blowing from up the mountain. There were too-early buds on the aspens, sure to die, and the grove was a swamp of part-melted slush. Twigs snapped on the drying hills and a few jaybirds were back home. I listened closely for my gypsy. She'd be angry and vengeful from nights outside my window, trying to

221

coax me out or to let her in. "It could be years," she told me. "He may never ever come back. Shouldn't we try reality for once, shouldn't we be seeking truth? We can find it, stinking as it does. See these years passing, my butterfly, months, what does it matter? And where do they go once they've gone? Could they die? Lord, no! Do they round the earth and return? Pray not—we'd have to live them again. Pity me now, little fairy, I'm weary, so cold." But I was afraid to let her in and it thrilled me to feel fear again. I blamed it on the change in seasons.

When I heard her scream from past the next meadow I was too weak to run so I paced my stride, long steps like a hunter, on the drier side of the road. There were rumbles beneath the ground, springs filling, the trees shook and pine cones dropped. Past the meadow I went in to the woods, carefully because she had traps and hypnotic powers to hold my eyes and break my defenses, as staring at a bony orphan would, such terrible beauty. I climbed and looked but I couldn't see tracks, so I turned back down to the road.

On the last crest before Marlette I saw her, halfway down, sitting on a charred stump, smacking her lips and waving. "My, you're bedraggled," she said. "Keeping your butt warm? It's a shame we can't hibernate—think how rested we'd be by now—though I prefer to live. And you, little butterfly? Oh, my, I see I've asked the wrong question. You have a popgun. Out for meat, are you? Haah! Never mind. I have a potion, as sweet as a peppermint stream, to tickle your tongue, and you like that. I've seen you hot, little fairy, your skin rashes so. You're a hard case, my soldier. Come down and give me your lips, bathe them in salve. You've only just tapped the well; now dive to artesian depths."

I kneeled and aimed, as Charley had taught me, with the stock against my shoulder, and fired. There was a splash of red; then she jumped down. "My soul! You're a

222

terror!" She ran limping into the valley. I wanted to see her face.

I could've turned back; she wouldn't come again. She was tempting but I was the one who chose; it wasn't revenge I was after but justice. She had nothing to offer but lies and I had her on the run, like a chicken stalking a coyote, or a crusader. I was cold and hard, a soldier, so I followed her down. There still was snow on the hill and in patches in the meadow. She was a shadow against white and the sun glare hid her well but there was no cover and too far to run to the brush on the slope. On the flat I shaded my eyes and fired again—a crack like sharp thunder through the valley; I shot once more just to hear the noise.

"Oh, sweet," she squealed, "haven't I given you enough? Such ingratitude. But never mind. In death I'll be soft as a baby's cheeks. You wouldn't ravage my carcass, would you, princess? Haah!"

She made for the same peak that Phillip had climbed. In the gulleys I could lose her so I ran faster, dizzy in the altitude; east seemed west and everyway. She weaved along so I aimed at the midpoint and fired my last rounds. After the thunder there was no other sound, quiet like I'd never heard it before, no summer birds or rustling in the brush, no wind through the trees or faraway hum of motors. She turned a fist to the sky and shrieked. Yellow tears welled in her eyes and a short wind blew snow and blew her down.

I ran up, reloading, but there was a deep hole filled with slush and black water. I poked in it with my rifle butt, but the bottom was too far.

Back over the crest and down I thought I heard her calling. "So we forge our own world, then? What did you do to deserve such freedom, my angel?" I fired once more, just into the sky.

Back in the cabin it was time for cleaning out all the

dust from the winter and things I owned, all the clutter. First there were papers, ripped-up magazines and scraps from my note pads; I started the fire with them. I went through the books Charley had brought, some that were Phillip's and some junk; I hadn't read any of them all through. There were old magazines from Walker's days, some that I'd made notes on, dreams I'd had and since forgotten; suicide letters to make Charley feel guilty and others to tell him he shouldn't; and sketches of snakes and packs of coyotes, rivers with temples across them, which wouldn't mean anything without the music. I burned them all.

I flipped through my sketches on ring pads and set them aside to kindle fires. Then I went for my clothes, burned all the frilly things Charley had brought, nightgowns and dresses he thought might cheer me, bright heavy sweaters he must've bought at the thrift shop, socks whose matches were lost or were caulking a wall, towels with frayed edges, all my underwear but one pair of panties, and the woolen things, handkerchiefs I hadn't washed and one of Charley's engineer caps. I tossed on old boxes I had kept food in, and empty jars to hear them pop and melt. The more I burned the more I wanted to burn; I ran outside and found trash where the snow had been, more papers and rags and clothes I had thrown down, old tea bags and a hatchet handle. The air was black from leaking smoke and my nose was clogged with ashes.

Phillip's notebooks sat in the corner where they had been since Charley brought them; I'd only touched the one. They were precious to me still, all that was mine from before. On days I felt frightened I had ignored them from fear and on days I felt stronger I promised myself I'd read them when I was sure of my strength. I stepped toward them, then jumped back, tried it again, but I couldn't touch them; so I went for my Bible instead, turned it open and closed my eyes, ripped out the pages and tore them in half, wadded them and threw them into the fire, till there was nothing left but the leather cover, which I sliced into small pieces that would burn.

There were just Phillip's notebooks left and the mirror and the things I need to live. I was remorseful, as though what I had thrown away were a fortune, but I had started a massacre and couldn't leave witnesses. In the mirror my skin was still raw from Pancho's beard, my eyes were red in the firelight, and my lips were muttering as if in rote prayer, but I wasn't praying. I grabbed the mirror and smashed it across the stove; glass chips and splinters flew everywhere. Some melted on top of the stove.

It was time to read the notebooks, I thought. I was afraid he might've seen our life so differently I wouldn't believe myself anymore; then I'd have to go back and start over remembering. There were things I wanted so badly to know: how many times he was angry at me; if he called me a woman or a child. I sat down by the stack, picked up a handful. On the front inside cover of each was a school year, 1965–66 and on. Perhaps before our year he had noticed me, thought he'd seen something special and written it down. That would thrill me, I realized, dangerously, but I was frantic to know all the things Phillip thought.

I scanned the first pages of our year looking for my name, but there was no mention, so I started reading more closely in case he called me something else: "Winning and losing are fates, not occurrences. Only the last time counts. A man might lose always, then win it all back. He has been a winner all along. And losers are afraid to win, sensing one day they will lose all they won." Just half-ass philosophy! I didn't need it. I ripped out the page and fired it off.

Next were quotes from writers I knew and writers I didn't, lists of the torments his mother had caused him, more tries at philosophy, godless, images of humans wheeling backward, their arms thrashing. There were notes for class lectures and pages tallying blackjack odds as high cards left the deck, but no mention of me, not one, till the next to last page: "Why do you ignore these devils, Jodi? Aren't they the soil against which you appear white? And isn't your whiteness a filth of its own, like underclothes hung against the sky?" I knew what he meant—that I was righteous and tight, that I couldn't understand what he did. I had thought he believed I was full of everything, and free.

I ripped out the page and burned it with the others. There was only one more—just blank pages following— one horrid word: ACTION. He wasn't my lover at all.

I crammed each notebook into the stove and watched them flare up and burn down to nothing, bitterly, then gladly, then sadly. I might've been wrong. Perhaps he thought me too close to write about. Or he thought it might make me too real. Or maybe he knew I'd read them today. No. He wasn't a spirit. He was just a poor man.

I swept up the floor, wiped ash from the walls and opened the door for air. As soon as the soot cooled I dug it out from the stove and buried it down in the meadow.

* * * *

June 20, 1972

Grandma came up yesterday to stay the week and then ride to L.A. with us on Saturday. She's proud that she was the first cause of my going away. She tags after me when she's not at the clubs, comes to my room at all hours to ask if I need a money belt, a special purse for my passport or a beret or panty hose. She bought me new Leatherette luggage. She has had no one to take care of for so long.

My mom still won't smile to give me her full consent, but because she speaks softly and brings me men's socks and extra blades for my razor I know what she's saying—that choices are hard and plans always change, that she'll work on my dad even after I write home about Phillip, and that even if he disowns me, she'll find a job and send her own money. This evening she wanted to take me to south shore to the new shops that stay open, but I came home too late and my dad was still out with the car. He stays away a lot when grandma is here, especially now that he can say he's meeting a client.

This week at school is for saying goodbye, for finals and last-minute makeups, but teachers skipped all that for seniors, gave tests early and let most everybody pass. It's a week of excitement and not taking roll, of longer lunch periods when kids go to the lake and come back late though we're not even supposed to leave during lunch. Kids talk in the halls and in classes about the results of college board tests, joining the army or going away to eastern schools or state colleges, and finding jobs maybe for the first time. A boy who always talks about model trains found work on the railroad in Truckee. Charley could try that, like his granddad.

Jill walks with me between art and math, tells me over and over again to send her my address wherever we land and that she and her boyfriend want to travel. She says she has false IDs so she can move out and wait cocktails, save up, so they can meet us and go to Greek islands and visit her cousins in Oslo. I want to ask her if she heard about the film or if she knows for certain that Aaron was behind it, but I won't because I can't afford that return of anger these days. In a hundred hours we'll be on the plane and the next day in Paris.

Mr. Lopez told me yesterday that I won a scholarship from the Incline Arts Council for $500 a year as long as I go to school. I hadn't even heard of the scholarship; he recommended me on his own and called my mom today to tell her and wrote up a notice for the morning bulletin.

Phillip is busy at school now, passing back papers, totaling up grades and hearing out students who think theirs should be higher, who need an A or B for personal reasons or the credit to graduate though they don't deserve it. Phillip gives them what they want. Being busy makes the time pass. I'm helping him pack up his books and clean out his desks and files, sorting exercises, tests and notes to throw out or leave for whoever takes over. Yesterday he hauled boxes to a shed in Mr. Beavers's yard; he wouldn't let me go along because he had to stop at his house for more and his mother was there, as always. She helps him pack, which makes me laugh because she thinks he's leaving with her.

Last night they fought because his dad called and said he didn't want the money and warned him not to come home, said that he could work another year and Phillip didn't owe them anything. But she was listening, grabbed the phone, shouted that he'd always undermined her, which was the cause of Phillip's rebellion. His dad hung up, and Phillip told his mom to take the money and leave the old man, give him a few years of peace before he died. He told her to go to a mission where cannibals live and she might do some good. She caught the Holy Ghost, started shouting in tongues and came at him with a dish cocked in her hand. He ditched the house, and at King's Castle ran his last few hundred dollars up to a thousand while my grandma was losing her dimes.

Today I asked Phillip to come with me to the lake, because the next few days I'd have to spend with my family and I probably wouldn't see him alone again till Friday night. We drove down to Reno, first to the library to return books and pay fines, then to his credit union, where he borrowed $2000 against his retirement, $4000 less the $2000 they kept back for his car loan. He'd leave off his car in L.A. for his dad to drive.

In the car he counted travelers' checks. "How long can three thousand dollars last, Jodi?" I reminded him about my scholarship and I told him again we could count on my folks. It didn't seem to ease his mind much, so I had him pull off the road and we kissed for a while.

He wanted to go someplace other than King's Beach because his mother might look for him there, though she complained that she couldn't walk a block with her arthritis. But King's Beach was the home we were leaving. On the south end by the park a Mexican family was broiling steaks and their children were throwing sand and Frisbees. Phillip had a phrase book, so we tried to translate but they talked too fast. We sat with our toes in the water, watching speedboats and crescents of spray which the dipping sun sprinkled with rainbows. There were clouds over the Rubicons and still high snow, and calm water reflected the trees on our side and mountains across. Kids played guitars and smoked grass on the point, an old man jogged with his belly churning and boats turned into Carnelian; guys I'd seen in the tavern with Charley drank wine on the pier; a flock of ducks or big black birds dove toward the flashing lights of windows on Dollar's Point. There were motors and shouts and sand, children and lovers and old women with big purses, and a squall out over deep water. Everything was here and I loved it so. I waded to the pier, skimming stones while Phillip watched back over our town.

I walked up to the taco stand. Phillip's mother came around the corner by the drugstore; I ran back and told him. I said we should shadow her, play detective. We ran up to the buildings to hide, then circled around the block behind her. She chewed out a panhandler; we couldn't hear what she said but the boy slinked away and she walked on, kicking sand from her shoes, shading her eyes and looking around. She turned toward the highway, then changed her mind and came back, so we had to duck behind a car, then cut across to the point to tail her to the next road and back to the highway and up the

229

hill to Stateline. She snooped in casino windows, then walked down to Cal-Neva, stood at the door for a long time, finally went in.

"Maybe we'll catch her at a table," I joked.

"No. She's looking for me. When I was in high school she'd find me at the movies on Friday nights and drag me out. I swear it."

At the back entrance we stepped just inside and peeked over the railing. She stared down the dealers, players, lookers; wherever she turned were eyes that saw her face and jerked away as though discovered in some seamy escapade. The club was dim, purposely estranged from God, I thought, a hideaway of lust for excitement, cheap laughter, boredom behind it all, because the highs and downs meant nothing but money, tedious games and the only thrill was in chance, fortune. I guessed I was watching through Phillip's mother's eyes, strange to me, hard and condemning though we believed in the same God. But belief was where the idea met the believer, which was why I didn't worry that there were so many different Christians, Paul, Pastor Sandoz, myself, Phillip's mother. All of us sucked the idea to meet our needs. Only the idea was pure, only Jesus.

Back in the parking lot Phillip's mother stopped a woman, talked for a moment, then climbed into the woman's car.

"What's she doing?"

"She's not shy, Jodi. She's asking for a ride, saying she's old and sick."

It was nearly dark, so we walked down the road to the hot springs. There were folks out strolling, a volleyball game, hibachis on condo balconies, but at the springs we were alone. Phillip stripped and plunged in while I looked around first for flashlights and shadows. Things had changed since I was so brazen. I knew we wouldn't get busted, and I thought if someone came to stare it was their lust if they thought I was sexy, not my fault, because I wasn't thinking of sex, except how to avoid it. I'm thinking a lot about purity these days, because of the lies I've had to tell. I feel the need to control myself rigidly, like a fast; I owe some debt to my soul. Besides, we have no private place to make love, and to search one out seems sneaky, another lie. And I also realize now that I can feel innocent and still be guilty, a terrible thing to know. If I could have one wish it would be to make that knowledge untrue, so I could believe in my feelings.

In the pool Phillip hugged me, ran his hand up my thigh and left it there, squeezing gently and kissing my neck.

"We can't do it here," I said.

"Why?"

"I don't know. Do I have to have a reason?"

"Where, then?"

"Maybe at Charley's or in the woods past your house—if it's so important."

He was hurt and I was sorry. He crossed the pool and leaned out. I wished I could see his face. Even when he turned toward me I couldn't see his expression in the dark, but I thought he was angry and that angered me. He kept jumping around the pool and wouldn't sit by me for long or talk much. It seemed we had so much we needed to talk about, but it was safer if we didn't with both of us tense and angry. I climbed out first and he came right after. While we were walking I said we should go to Maggie's mother's, to tell Maggie goodbye.

Maggie seemed nervous with Phillip around and couldn't keep her eyes off him. "You guys should have a baby; they're really fun. I don't even mind changing diapers much or staying home nights, except sometimes, and then mom helps me; with two parents you could get away with a lot. Jodi, do you think I should ever let Paul take her? I think he might kidnap her. He found out I went to a dance last weekend and that a boy brought me home, so he threatened to take me to court. He thinks a judge will give him custody because I go to dances. He's really gone. He'd probably tell me if I wanted her back I'd have to live with him. No way for that! Does he still ask if you think I'll come back? What do you tell him? I hope it's no, because maybe he'll give up. You know he says we'll be married forever. Isn't that a crock? Mom says she thinks I could get an annulment. Do you know anything about annulments, Mr. Oswald?"

Phillip said he didn't. Maggie kept talking about her own life; there seemed no room for us. I told myself that times were frantic for her, but I couldn't sit listening, so I said we were due to meet Charley.

It was Charley's night off. He was on the porch needling Paul. "What I do is not gambling. I cheat, so that makes the difference. If a guy's wrong for gambling, then the guy who cheats him is in the right, right? I mean somebody has to be. Hi, Jodi. Hi, Mr. Oswald. Hey, I want to talk to you. Come on in, I'll get us beers." He took Phillip off by the arm and left me outside with Paul.

"You see Maggie?"

"Yeah."

"Give her more reasons why she shouldn't come back with me?"

"She's got plenty of her own reasons."

"Yeah, and she got them from friends like you. Oh, you don't know how hard it is doing what you believe is right and having people you love hate you for it."

"Don't I?"

"You don't know what it feels like to have your child taken away. When Charley can't see his baby it tears you up, but with me you think it's O.K. You want to know the difference between you and me? What I think is right comes from the Word. What you think comes from demons, else you'd come back to studies after the Lord touched you again. That night, at—"

"I know what night!"

"Then why do you keep doing like you did before?"

I just shook my head. I didn't want to argue. I wanted to remember Paul as the boy who first showed me Christ and forget all the rest. If I hated him it would be another wedge in my faith.

"You're nothing but a hype, Jodi." He walked out the gate and up the street.

Charley came back out with Phillip. "I can do it, man," Charley said. "I've done it before and I owe you, right?"

"You only owe what you want to," Phillip said. "And what about floor men and the eye in the sky?"

"They're blind. Ask Jodi what she thinks of the place. You can't stay there all day and see clearly. You ought to know that."

"You're not going to cheat, are you, Phillip?"

"No."

Charley shrugged. He asked us where all we'd go in Europe, how long we'd stay, all the old questions everybody asks; we didn't have answers or even guesses, so Charley scowled as though he thought we didn't want to tell him. When he looked away Phillip nudged me and motioned inside but I made believe I misunderstood, got up and told Charley I'd see him before we left.

Down the block Phillip stepped off the sidewalk toward the street which led up to the woods and the creek, where there was a meadow beyond the last house. But I told him to take me home, that Danny was due to call, half wishing he'd call me a liar so we could fight it out. But he only sulked in the car.

★   ★   ★   ★

June 21, 1972

I don't want to see my dad again after what he did tonight. Not ever. If a strong man can't help himself, can't

233

hold back from attacking a weak man, can't wait a day or an hour till he can ask questions and think about the answers, can't believe enough in his own daughter, whom he has pretended to believe in all along, to even ask her side—if he hasn't learned this much in forty-seven years, he doesn't deserve to be forgiven. Not by me. Once he hit a father from Danny's Little League team and once he hit a laborer he had fired who came to our house to tell him off, but I didn't know he was a bully. He got what he deserved. He wouldn't speak on the way home and no one would speak to him. Now he's gone, probably drinking. Mom went to bed without saying good night; grandma wanted to talk but I was too angry, so I came up to my room and now grandma is mad and her lights are out. I want to go find Phillip but I don't know where. He calls it bad luck to gamble the same place twice in a row, so tonight he's probably at south shore, but Charley hadn't seen him when I called Harry's. He did see my dad, first at the showbar and then at a blackjack table, but he disappeared into the slot rows. Maybe he's lost forever in an eternity of cranks and bells and old ladies from Lodi. I'd like that, but grandma could find him. She knows the lay of the land.

Friday is graduation. Tonight we had to go to the awards banquet because of my scholarship. I had the feeling there might be trouble but not so much, not such a massacre. While we were dressing dad called to say he had to meet a client in Markleville, so he wouldn't be home in time to take us; he'd meet us there. Mom called a neighbor for a ride. Grandma ordered me out of jeans and into a low-backed summer dress she had bought me for Paris. Phillip had saved us places beside him, next to Mr. and Mrs. Beavers. Grandma bitched about the watery spaghetti sauce, the cereal meatballs and the wilted salad. She asked Phillip if he had seen my paintings or sketches; he must've thought it was a loaded question because he stammered, then finally said no. Grandma stared him down and after a while he asked why she was staring.

"Honest people," she said, "look at your face but not in your eyes. Most people look away, to tell you you're not important. Crooks and salesmen stare you in the eye."

"So are you a crook," Mr. Beavers asked her, "or a salesperson?"

Grandma didn't laugh. "Mr. Oswald won't look at me but he's infatuated with Jodi. Observe how his chin points her way. As a teacher, Mr. Oswald, surrounded by young ladies, do you find it difficult to keep your mind on your work?"

"I do," Mr. Beavers cut in.

"She's teasing," I told Phillip.

"Surely," he said; then he reached into his pocket for his wallet, looked in, then stuffed it away.

First were the sports awards. Bracken, Fabriano and the rest of the coaches went up from their table to the stairs on the stage. Mr. Furby introduced them chronologically—football, cross-country, skiing, wrestling, track, baseball, tennis, swimming. Each coach called out the awards for his team—all-league pins, varsity letters, J.V. letters. Grandma was anxious to leave for the clubs. Mom was watching for dad. Mr. Beavers took Phillip outside. On stage, it seemed from their gestures, Bracken and Fabriano were arguing. Phillip came back with wine on his breath. He kept rubbing his chin and squeezing his nose, scratching his head and bouncing his knee, tapping his heel on the floor. Grandma asked him how long he had been teaching. He said this was his last year. She asked where he was from. He said he was ready to move.

Grandma snapped. "Why won't you answer me?"

"I did," he muttered. "This is my last year."

Grandma was furious. I thought she'd kick him beneath the table, but she took out her compact instead and caked more powder on her face. I tried to figure a way to get Phillip alone, but grandma was unpredictable; she might make a scene. Mr. Lopez came up from behind and I nearly wet my pants, partly startled and partly sure he'd give us away.

"Phillip. Jodi. Say, tomorrow I'll give you those addresses in England and Barcelona."

I tried to give him a sign and he walked away confounded. When the sports awards were over Bracken, Fabriano and the other coaches came back to their table. I asked Phillip why Bracken and Fabriano sat together if they hated each other, but Mr. Beavers answered. "Machismo. In the marines men would stalk each other for weeks."

Bracken hissed something at Fabriano. "Broken nose," was all I caught. Mom was still watching for dad. She whispered that I shouldn't be disappointed if he didn't show, that he was avoiding grandma, not me. Grandma asked mom what she said, but before mom could lie, Miss Waterman came from nowhere and asked mom to step outside. Phillip turned after them but I held him back and whispered that mom would play it well. Grandma asked what I had whispered to Phillip and what mom had whispered to me. I just winked and said, "Secrets."

"I want to leave this place," grandma huffed. But mom had come back in.

"Now, Muriel, it's Jodi's night."

"Crap" grandma said.

There was a break between the club awards and the scholarships, so I said, "Shall we go smoke, Mr. Oswald?"

"You don't smoke," grandma said, scowling, but mom asked her something and Phillip and I slipped off. On our way toward the patio door Coach Fabriano charged

236

past with Bracken on his tail. By the time we pushed our way outside they had squared off; baseball players lined up behind Bracken, football players behind Fabriano, guys on both teams milling around.

"This is not the place, Coach Bracken."

"But it's time, Mr. Fabriano!" They each took a step and stood nose to neck (Fabriano is a giant), but two coaches grabbed each and pulled them back. Kids booed and grumbled.

A girl named Ginger ran up to us. "Mr. Oswald, you know that extra credit I turned in about Mary Shelley . . ."

I walked away and stood by the fence. It was a glorious night, the moon straight above Mount Rose, balmy air from the Carson Valley, wind through the trees and houselights all golden, a faint smell of wood fires. Sometimes I loved darkness, wanted to step out into it where people could pass and not see me and I could hear more things, as I could with my eyes closed or if I were blind. I saw Aaron coming and tried to walk off, but he called to me.

"What?"

"Did you hear I got a scholarship to Oregon?"

"Like you need it, right?"

"Hey, I worked for it."

"Yeah."

"How about you?"

"I plan to disappear. Next time you look I'll be gone."

"Jodi, no hard feelings, huh?"

I couldn't stand for that and let him off clean. "None, rich boy. Just move back where you belong, where there are lots of poor folks to walk over and theatres you can show your films. Go make all the films you can, asshole. It might make the world end sooner."

"What?"

"You think I don't know just because I didn't come

after you? You couldn't just sell that filth in Reno, you had to pass it around to my friends, give it to Paul. I didn't try to hurt you!"

"Paul who? What is this, Jodi?"

I went for his eyes but he slapped me hard and when I tried to kick him he threw me down. Phillip came running. I lunged to push him away but he stepped back and fumbled in his pocket, yanked out his knife, punched the button and the blade snapped free, six inches long and polished. His shoulders quaked and his lips curled inward.

Aaron backed against the fence. I couldn't tell if he was scared. "Stop still, fucker! You want to die or what! Look over here!" he shouted. "This guy's crazy, he's a killer!"

I don't think Phillip heard. He puffed out a breath, lifted the knife, drove it toward Aaron's shoulder, weakly, as though he weren't quite sure, so Aaron just had to lean and Phillip slammed against the fence. I jumped to Phillip and took his shoulders. "I *do* want to stab him," he whispered.

I folded his knife and threw it over the fence. Aaron was gone. Some teachers, parents and kids stood staring. I pulled Phillip through them and back inside, hoping it had mostly gone unnoticed. I was proud of what Phillip had done, but afraid of it, too. It all had happened so quickly, for a moment I doubted it really had been. Phillip's hand was sweating. His face was gray and feeble. "It's over," I whispered. "I love you." Bracken waved to us glumly, sitting by himself behind our table, next to the main door.

For the scholarship awards Mr. Furby asked parents to stand up while their kids came forward. National Merit was first, then Nevada State, then Bennington and Vassar, Stanford, Aaron's to Oregon, later the Sons of the West, American Legion, one from the D.A.R. Then small

238

ones, like mine, from business, the marketing club, from the symphony in Reno.

My dad walked in loosely and took the seat beside grandma; he grimaced at me like a kid about to be scolded. I introduced Phillip as my English teacher. Dad shook his hand warmly.

Mr. Furby called my name. Aaron's dad tapped my arm as I passed down the aisle. Mr. Furby gave me a certificate and said he was sure I'd someday be great. If I were Dali, I thought, I'd paint Mr. Furby with a corkscrew in his ear. I bowed toward the Incline Arts Council, and because my mom's ex-boss from the gallery was one of them, I didn't go over and shake their hands as I was supposed to. Mom grinned at me and pulled out my chair.

Phillip was twitching and his eyes stayed upturned as though he were entranced by the red, white and blue streamers from the ceiling. Between Phillip and my dad, with grandma watching us both, I couldn't take the chance of trying to comfort him. Mr. Furby said now we should recognize three beloved teachers who were leaving the school. First he called Miss Waterman; she warned us against illiterates and girls who didn't wear panties. "That's a feisty old bat," my dad said to Phillip.

Next Mr. Furby called Mr. Krinke, who said he'd remember Mount Rose as the pinnacle of forty years' teaching. "You're next," I told Phillip; then Mr. Furby called him. He didn't budge, so I shook his arm. He stared at me thoughtfully, strangely peaceful, then he jerked and stood up, sat down, bounced up again, waved at Mr. Furby, then slouched back into his chair. People around us were staring and tittering.

"It's O.K.," I told Phillip. He looked at me puzzled—then he saw Miss Waterman behind us, tapping my dad's shoulder, asking him to step outside.

Phillip wheeled his chair around but I stuck out my

arm to stop him. From the doorway Miss Waterman pointed sternly at us—there wasn't even time to pray for a miracle—then said some cross things, it seemed by her twisted mouth. As he stood firm in the doorway, Miss Waterman gone now, my dad's face was flushed and squinting, legs spread and shoulders squared, arms tight at his sides.

I took Phillip's hand. We stood up. My mom yelped something and grandma did, too, but we started for the door with steps short and slow as in a wedding. My dad sidestepped to meet Phillip's eyes. "Jodi?" he said, as though hoping for a lie.

Phillip nodded and folded his hands at his waist. My dad rubbed his eyes with his fists—I reached for him but he shoved me back away, grabbed Phillip's tie, drew back and mashed Phillip square in the jaw. Phillip back-peddled, moaning breathlessly, but he was still standing. Then he reached for his pocket.

"No!" I screamed, though there was no knife anymore. It was all too terrible. If I had the knife I'd have gone for it, too. "God, no!"

My dad stepped toward Phillip but Bracken jumped out from beside the wall. He wheeled my dad around and smacked him in the eye, again in the stomach, again in the face, again in the back of the neck. My dad hunched over and fell forward.

When I ran to Phillip he shoved me off and walked for the door. I followed him, grabbing, but he turned and straight-armed my shoulders. His face was like sculpture, rigid and sure, cold as a dealer's or assassin's. "It doesn't matter, Jodi. Just go home." He and Bracken walked together out to his car.

My dad was a mess, his eye already blackening, a tooth loose and bloody. He was still on the floor. I wanted to kick him so he wouldn't get up. We could've left him there but he had the keys; grandma helped him up.

I can forgive Phillip; Aaron pushed him too far. I can

240

forgive Aaron; he might not have made the film. And Bracken was only helping a friend. But I'll never forgive my dad. He made me and made me believe in justice, then he tried to take it all away.

I know I can't sleep tonight. By the time it will take me to walk to King's Beach Phillip might be coming home. I'll take my small suitcase. This will be the last line in my journal, because I'm leaving it all behind.

* * * *

June 22, 1972

Last night late Phillip's car was still gone. The bedroom lamp was on though it was near 3:00 A.M.; there were wispy clouds across the moon, streetlamps dim as though in haze, classical music droning from some house, a T.V. too loud from another and dogs everywhere barking angrily.

I tried to read on the curb beneath the streetlamp but a sheriff turned the corner and saw me before I could duck. I asked him to turn down his radio but he scowled, threatened to bust me for curfew, wrote me up, then told me to go home; he said he'd drive me but I pointed to Charley's house. He told me it was a dangerous place to live, dangerous people. I said I was leaving tomorrow.

When he left I started up the street for a flashlight from Charley's truck, then remembered Charley was working graveyard, so I went back to the church steps and curled up in the dark against the door. It seemed cold, hard like teeth, the mouth to something living, like Jonah's whale. The doors might be open for sanctuary but I didn't have the nerve to try them; in there anything could happen, I could lose my conviction and repent of things I didn't believe I'd done wrong, like deserting my folks; then I'd have to go back home. I could still see my dad's flushed face and his hand on Phillip's collar. Remembering made the time pass till all the noise quieted, the light in Phillip's house was shut off and the dogs quit barking. An early rooster crowed long before dawn.

Phillip might lose all his money; running might cut off mine, but we still had the one-way tickets. We could trade for a different flight, maybe from San Francisco so my folks wouldn't find us. If we went to Paris broke we could sleep in fields and steal peaches, walk south when it turned cold—a blessed freedom after all these people, all these lies.

Still in darkness, when house lights began to flick on, I stashed my suitcase and walked to town for coffee, but I had to sit outside the café and wait till it opened. I have always loved sitting on curbs, since we lived in Bellflower. Cars seemed futile, passing that way, then back this way, and it made me feel strong, above them, attached to the earth. Down the alley was the lake, always. They could cut down trees and roll back the hills but there was spirit in the water, permanence. I crossed over and walked out the pier. Nowhere was a lake like this, nowhere such depth and solitude except on the sea, and the sea was turbulence, boasting waves.

After coffee I checked again for Phillip's car, then took my suitcase and hitched to school. At the gate I met Mr. Furby. He asked about Phillip and my dad. I told him I hadn't seen either one and he said he was sorry, that I should come to his office if I needed to talk, but I went looking for Phillip. His classroom was locked still and the office said he hadn't called in. A coach said Bracken hadn't showed up at the gym yet either, so I walked on the track, then checked the classroom again. Kids were on the lawn waiting for a substitute and a couple asked me about last night. I told them it was all a prank—the fight was entertainment. In the art room Mr. Lopez gave me addresses, then followed me out and shook my hand. He wanted to kiss me, I thought, but he didn't try.

Because of my suitcase I caught a ride with two boys

who thought I was traveling. Both eyed my breasts and legs and one reached for my knee but I stared him down furiously. They dropped me in Stateline and I ran down the hill to Fox Street. Phillip still wasn't home and Charley hadn't seen him all night. I looked up Bracken's phone and called but he didn't answer. Charley was shocked that someone had beat up my dad, said Bracken must've caught him off guard. When I told him we'd leave as soon as I found Phillip he sat in a stupor for a long time, drank one beer, then opened another.

"Strong lady like you, I guess you never needed me."

"You didn't need me either, Charley."

"Naw. I'm tough, you know, mercenary."

He said he'd leave his keys in the truck in case I needed to use it. I sneaked through the church grounds in case Phillip's mother was outside, and curled up in the garden beneath the church steps behind the juniper. Phillip's mother was staring out from the kitchen. I wished I could see her closer, but I didn't dare for fear she'd see me and chain me up or God knows what, chase me shouting the Holy Ghost, call out the neighborhood and Pastor Sandoz. I wondered if she'd spoken to him; it seemed as though she should have with the church so near. Birds all around chirped lightly and I remembered what Phillip said was her favorite scripture, the eagle in Midheaven calling "Woe, woe, to those who dwell on earth." I wondered if we could be two different species, actually, genetically. There were men who could rape, then kill what they'd touched, tyrants who sent men to war for greed, soldiers who chopped necks and held up the heads with their swords. I wondered if Phillip's mother had ever watched a sparrow rise up or seen an eagle stop still in the sky without calling it devilish or a deadly omen.

It could be, I thought for the first time, that Phillip might have left already, might be down with his dad or on the way. He might've left word with my mother, but if I called home we'd fight for sure. A clean break was better. I just needed patience. My mother would call Charley eventually if I didn't come home.

Down the street my dad pulled up at Charley's. He ran to the door and pounded but Charley didn't answer, so he stopped next at Phillip's. His shirt was unbuttoned and his coat over his shoulder, though it was past noon and hot. I couldn't see Phillip's mother behind my dad but I guessed she was telling him off, thinking him a friend of Phillip's, threatening; I hoped they'd hit each other. But she might know where Phillip was and tell my dad. I ducked out and ran up to Charley's; when I brought out the truck my dad was pulling away.

I stayed a couple of blocks behind, ready to run if he spotted Charley's truck. In Incline he turned down to King's Castle. I parked up the street and walked. The guard was a guy I knew, Pancho's friend Mick, so he let me in. I stepped inside about three feet, then saw my dad with a drink and a woman snuggling, an off-duty keno girl with messed-up hair and a sweater with spangles. I stomped on the floor, hating, frantic, trembling. He was a cheat, a weakling, needed someone to soothe him, to make him feel strong, the macho prick, while he should've been looking for me. All my gods were dead or dying.

"Hi dad!" I screamed.

Then I ran out the door and down through the grounds to the beach, around the fences in the water just past the club, the big homes, the mansions, all the way out of Incline. I hitched back on side roads to get Charley's truck at King's Castle, then cruised around just looking and cussing my dad out loud. At Charley's I took some books from my suitcase, then went to the church, behind the juniper. One book was about Egyptian treasures in the Louvre. I hadn't been in many museums before, except ones for Old West stuff. I wondered if they'd let us panhandle outside the Louvre and how

244

Phillip would look panhandling, whether he'd like that kind of humility. The other book was by Hemingway; Phillip had given me a few of his that took place in Europe. The beginning was military and I wasn't in the mood, so I flipped ahead. It was O.K. but the love scenes were corny.

Pastor Sandoz came back from somewhere and found me. The books must've involved me more than I thought because the sky was red over Phillip's house and Pastor invited me to his apartment behind the church for dinner. I'd never been there before. It was one room with hardwood floors, a cluttered desk and a hideabed. He had pea soup simmering; he brought me a bowl and a thick slice of bread and sat on the floor across from me, staring, thinking of sex, I believed. I was probably wrong, but anyway I didn't mind. I felt there were wires attaching us and going out to all the people; I wanted to hold them all, but whenever we came close, me and anybody, the wires tangled and shorted. Still, it was a sweet feeling, tenderness toward everyone, something I needed lately, and sex was just touching, just mixing our hearts. There was no violation, only togetherness—or selfishness. But I couldn't hold the feeling.

"Pastor, why is there sin and cruelty?"

"Only because of Satan, Jodi."

"Then why didn't God kill Satan?"

"He will. Meanwhile I suppose we need to be tested."

"So we're set up, right?"

"Not precisely."

"Yes we are! We're framed!" I was tired of guilt, tired of trying so hard. God was a tease and coldhearted, a bloodsucker. Jesus was the son of a madman, a dope for not knowing and telling. Phillip's mother was right; everything kind was a deadly fraud.

"Please be patient, Jodi. You can't understand the world in a year."

"How many years since you were saved?"

245

"Twelve since I believed."

"So you don't believe now?"

"I didn't mean it that way."

"O.K. then, after twelve years you tell me just one thing and I'll be satisfied. Why should I be good? Why should I care? To glorify God? Didn't He just make us to give Himself glory? All through the Bible: 'Praise God, He did this and made this thing and burned this to the ground, praise the Lord in His righteousness!' He's just righteous because righteous means whatever He wants it to. It's crap and madness. Like I'm supposed to be what my parents want so they'll be proud? What did they do to deserve it—love me? I loved them, too! So what? They don't jump when I say so!"

"I can't answer anger, Jodi. You're upset . . ."

"Yeah I am!"

He came to me with his head cocked sideways and his mouth drawn tight, a clown. He reached for my forehead.

"Don't touch me. Damn!"

I ran out and away, a mile through Brockway before I came to my senses. He wasn't a lecher. My God, I can't think anymore.

★　　★　　★　　★

I had a dream. Charley and I were with Walker in his hospital. Charley lay back on the bed, pushing the lift and lower buttons; I was in a wheelchair whose motor buzzed; Walker was his old self in a stubble beard and engineer's cap, stretching his bulky arms, pacing the floor and telling a story I hadn't heard before:

A Paiute sorceress lived on the south slope leading to Job's Peak at the lower end of the basin a hundred years ago, in Walker's granddad's time, when the Paiutes were a tribe and migrated seasonally, but this lady was alone

246

and stayed year around. It was rumored that she knew foreign languages, world geography, the working of tarot cards, voodoo, most everything. She lived on rats, badgers, bark and herbs.

Walker's granddad was curious. He climbed up on foot so she wouldn't hear him coming, found her shelter and hid on a ledge above it, waiting all day, sure she'd come from below because above was just gray dirt and granite. But she tricked him, came from above silently and before he could fight she had roped him in leather. She shoved him along down a path to her shelter. Inside was an iron pot, which she filled with water and boiled on a fire while she played a tune with sticks on the side of the pot. When the water boiled she unlaced granddad's legs, yanked him upside down and stuffed his foot into the boiling water. He howled and sprang free, ran out and down and away, still tied in thongs from his hips up. She threw stones and cackled and screeched, chasing behind him till she tired of the game.

"What did she look like?" I asked Walker.

Charley grinned. "Think she might be your gypsy's grandma."

"Please don't make fun of me, Charley."

Before Walker could answer nurses came to the ward to shoo us out, but we stayed at the door to watch. They jammed a needle into Walker's arm, and in a flash he dissolved, to the gray-skinned corpse he really is.

I had another dream. Phillip and I were in a bookstore. As we turned to leave a man walked in, stern, sweating, in a gingham sport shirt open in front, corduroys and high-top tennis shoes. He ducked behind a shelf, then came out like Superman, renewed, holy, genial.

Phillip dropped to his knees. I laughed at the sight. The man began to sweat again down his forehead and into his eyes, which he wiped with a gingham sleeve. "Oh, sweet the death of a man," he cried joyously, "when he has risen up from the tomb!" Then with a ponderous frown, "But have you the courage to kneel before Christ?" Phillip covered his eyes. "So you are not a man but an angel," the stranger said, "and for you Christ will not intervene." He walked out, shaking his head as though he wished it were not so.

I don't know what that means. I don't know what anything means, and on these days with the earth turning slowly, the wind blowing fierce down the mountain and the stream high into the meadow, washing the winter away, I'm learning not to care what things mean. Who is to say we're wiser if we know?

Before he left for Mexico, Pancho brought me a HONK IF YOU LOVE JESUS bumper sticker. I glued it on a board, climbed a cedar and hung it on top, facing the sky, hoping it would catch the eyes of geese bound for Canada. Lucky Jodi, I don't have a horn—I'm a quiet spot in a world which goes honking along.

I'm learning to laugh again and waiting for Charley.

248

Part Four

A FEW MORNINGS AGO I started early and took my rifle and climbed the mountain. On the hill before Marlette I rested, wondering about the flumekeeper who shipped the boat he had built to the coast and sailed away. He could still be alive in the South Seas or up the Amazon. Nobody knows.

On the south side of the south peak where the climb is more gradual there were rocks to grab when I slipped on loose gravel. I made it in one long climb, sweated dry inside till my head was spinning and the ground crunched all around, loud in the thin air. At the very peak was a great smooth boulder jutting out into the sky, shaped like an arrowhead angled up. The boulder was slick, so I crawled to the point, found a basin the right size for sitting with a groove on one side for a handle as though someone had chipped it there. The drop was a thousand feet to a cutaway ledge with a wash like a dry waterfall, then a stone bed to a gulley which ran on to Carson Valley. From the grasslands and feed crops and pastures heat waves rose; the west was green to the horizon, except for peaks which were still white-capped and bays of turquoise lakes, and Tahoe, where every color lived.

Beneath the snow cross on Mount Tallac was the inlet

251

to Emerald Bay. I stared hard till I could see telekinetically, as though I were skimming above it, flying low, charting the ragged lines where colors changed depths, royal blue to silver-blue to transparent and flecks of gold far beneath. A boat came out from the bay. A jet dipped down toward South Lake. Closer, near the cabin, a red speck was moving. I fired a shot in the air but the wind whooshed the sound away and the red speck kept climbing toward the cabin.

I crawled back off the point, slid down the way I had come, ripped the pocket off my jeans, bruised my legs on stones, left my jacket where it fell. In the valley I fired again, and again when the first echoes died. I checked the clip and reloaded, wondering how close I'd have to shoot to frighten the person away. There hadn't been anyone up to see me since Pancho left for Mexico. He might've told Maggie, or it could be my dad on a hunch.

Once more I fired a warning from the top of the hill; then I ran down north of the stream, away from the road, and caught the ridge trail. It was rough with branches fallen in winter and cuts from runoff in spring. After I turned my ankle each step was a spike of pain and my foot started to swell till my boot was too tight. The pulse in my neck came too fast, frightening me, and sometimes it seemed to skip, but I still ran till I reached the hill behind the cabin. Whoever it was hadn't passed on the road (I had watched it all the way) and wasn't in sight, so I hid and watched, thinking at first I could wait till dark if I had to, then take what I needed and live farther up, on the shore of Marlette in the wreck of the flumekeeper's home, but that was madness.

I crawled down the hill and ducked behind the cabin, peeked through the window and came around front. There was no sign; even the birds chirped as always through the morning. Something small whopped the back of my head. I spun and yanked the rifle to my shoulder, trembling.

252

"Kid!" Charley called from our fir tree. "You've been king on the mountain too long."

He drilled me again with his slingshot, then swung down with a whoop like Tarzan and landed in the mud beside me. They couldn't keep Charley in jail. He walked away from a road crew near Minden. He makes his own laws.

Every morning we bathe in the stream in the shallows through the meadow where it's warmer and sandy. We lean on our elbows, Charley stretched upstream and me downstream and we stare at each other and reach back to tickle each other's toes. Charley is peaceful these days, and happier. Before he came up he stopped to see his friend Lucky and picked up an ounce of heroin. He says it's almost pure.

When I tell him I shot down my gypsy he calls it a lie; he says I'm too tender to shoot a beer can but I argue that it's not true, that I haven't a conscience, because Phillip said that no one with a conscience could believe the Bible.

Charley tells me I shouldn't believe what Phillip said, that Phillip was compulsive, obsessive, that he made up his own dilemmas, as on that last night. But I say that Phillip just wanted to win, the way Charley wanted to give and I wanted to love—too much, too soon, for all of us.

I gave Charley my journals to read and last night he asked me, "When you burned his notebooks why didn't you burn these, too?"

"You bastard, Charley," I said. "You think I need you to tell me I'm selfish?"

Then while he slept I lay awake thinking about what I've written. It tells Phillip's story if anyone's, not mine; mine has hardly begun. So I woke Charley up and fixed him coffee and told him to tell me again all he remembered that I hadn't seen. Charley isn't selfish. He'll give up even his dreams for me.

* * * *

My last night down the mountain I ran from Pastor Sandoz, spent hours walking furiously on the highway,
to the beach and around the blocks nearby, back to
Charley's, though I didn't go in because his truck was
gone and Paul was home. I walked up to Stateline,
checked the clubs there, except Cal-Neva, where I
couldn't get past the door guard. I hitched to Incline and
searched King's Castle, where I saw grandma pumping
slots just as though nothing had changed. Past midnight I
tried to call Charley at work but they said he was gone. I
sat beside the highway watching cars speed by and angrily throwing stones at the tires. Then I went home to
my folks' house.

My dad's car was there. I used the ladder to climb to
the roof and from there to my window and in. With the
night-light behind my bed where it wouldn't show in
the hall, I wrote in my journal and wondered why I had
hoped for comfort at home—there was none anymore.
There were footsteps on the stairs, my dad and my mom,
but no voices till a car pulled up: grandma in a cab. Her
talk was muffled and shrill. My dad shouted back he
didn't need her or her lip; then he ran upstairs, tossed
things around in his bedroom, then clomped back down,
slammed the outside door. His car squealed from the garage and bottomed out at the road.

The house was silent again, though the lights were
still on downstairs and grandma and mom hadn't come
up, so I guessed they too weren't speaking. I felt bad
about mom but I wouldn't go down. My family was over
and I was already gone far away. I heard Charley's truck
and I jumped to the window. Mom rushed out the front
door, met Charley at the front steps and told him something. Charley squeezed her shoulders and left.

I climbed out on the roof, back down the ladder, ran

down the hill to the highway. It was useless to hitch in the shadows of a night so dark, with only the moon and a few stars dim and eerie through the misty clouds, so drivers were startled and swerved when they saw me. I jogged, in a trance from exhaustion and the hypnotism of headlights and taillights and the slap of my feet on the ground. In Stateline the streetlamps were golden and their beams were full of dust, the clubs still busy at 3:00 A.M. I ran down the hill, straight to Charley's. He was drinking beer in the kitchen.

"Did you find Phillip?"

"Yep. He was rich. Shit, if I had that money he won—but he wouldn't leave. You know what that means."

"Let's go. Please, Charley. Let's go right now."

On the road I kept shouting to go faster but Charley's truck was old and clumsy and I was too frantic, so he pulled off, said there was no reason to worry, Phillip was O.K., probably not so crazy as to lose it all. "Even if he did," I said, "so what?" We still had our tickets.

Back on the road Charley told me about the night, all the details, but I couldn't pay attention, though I kept asking him to repeat what he had just said, which must have drilled it all into his mind, because he remembers it still, even down to the cards. I wanted to hear, groping for clues about what would happen to us, what kind of man Phillip was when I couldn't see him, those times when luck was his angel. I was afraid of the clubs, that other world which had lived alongside the quietness of mine since the first day we came to the lake. But I couldn't hear Charley while my head spun with premonitions, vague and mysterious, of doom and irreversible changes. I kept looking to the next turn, then the next, trying to count the miles left.

Charley had first seen Phillip at a keno seat, about 9:00 P.M., bug-eyed and watching the board. Bracken was passed out beside him.

"Go call Jodi!" Charley said.

255

Phillip rolled his head and rubbed his eyes. "But I can't call her yet. I have nothing to say. Midnight—what time is it now—midnight I'll call her. Oh, I'll make her happy. I'll keep her well, Charley, I swear to God."

"She doesn't want to be kept. She just wants to be gone. You're losing, right?"

"No. Not at all. I'm winning. More earlier—eight elevens I doubled and hit tens."

"Wonderful. Now listen, you go get a room and I'll bring Jodi back by morning. You'll be fresh, you can still make your plane."

"But I haven't won enough."

"What's enough, boy scout? You think you might break the bank? When did you sleep, man—you look like a ghoul. They could spot you coming from Fresno, and drifty as you look, you couldn't recognize a mechanic if he snatched an ace from under your chips. Look around. A thousand people here want that money and they're all on the payroll. This is no Rock Candy mountain."

Phillip took a grease pen and marked a keno ticket.

"You're not just playing keno?"

"Oh no. I sat down here because I don't know what to do with my friend. He's drunk. . . . If I leave him here while I play, will they take him to jail?"

"Sure. Look, I've got twenty minutes more break. We'll get a room, you and him can both sleep. When I get off at midnight I'll find Jodi and bring her back. If you still want to play then, do it."

"Yes. We should take Bracken upstairs."

"Bracken? This is the guy who whipped Mr. McGee? Some lucky punch." Charley pulled Bracken up by the shoulders.

"Not luck," Phillip said thoughtfully. "Fury, perhaps. Or will power. Do you suppose?"

"Who cares? Help me here." They dragged Bracken to the hotel lobby. Charley signed them in and found a bellboy who helped carry Bracken onto the elevator. Charley tried calling my folks' house, but my dad answered, so he said he was just checking if they had found me; then he called his house and told Paul to run down the street and look for me at the church or hanging around Phillip's, told him to check the beach and the pier and the park.

The club was wild from a convention of Elks or Rotarians—Charley wasn't sure—and their wives and whores and girl friends. Beside the show band and the clang of machines, howls of winners, paging for phone calls, growls of the losers, burps of the drunks and the barmaids' shouts, there were party favor horns and cowbells around gamblers' necks, shrieks of women goosed unexpectedly, hard backslaps and bragging across the rows. From a table at the far corner came sporadic yelps of a crowd surrounding some Arab prince at baccarat, playing one to one, with the limits lifted and tipping in hundred-dollar chips.

Charley saw Phillip pass the show bar and disappear behind a craps table. He asked for an early break but the floor man said no. When he next spied Phillip he pointed him out to a waitress, asked her to bring him over. Phillip came, sat down at a seat just given up, looked hard at Charley, then placed a small bet. Charley played straight but gathered the cards slowly, making them easy to count. After he won two, Phillip bet $100, called for a hit. Charley bent back the top card, a low one, then dealt him the second, higher. Phillip won, let the bet ride and split aces on the next hand. Charley held twenty; first he threw Phillip a legitimate ten, then had to use the second, which came up a nine to push. Now at $400 Phillip let the bet ride again. He stayed on low cards and Charley busted.

Phillip dropped his bet back; Charley played clean and beat him twice before his relief came. Charley walked across to the bar, from where he watched Phillip, who

257

had stayed at the table. The break dragged on and Phillip still played, losing now—Charley could see it in the sharp jerks of Phillip's head and his hands gripping the table. Charley called the same waitress and slipped her ten dollars to go for Phillip again. When Phillip came he leaned on the bar with his face in his hands. "I'm very tired. Do you have a pill I could take?"

Charley ignored him and whispered, "You playing with me or not?"

"What? You weren't cheating?"

"Yeah. How do you stand?"

"I have five thousand dollars."

"How much do you want?"

"More."

"Then when I come back we blitz. Two thousand each hand. Unless they clear my rack before I go back, or somebody wins a bunch, I can pay three times without calling for a new rack. I'll cover it with the pit boss later. He owes me. If a crowd or a floor man shows, drop to ten, we'll wait them out. When you're three hands up, you're gone, right?"

Phillip looked out over the strobe lights in the show bar, the spinning wheels, smoke rising, sophisticates with gaudy ladies, simple folks with great wide eyes staring like sea tramps at a new land; rolled with the noises—the howls and whirls, clangs and thuds, hisses, shouts of bargirls, grunts of bartenders, the giggly ooze of the line just entering the cabaret.

"I can't play two thousand. I'm a nickel gambler."

"You can. This isn't gambling, man, this is crime."

Charley left him and went for coffee. At the end of his break Phillip was waiting at the table. First bet he played $3000. Charley checked around; the bosses weren't noticing yet, so he dealt. He had never yet cheated for himself, only for strangers he felt kinship to, but this was his night as well as Phillip's—maybe his only night if the pit boss named Zed caught on. Charley could only bully him once about talking in court. Then he'd have lost his chance to be anything but poor. He held eleven. His hit card was a queen so he dealt the second instead—a four—then the queen on top to bust. Phillip had $8000.

Phillip folded his arms, pinched them tight against his chest, left four thousand to play. Charley grimaced and shook his head but Phillip didn't see. Then came the floor man and Zed. The eye in the sky was on him, Charley knew, and the floor man wasn't his friend; he had to deal straight. He laid them down slowly—twelve for himself with four showing. Phillip split sevens, battling the odds, grinning furiously; he threw down his last $4000. Mad guts, Charley calls it, and foolish.

Charley topped the first seven with a six. Phillip scratched for another and Charley gave him a seven for twenty. Charley threw a three on the next seven, then an eight, for eighteen. At the last player the deck ran out. Charley shuffled working the face cards to the bottom, the deck mostly hidden by his big hands, so after Phillip cut the tens would be on top where Charley could draw one to bust, but Phillip cut high in the deck. Charley drew a six for eighteen—a push on one hand, Phillip's win on the other. Phillip had $12,000. He scooped his chips frantically, filled his pockets and stumbled away.

On his next break Charley looked but couldn't find Phillip. He called my house again, then his house, then finished his shift and past midnight found Phillip in the bingo room.

"Why are you still here, man?"

Phillip glared at Charley as though he had asked a stupid, annoying question. "Do you think I have luck like this every night? It might not happen again for years."

"Luck is nothing but leaving when you're up, man. Moving on before they get you. Just like in real estate, stocks, any of that shit."

"I believe that. I can see my fortune. I'll know when to leave."

"Ah, right, I forgot these hotlines to the Almighty. Did Jodi teach you?"

Phillip smiled condescendingly. "Common sense, logic—those things are descriptive, after the fact. Can you understand? If Jodi has faith, why shouldn't I?"

"Because Jodi can take a fall. I don't think you can. Go look at yourself and listen to what your saying. If it's luck, you're clean. You don't have a choice, it's predestined. You can't fuck up, you can't fail, you just lose, right?"

"Surely. And if I win?"

"Luck and guts. Sure. I know you; you want to be a blessed hero. Look, anyplace you play tonight they'll run in a sharp mechanic, very sharp, much better than a half-assed cheat like me. He'll let you win low and knock you down big. He's got his mind on straight and it's not his money."

"But I'm playing your table."

"I'm off. They'd pull me, anyway."

"Then I'll play another."

"You don't hear me, do you?"

"No. I don't believe they're as wise as you think they are. And I'm not an idiot myself."

Charley ran off to call me, but he still couldn't track me down, and when he came back Phillip was gone. For an hour he checked all the clubs, the hotel room, the streets as far down as the lake. Then he drove home.

Later, as we climbed toward Spooner Junction, a slight fog yellowing the car lights made Charley slow down. I told him Phillip's money was mine, too, because Phillip called me his luck, and I promised Charley I'd give him some. Charley scowled and called me a jerk, said there was no luck, just bum odds against shrewdness, and as dull and arrogant as Phillip was, he might be rolled or anything. I told him to shut up, that he only believed what he did because of bitterness and as long as he thought on things so harshly, that was the way they would happen to him—payment for the contempt he had.

He laughed at me angrily and we drove on in silence, down off the mountain. The night was horrid, great dark things behind pools of darkness and even the brightest lights were lost in it all. Beauty and terror were tied like loving and nighttime; the lake was a bottomless hole where dead men floated forever while their spirits cried.

In Glenbrook Phillip's car came like a ghost from the fog, cut the corner too wide and ran us onto the shoulder.

"Catch him, Charley!"

He spun the wheel and gunned the motor but the rear tire caught a rut and dug in. We tried to rock loose but the mud was soft. Charley hopped the guardrail and found a fallen limb, wedged it under the frame and had me drive till he pried us free. He jumped in and I sped off down the white line but I couldn't drive as fast as Charley, so I pulled off and gave him the wheel. The truck rattled and creaked and Charley bent against the glass to see better. First light hinted and at once I felt rested and confident, faithful and thankful even for the frantic times. It was done and I thought harshly of no one, even my dad, even Paul, even Phillip's mother. They were all poor people.

Charley drove past my folks' house in case Phillip had gone there. The lights were still on. Mom was at the front window. I ducked and Charley sped on.

Between Incline and King's Beach commuters and delivery vans were out already, late gamblers weaved home and early-rising tourists strolled toward the lake. When I saw Phillip's mother I'd greet her smiling so warmly that she'd stand still, astounded, while we walked to the car and waved her goodbye. But first I'd kiss Charley, squeeze him and promise we'd always be best friends; then Phillip would hand him money so he'd never have to cheat or steal again.

261

When we turned the corner to Fox Street, Phillip was pulling out from the curb. There was another person in the car. Charley bore down and I leaned out the window screaming "Stop! Faster, Charley! Phillip, stop!"

Church Street meets the highway; straight across is the alley, and the alley leads down to the boat ramp, the pier. Brakes squealed on the highway and a car spun out, slammed into the bench by the taco stand just as we turned the corner. I screamed, thinking it was Phillip— but Phillip's car was in the alley and speeding straight ahead. Charley stopped at the highway.

Phillip gunned down the launching run, up the ramp to the pier, bumping, swerving, sparks flying from beneath his car. Then, while I sat gaping as though this were a stunt for my pleasure, his car flew up, stopped as a blot against the Rubicons, silent, stalled in the air. Then it went down. A fountain rose, dark water, gleaming in the tip of the sun.

"Charley, that's Phillip! What's he doing? Oh, Christ!"

Charley's truck bogged in sand beside the pier. I ran out to the silt and the gurgling sound, screaming for Phillip, wheeling my arms in the sky, pounding my legs against the water which slowed me down so I felt myself lame. There were no heads above the water. I spun around, thinking he might've climbed to the pier, but only Charley was there, and on the beach only a pack of dogs. Charley dove over me toward the car. The back wheels were out of the water, one still spinning. Water was up to my neck. I kicked with my feet, reached down trying to feel, then blind and breathless I dove through the silt. There were sharp things, glass or metal, pain in my hands. I shouted, choked, jumped up for air, dove again. On the first reach I touched a leg.

I followed it up. The door had pinned him. I could feel the gashes and the water thick with his blood; his neck stretched a foot long; his teeth bared.

I sprang out screaming and heard Charley shout, "There's an old woman! She's alive."

Then all I remember is the clack of a screen door opening across the beach in a cottage, two little boys with big dark eyes running down to the sand with buckets. Out past the bay the lake had never been so glassy and calm, the mountains never so tall and green, never such peace, never such glory, never again.

*   *   *   *

"Is it he?" quoth one, "is this the man?
By Him who died on cross,
With his cruel bow he laid full low
The harmless Albatross.

The Spirit who bideth by himself
In the land of mist and snow,
He loved the bird that loved the man
Who shot him with his bow."

The other was a softer voice,
As soft as honey-dew:
Quoth he, "The man hath penance done,
And penance more will do."

Every week Charley goes down the mountain, sells heroin and brings some back for himself. Just enough, he says, never more. Some weeks he brings me back news. Mark, my brother, is home from the army. Paul is living in Sacramento. Phillip's mother moved to the lake, to Phillip's old house, where she lives alone. I could kill her. I've matured. That's one of my secrets.

There are snapdragons in the meadow and crimson columbine, wild daisies on the bank by the road. Inside I'm painting a mural on the whole north wall—a canyon and beyond the canyon a row of cedar decked out with golden and silver bells. Between the canyon and the cedar is a garden of fruit, bright blossoms, paths lined with flowers that glow and a new moon each evening, twelve new moons so far. At night while Charley lies awake the bells play tunes, lovely tunes, lullabies. I shake him and tell him to listen. His eyes are open but he won't hear my bells.

I tell him that God speaks in actions and signs—like him being here with me now—and the Holy Spirit decides what we dream. I tell him we're waiting here for the cycle to turn and Jesus to rise up, burn the casinos, snatch airplanes from the sky, order the lake to give back its dead and the mountains to grow bushes full of plum-sized berries, waterfalls everywhere and trout jumping grandly, more of a home than Eden was. Phillip will be an angel, watching out for Charley and me. When I think of Phillip I think of my dad, Walker, Pastor Sandoz and Charley. They are all still my men. That's another of my secrets.

During the day Charley climbs the south hill to one of the washes where a stream used to run. He fills buckets with dirt and carries them down to our stream to pan through. He has gathered some dust he believes is gold, keeps it in my pouch that used to hold pine nuts. I watch from the bank and tell him he's wasting his life, that even gold turns to mud in his hands so he knows it will all come to nothing. He laughs, says he knows lots of things that aren't true, same as I do. I bring him lunch if he feels like eating. I tell him if he gets any skinnier and me any stronger, then I'll have to dig while he cooks and hunts for berries.

He won't admit to a habit, because he skips some days, but on those days he's restless, wants to leave the mountain, steal his son from Maria and take our chances somewhere else. But I say no, at least up here we're safer and we can dream with no one to tell us our dreams are sinful or madness. Charley won't shoot up in front of me so I leave him to do it alone. We believe that what he needs is his business and what I need is mine. I just tell him to be careful when he goes down.

Yesterday I walked a mile down the mountain to check for berries, but they were still buds, tiny and green. I had just turned back when a dog came up the road, an Australian shepherd. I hid behind the vine because I was afraid someone might be with him. He saw me and came for me, snarled and bit for my arm. I jerked away and ran through pine nests and thorny bushes but couldn't lose him, so I grabbed a branch and smacked his head. He bared his teeth, crouched and sprang. I hit him again, then picked up a rock and clubbed him. He fell, bleeding from the ear, whimpering, cowering. I stroked his fur, pulled stickers from his coat and stuffed grass beneath him. I took off my shirt and ran to the stream to wet it, wiped his blood and laid my shirt beneath this head. Then I ran back up for Charley; we made a stretcher, but when we came back down the dog and my shirt were gone.

This morning I cleaned all the trash from the meadow, kicked grass over the path we had worn and tore down the platform in the fir from where we fired on pinecones with our slingshot. Later we'll knock down the outhouse, in case someone comes up behind the ridge. Charley is weaving more vines in the vines that shelter the cabin. When I finish my writing I'll call him. He loves to lie beside me and watch me while he rests, but he doesn't need me often, with junk in his veins. Still he comes when I call him. When I speak of a baby he laughs. "Too bloody," he says.

I love Charley's laugh. That's enough.